# Trafficked:

## *Two Sisters Lost*

**A Novel**

*Love to you all
from Lois
( Lois K T.)*

Lois Kenna

# Tripodi

PISCATAQUA
PRESS

Also by Lois Kenna Tripodi

*To Take Shelter*
(A Novel of Domestic Violence)

Trafficked: Two Girls Lost

©2014 by Lois Kenna Tripodi

Published by Piscataqua an imprint of
RiverRun Bookstore, Inc.
142 Fleet St. | Portsmouth, NH | 03801
603-431-2100
www.piscataquapress.com | www.riverrunbookstore.com

Ordering Information:
Quantity sales. Special discounts are available on quantity purchases by corporations, associations, and others. For details, contact the publisher at the address above.

ISBN: 978-1-939739-22-3
LCCN: 2014935094

Printed in the United States of America

Once again,

For Rob

The danger was not that I should do ill,
but that I should do nothing.

—Montaigne, *Selected Essays*

# Prologue

*Somewhere in a city on the California/Mexican border, fourteen-year-old Carla sits against the backboard of the narrow bed, knees drawn up, and fingers in her ears. She croons tonelessly as she rocks back and forth, twirling a lock of her dark brown hair distractedly. The thin bedspread on which she sits is stained, almost colorless, as is the window curtain and frayed carpet.*

*A scarred, laminated dresser is topped by a single-burner hot-plate. Sharing the space are several opened cans of soup and single-serve boxes of cereal. The latter have proved enticing to a half-dozen, well-fed roaches which dart within a foot of the girl, who doesn't seem to notice.*

*In an alcove can be seen a cracked toilet with a broken seat. Water puddles around its base. A stained sink in equally poor condition shares the tiny space.*

*The walls between the units are thin; so thin that they do little to block any noise coming from next door. The girl is painfully aware of a deep male voice apparently cajoling and then chastising, alternating with the chilling sounds of a very young female—pleading, begging, and finally, screaming.*

*As the sounds permeate Carla's squalid room she moans "no" over and over, as tears course down her cheeks. Finally she can stand it no more. She slips from the bed and kneels beside it, her hands clasped in prayer, a prayer full of bargaining and promises if only He would intercede and make the horror of her life go away.*

*Sometime later—a few minutes, a half hour, maybe more—*

*the outer door is unlocked and the motel owner's wife, a frumpy, homely, Hispanic woman with a pock–marked face, comes in and half-carries, half-drags the teen's younger sister to the foot of the bed. A bedraggled yellow Easter bunny dangles from her limp hand.*

*In broken English the woman says, "Clean her up and get yourself ready. Nestor here soon for you."*

*As soon as she leaves Carla cradles the child to her and murmurs over and over, "Serena, I am so sorry."*

*The child whimpers, but there is no other response; no sign of recognition. She appears dazed—possibly in shock.*

*Carla lays her gently back with her head on the filthy pillow, noting with sorrow but not surprise that her shorts and panties are missing, and there is dried blood which has trickled down from between her legs. Her pink tee-shirt is bunched up around her neck—the LITTLE PRINCESS letters looking obscene under the circumstances.*

*Serena stirs a little as big sister washes her gently and puts her in a favorite Hello Kitty sleep shirt, but the few words she utters are worse than the silence. "That man hurt me a lot," she whimpers. "I want to go home. Please, Carla. Please!"*

*Carla feels her heart break. She turns to the TV and selects The Disney Channel. "We'll talk about it later. I have to get dressed now."*

*"You're going out? Don't leave me," Serena's voice rises in panic as she clutches her sister's arm.*

*Carla ignores the pleading. She puts on a tight red blouse with a low neckline over a push-up bra, paring it with denim short shorts and high-wedged sandals. With make-up, heavy on the lips and eyes, and long, shiny hair, she could pass for eighteen, even older. That's what many of the servicemen seem to like; barely over the age of consent, and a little trashy. That's why she brings in the money that so far keeps her and her sister alive.*

*There is a series of loud knocks and a gruff male Latino voice calls out angrily, "Don't make me come in there!"*

*Carla gives Serena a quick hug. "Remember, I'll always come back for you," she murmurs . . . and then she is gone.*

# 1

"Got a minute?" The deep baritone voice startled me.

I had been so engrossed in the weekly crossword puzzle that I hadn't heard the copy editor approach and lean into my cubicle. Frank was in his late forties; a bear of a man, well over six feet tall, with a neatly trimmed brown beard and brown eyes that most often crinkled with good humor. He had lettered in several sports in high school and ended up playing football for a few years with the San Diego Chargers until a blown knee ended his career.

"I'm impressed! Looks like you're almost finished, and you're even using a pen, but obviously you have far too little to do around here!" he said, with a big smile.

At most any other time we would have been subjected to the cacophony of sounds coming from a small but busy newspaper. However, the weekly issue of *The County Voice* had just been put to bed, and we had the place pretty much to ourselves. Ours was a no-frills operation housed in a strip-mall with Nick's Pizza on one side and The Joyous Swan nail salon on the other. Nevertheless, the paper had a good reputation and was still managing to turn a profit.

I motioned Frank to the extra chair. "Despite what it might look like, I am doing this difficult puzzle in order to improve my brain while waiting for our esteemed editor to arrive and give me my next assignment. Doing crossword puzzles improves my verbal skills and thus my value to this enterprise. Malcolm has asked me to consider doing a blog," I added. "But, speaking of earning one's keep, shouldn't you be running down the next front page shocker instead of sneaking up on the help?"

"Malcolm didn't come in this morning. Sounds as if he'll be out for a few days with the flu so he asked me to run this idea by you," Frank explained, his bantering suddenly replaced by a serious tone with an expression to match. "How would you like to cover an important local event, contribute to a good cause, and get in some exercise at the same time?"

"Sounds intriguing. Tell me more."

Frank was all earnestness now. "Erin, have you ever heard of the North San Diego County Human Trafficking Collaborative?"

I shook my head. "Can't say that I have, but I do remember seeing a film on television portraying a group in Thailand, I think, who rescued young girls from brothels. I do occasionally contribute to UNICEF, which advocates against exploitation also, but I wasn't aware there was a San Diego connection."

"The problem is worldwide but we have more than our share of exploitation right here."

This was news to me and I'm sure I looked skeptical.

He went on. "I understand you've been in San Diego for about two years." I nodded. "And like so many others, newcomers and visitors particularly, you probably think America's Finest City is just about perfect, right?"

"Well you can't beat the climate, and the beaches, and the lush landscaping, and the restaurants . . . but what are you getting at? Was that a trick question?"

"No trick and everything that you noted about southern California *is* true; but unfortunately there's another darker side. The FBI has identified San Diego as a high intensity child prostitution area and a gateway to international sex trafficking. In fact they say it is one of the top ten cities in the nation with the highest incidence of this type of crime. And this problem extends for many other county cities as well, from El Cajon and National City on the border, up the coast to Vista and Oceanside.

"This has been going on for decades, with the bad guys winning more often than not, but lately there have been a few encouraging breakthroughs. Malcolm is thinking of running a series of articles highlighting the whole subject. We both thought of you when it came to asking someone on staff to check it out."

Real reporting! Of course I was hooked. I was grateful to have my job—Malcolm had hired me based largely on the recommendation of a former classmate of his, my boss at a small newspaper back in Rhode Island—but I was sick of doing fluff pieces; covering city council meetings, society events, and the like. "Thanks for the vote of confidence," I said. "Tell me more."

"Well, for quite a few years now the Collaborative I mentioned has sponsored an awareness event, including a walk, and this year it's scheduled for next Sunday at the Avo Playhouse in Vista. I thought you might be interested in attending as a way to get your feet wet."

"Sounds perfect," I said. "Where do I sign? And do I get a press pass and will the paper want pictures? I've been practicing on my smart phone."

"I like your enthusiasm," he said, giving me a thumbs-up. "I'll get you some official ID, and pictures are always helpful. I take part in this event every year myself," he explained. "I'll introduce you around."

With that he stood up and pushed his chair back. "Well, it's time we get back to our other lives. I think we're the last ones here. I'll lock up. I have a Spring Valley high school basketball game to cover this afternoon, and Gonzaga plays San Diego State tonight—not bad assignments for an old sports nut like me."

Frank didn't need the money but he and the editor went way back. And it did lend cachet to the paper to have a former pro athlete on the staff. Besides, he just loved being around sports—at all levels.

I grabbed my backpack and followed him toward the outer

door. As we walked along together he said, "Oh, by the way, I can pick you up Sunday or we can meet in Vista about eleven. Maybe your fiancé might even like to take part. In any case let me know if you need a ride. You have my cell number."

I thought it unlikely that my fiancé would care to become involved, but I could be wrong. Ours had been a whirlwind courtship, however there were times when I felt that we were still in the getting to know each other stage of our relationship.

As I slid into the metallic-grey leather driver's seat of my leased, late-model silver BMW, I reflected on how far I had come since my friend Amy and I had headed to California from Rhode Island over two years ago. My car then was a high-mileage, nondescript, fourteen-year old Volvo station wagon and I was its third owner, but it was the first car I had ever owned, and I loved it.

The car I drove now was just one symbol of my change in status from those early days when Amy and I were living in a dingy rent-by-the-week motel room near the harbor in downtown San Diego. We were down to our last few hundred dollars and working in a hole-in-the-wall restaurant for impossible-to-please owners and mediocre tips. Hardly the bright new world we had imagined when we headed west! But we eventually got better wait staff jobs in a friendly, family-owned restaurant called Bella Italiano and regular paychecks from our second jobs as motel maids.

Together we had made enough to move into a tiny apartment of our own in a better part of the city. I still planned to pursue other employment, but for a while our new life wasn't bad, and there were the beaches, and what seemed to us to be a vibrant nightlife. The fact that it was a college, tourist, and navy town, was a plus for two twenty-something, small-town Eastern transplants.

Since those days, my life had improved considerably—hers,

not so much—and I felt more than a twinge of guilt that I hadn't made more of an effort to keep in touch regularly. We had spoken a few times but it had been almost six months since I'd seen Amy. So I was really looking forward to her visit. There were no secrets between us, no need to keep up appearances—just two old friends sharing a homemade lunch.

Traffic on the multi-lane interstate was heavy going north, but it was flowing smoothly and I hummed along while playing the White Stripes on my CD player. I turned off on La Jolla Village Drive heading for the impressive Heights townhouse Michael had purchased as soon as I had agreed to move in with him.

My fiancé was a financial advisor at the Morgan Stanley office in the famous quaint La Jolla Village itself. He was very good at what he did and as the fortunes of his clients grew, so did his as well. He had also pointed out logically that the new living accommodations afforded a welcome end to his previously long commute from the North County. Still, the hefty mortgage payments on the townhouse made me nervous. The financial world had been a notoriously unstable one for a number of years.


Once home I changed into jeans and got ready for my guest. Soon I heard the familiar sound of my old car coming from one street over and went out to greet Amy, gesturing for her to park next to my new vehicle as she came into sight. "Glad to see it's still chugging along," I commented, as she stepped from the car.

"The mechanic says she's good for another fifty thousand at least. Are you sure you don't want her back? Even swap?" Amy asked mischievously, looking appreciatively at the gleaming Beemer.

"Don't tempt me. You know she's like an old friend," I answered, only half in jest. "Come on in." We hugged and then she followed me along the flowering plant-lined walkway and up the front stairs. Once in the foyer her eyes widened as she noted the huge crystal chandelier and the curving staircase that led to the upper level. "It's even nicer than you said it was," she exclaimed.

Modern elegance was how Mike described the complex and he had furnished our unit accordingly. Most of this was accomplished before I had moved in and, though it *was* beautiful, I found the dark leather pieces and generous use of chrome and glass to be a little austere. I planned to add some homey, colorful touches, little by little.

Of course Amy wanted to take a tour. She was particularly impressed by our king-sized canopy bed and dual walk-in closets, the Jacuzzi in the master bath, and the mahogany table in the formal dining room which could seat fourteen. She shook her head in disbelief at the living room, with its surround sound system and giant TV, and the luminous marble countertops and custom tiles prominent in the eat-in kitchen.

"Erin, don't you have to pinch yourself every so often at the way things have turned out?" she asked, as she looked around admiringly. "And Michael obviously adores you. I'm so happy for you!"

There was no trace of envy in her voice. Amy tended to be on the chunky side, and she did little to enhance her rather plain face, dishwater blonde hair, and pale blue eyes. Though, at her request, I had made suggestions but to little avail. As for my looks, since childhood my strawberry blonde hair had drawn admiring comments, and I had long ago learned to style it in a variety of flattering ways. Blessed with good skin, I also knew how to enhance my features with a judicious use of  cosmetics. But Amy had two secret weapons—her smile and her sweet nature which endeared her to anyone who was fortunate enough to get to know her.

I gestured for her to sit on one of the stools that fronted the center island. Then I plugged in the electric griddle, took cheese and tomato slices out of the refrigerator, and put pre-cooked bacon strips in the microwave. "Just to show you that I haven't forgotten my roots and gone uptown on you, I'm making grilled sandwiches for lunch," I said. "And there's a jar of dill pickles, a bag of Doritos, and some leftover Christmas paper plates. Feel free to help yourself."

For the next hour we ate our simple comfort food and regaled each other with stories, many of which began with "remember when?" Now in our mid-twenties, we reminisced how, within one month of each other, we had been placed in the same Rhode Island foster home. I was thirteen, and Amy twelve, sharing a similar background of neglect and worse. In some ways we were closer than many siblings.

Suddenly, Amy checked her watch. "Yikes! I'm out of here. Bella Italiano is calling. My shift starts at two. Promise me you'll stop by soon. Tony and Yolanda still ask about you."

"Will do. Say hi for me and don't forget to remind them of how lucky they are to have you still working for them."


The house seemed so empty after she had left. However, there was little time to dwell on that, since Mike was meeting new clients at Roppongi's, in the Village, and had asked me to join them for dinner.

I dressed carefully in a cobalt-blue crepe wrap dress and added matching patent-leather heels, together with blue and gold dangling earrings. I was going for sophistication, so I put my long hair up in a chignon, teasing out a few tendrils and a wispy bang around my face to soften the effect. Michael would approve and I had to admit that I enjoyed playing the role of a fashionista now and then.

I left my car in valet parking and entered one of the area's most intriguing restaurants. Roppongi's served fresh Asian fusion food, exquisitely prepared, featuring outside patio seating around fire pits, in addition to several very attractive choices of indoor dining rooms.

The hostess recognized me and I followed her to one of their more private rooms. Mike stood up when he saw me, as did a distinguished looking older man. My fiancé gave me a chaste kiss and the gentleman shook my hand vigorously as I was introduced to the Nelsons from Omaha, Nebraska.

The woman smiled warmly, and then said, "You're even prettier than your picture. I don't mean to be so forward, dear, but we were showing off pictures of our first grandchild and asked Mike if he had a recent snapshot of both of you. You two should be on the cover of a magazine!"

They each had a drink in front of them and the arrival of the margarita Mike had pre-ordered for me saved any further embarrassment. Actually I was flattered by the compliment. I looked appreciatively at my handsome fiancé, impeccably dressed, with his coal black hair, dark eyes and his high cheekbones, compliments of his Spanish heritage. He had worked hard to put an impoverished past behind him and it had obviously paid off.

The Nelson's confirmed that they had chosen to meet with their new financial advisor in good part because they could swap the frigid Midwest for a brief vacation in California

"We visited your fabulous San Diego Zoo earlier today," Mrs. Nelson exclaimed. "And Mike suggested a trip to tour the Midway Carrier museum tomorrow," her husband chimed in.

The excellent food and service made for a pleasant evening. Conversation flowed easily and the Nelsons seemed in no hurry to get back to their hotel.


I followed Mike as we drove home. It was nearly ten when we pulled the cars into the garage. Once inside I kicked off my shoes and removed my earrings. Mike hung his suit jacket in the hall closet. "So what did you think?" he asked, coming closer and looking directly into my eyes.

"I had a good time," I answered honestly. "They seem like very nice people." Then I hesitated. "I only wish . . ." No, I told myself. Why spoil the mood? "It's nothing," I said. "Let's go to bed. Don't you have an early tee time tomorrow?" I yawned for emphasis.

He ignored my question. "Wish what? Come on, Erin. Thought we had agreed to be totally honest with each other. I know I can be a little overbearing at times, but you know I respect your opinions. What's bothering you?"

"OK, it's just that when Mrs. Nelson and I were in the ladies room she praised me for being a partner in an old-fashioned bookstore, helping to preserve what she called a "vanishing noble enterprise." And she also seemed to have the impression that I was a reporter for a major newspaper. Where do you suppose she got such ideas?"

"So I exaggerated a little," Mike said, with a shrug. "If you'd let me put some of my money—*our* money—into the bookstore you *could* be a partner instead of a temporary clerk, and you *are* a reporter. Besides, she got the beautiful part right," he said huskily, cupping my face in his hands. "I like the dress, but I'd like it even better if you'd take it off. I don't have to get up *that* early!"

We made love on the living room couch for the first time. I had to admit that the suppleness of its luxurious surface was a plus, though I don't think the location would have mattered, what with the passion we were feeling for each other.

"That was good," Mike said, with a sigh. "Am I forgiven?"

"It was better than good, and you know it!" I said, breaking the mood with reluctance. "And I accept your apology, but it *is* late and I'm sticking to the leather. Go take your shower. I'll take mine in the guest bathroom."

# 2

*"You're a skinny little thing," the blonde, pigtailed girl comments, looking down at Serena as she huddles on a mattress in the corner of the communal sleeping room. "And you sure do snivel a lot!"*

*"Leave her alone, Tara," says a second, golden-skinned, young girl in accented English. "You're such a bully. As if you didn't cry a lot when you first came."*

*"Well, she's got snot coming out of her nose—disgusting! And, anyway, crying gets you nowhere," the girl called Tara replies, with a toss of her long, blonde hair. Serena sits up and, since no one offers a tissue, wipes her nose on the back of her hand.*

*"Don't mind her," the dark-haired, kinder girl says, glancing at Tara dismissively. "My name is Alicia. You look rather shaky. I think they drugged you. They do that sometimes—makes less of a fuss getting us here."*

*Shakily, Serena gets to her feet. She has only the haziest remembrance of the past few days. Where is she? And where is Carla?*

*"What is this place?" she asks, as she tries to make sense of the situation. There is very little light coming through what appears to be a single window, high up on a concrete wall, making it hard to tell if it's day or night.*

*"This is a fancy hotel, of course, you ninny," Tara says. "Why don't we order room service? I'll start with pancakes and strawberries and lots of syrup and ..."*

*"Stop it, Tara. Don't be so mean. The poor girl is probably starving," Alicia breaks in.*

*Serena does indeed feel strong hunger pangs. When did she eat last?*

"*Someone should be coming in with food soon,*" Alicia says. "*To answer your question, we really aren't sure where we are except in the basement of some sort of factory somewhere in San Diego. Where do you come from?*"

"*Carla and I live in Campo with our abuela—our grandmother,*" Serena answers automatically in the present tense.

"*Used to,*" Tara spits out. "*Used to!*"

"*And she will again,*" Alicia says soothingly—enclosing the trembling newcomer in a warm embrace. "*Now, I am from far away. From Jamaica,*" she explains, in the most beautiful voice Serena thinks she has ever heard. "*Do you know of my lovely island country?*"

*Serena shakes her head, careful not to move and break the spell of the first kind touch she has felt in ages.*

"*Someday I will take you,*" Alicia says dreamily.

"*Why do you lie?*" Tara is in their face now. "*You know none of us will ever be able to go home!*" And then she begins to cry deep, gulping sobs, and Alicia opens her arms to welcome her in as well.

*Serena is alone again. She had fallen asleep and only vaguely remembers when the other girls left—telling her to be brave and assuring her that they would be back soon. She goes into the adjoining crawlspace to relieve herself in the bucket supplied for such a need. A cracked wash basin topped by a wavy metal mirror comprises the only amenities. She can hear muffled voices, heavy footfalls, and the sound of machinery coming from above.*

*She's beyond tears at this point—feels just a huge emptiness as she tries to keep the fear away. She fondles her beloved tattered yellow Easter Bunny, all she has left of life before . . .*

"*Okay, little one. Time to earn your keep.*" Dion's deep voice breaks the silence. The big man has to duck his head as he descends the narrow stairwell. Serena is afraid of him. His dreadlocks and the long scar on his cheek give him a menacing look. She *has also noted that, though he laughs a lot, he has cold, hard eyes that do not smile.*

*Dion claims to be Alicia's uncle, but she says that's a lie; that her family sold her to him because there were too many others at home to feed. How can someone sell a person? Serena wonders.*

*"Put these on," he says, thrusting shoes and a bundle of clothes at her. Serena notes that they look to be for someone smaller and younger. "And remember, if he asks, you're eight, not ten. Now hurry it up and brush your hair."*

*"Call me, Daddy," the man says after Dion has left the motel room. "And I'll call you dearie. Look, I brought you some Gummy Bears and this little pink unicorn."*

*The tall, balding, older white man is standing only inches away, his garlic breath causing her to gag. "Don't be afraid," he says. "I don't want to hurt you. I just want to love you."*

*Serena notes that he is quite heavy and that he perspires a lot.*

*Later, when he has slowly stripped her naked, and neatly folded her clothes and his, he asks her to kneel in front of him.*

*Serena does as she is told, but she is barely aware of the groans coming from the man as she shuts her eyes and retreats to her special place. She and Carla are running through a field, holding hands and laughing. There is a friendly dog, kites, dolphins playing in the nearby surf, and ice cream.*

*"That was good, honey," he later says. "You showed how much you love your Daddy. Now I want to take some pictures of you because you are so beautiful. Scramble up on the bed and put your thumb in your mouth. That's it, and now let's put on a little music. You do like music, don't you?" She nods, and with that he takes a camera and a small boom box out of his duffle. As he snaps picture after picture, pausing to pose her just so, Serena hears a woman's voice—so like her mother's—singing the familiar nursery tune*

*"Mary Had a Little Lamb" and several  others over and over. She is three years old again.*

*In the car driving back Dion says, "Mr. Smith liked you a lot." He looks down at the unicorn in her lap. "He says he'll bring you something really nice next time."*

*"Bologna sandwiches again!" Tara wails, as she throws a sand-wich across the room. Her eyes are red-rimmed. It's obvious that she has been crying.*

*"But at least there's a whole plate full," Serena offers. "And applesauce."*

*Alicia picks up the white bread and meat and puts it into a covered metal container. "You don't want the rats to come back, do you? Now come on and eat with us. If you don't, you'll turn into a shadow."*

*Tara manages a wan smile. Alicia is joking. In fact, Tara is a chubby eleven-year-old, with a tummy roll of what she calls baby fat. But with her platinum blond hair and aqua-blue eyes she is a favorite of many of the men who pay for the girls.*

*When Tara leaves to use the bucket, Alicia whispers to Serena, "We need to be especially nice to her tonight. At the motel earlier two of them took turns with her. I guess it was really bad. Here she comes."*

*"Will you tell us some stories?" Tara asks, in a little voice, as she settles down on her mattress. Her fair skin is flushed and she is sniffling back tears.*

*"Sure," says Alicia. "And why don't we start with the beautiful princess who lets down her golden hair so the prince can climb up and rescue her?"*

# 3

The more I read about human trafficking online the more appalled and angry I became. The personal stories were devastating. Sunday couldn't come fast enough. It wouldn't be just another assignment. I was truly anxious to get involved. Recent statistics claimed that three of the top ten worst child sex trafficking areas in the country were in California; one of those being in San Diego County.

By the time Mike came back from the Torrey Pines golf course I had a stack of articles I was anxious to show him but I vowed to lead into the discussion carefully. By the time I heard his car in the driveway I was much calmer.

"How go the golf wars?" I teased, as he dropped his bag in the hall closet. "You look beat."

"It's a tough job but somebody has to do it," he said, sighing for emphasis. "Not a fun game. Those guys were out for blood."

"Your kind of game and you know it," I commented—Mike thrived on competition. "I'll have lunch ready as soon as you finish showering and then I'll tell you about my latest assignment."

"Let me guess. They've finally given you the restaurant review job. The woman who does it now sucks. I've always wanted to be the anonymous dining companion," he said.

I shook my head in feigned annoyance. "No such luck. But hurry up and shower and I'll reveal all."

A few minutes later I heard his steps coming down the stairs. "Hmm, you smell good," I enthused, as he came up behind me in the kitchen and gave me a big hug. The hug led to a series of mutually satisfying kisses.

"One of us *has* to be strong," I stated breathlessly, a few minutes later as I came up for air. "Either your ham and cheese Panini is going to get cold or the Amstel is going to lose its chill."

He groaned. "You're *such* a romantic, but I *did* pass up lunch with the guys in order to have lunch with you, and playing eighteen holes on the South course always gives me an appetite, so . . ." He reached for his sandwich. "I hope they put plenty of mustard on this."


When we had finished eating, Mike asked, "So tell me about that new assignment you're being so secretive about."

"I'm not really trying to be secretive, but it will mean a big departure from what I'm usually involved with. Here," I said, handing him the printout of the upcoming awareness event. "Malcolm wants me to cover this and then turn my observations into the first of a series of articles."

He scanned the material, and then remarked, "I don't like the sound of it."

I ignored his comment and went on hurriedly, deciding to let facts strengthen my case. "Did you know that the Family Justice Center in San Diego claims that over 150,000 young American women and men are subjected to commercial sex exploitation annually? And that the *average* age of victims first being trafficked is *eleven years*?" I asked, jabbing my finger at one of the papers.

"And that the usual time served for traffickers, if they are even prosecuted, is three to eight years, with 50 percent only doing half their sentence after good behavior? Damn them!" I added vehemently, barely refraining from throwing my highlighter across the room in outrage at that travesty of justice.

Mike had been following my 'lecture' attentively. Now he looked at me with a mixture of surprise and concern. "Take it easy, honey. *Please.* It's a sad, sick situation, I agree, but also potentially dangerous for anyone who tries to get involved. My advice is that you should leave it to the professionals."

"But that's part of the problem, don't you see?" I was getting agitated again. "The bad guys are winning! Things will never change unless more of us civilians get on board. I think there's a real danger in doing nothing." Tears of frustration stung in my eyes. "I'd hoped you'd be more supportive."

"I'd like to be, honey, you know that, but I can't help worrying about you. Remember, I grew up in gang territory. They play rough. Human trafficking is just one of their illegal enterprises. Dealing in illegal drugs and guns are two others."

He reached for my hand but I pulled it back. "I had even hoped you might come with me tomorrow but I can see that won't happen," I said. "Frank, from the newspaper, offered to pick me up and introduce me around. I imagine that you also would prefer I didn't leave the BMW unguarded in a rundown part of Vista anyhow." My self-righteous anger abated somewhat as I saw the look of sadness in his eyes.

There was an uneasy pause, then Mike said, "You know your kindness is one of your most endearing charms, right next to your passion for life in general, but I'm really afraid that you are setting yourself up for a major heartbreak, perhaps even physical harm. Of course you must do what you think is right. Just promise me you will be careful. And remember, I'm here for you." I nodded.

"How about a kiss?" he then asked. "And weren't we supposed to be meeting with the wedding planner this afternoon?"

Late Sunday morning Frank picked me up in his old gray Chevy minivan and we headed north on I-5 to Vista. "Did I say that today's event is hosted by the local branch of Soroptimist International?" he asked.

"I don't believe so, but good for them!" That name brought

back pleasant memories for me. "Guess I never mentioned, but in a way, those philanthropic businesswomen made it possible for me to get my newspaper jobs."

"How so?" Frank asked, as he skillfully passed several large delivery trucks slowing down for an upgrade.

"In my senior year in high school one teacher knew of my foster care situation and how much I hoped to do some college work. I got a few hundred dollars from a local business in scholarship money and the Soroptimists added enough so I could take journalism and computer science classes at nearby Brown University. I'll always be grateful though I had no idea they had anything to do with human trafficking."

"I think they formed a local focus group about ten years back and ultimately joined forces with the San Diego North County Human Task Force when it was formed in August, 2010," Frank explained. "They're composed of a pretty impressive group of business and professional women; they certainly give volunteering a good name.

"Well, here we are," he said, as the car was waved into a parking lot on Main Street by a young woman wearing a sash emblazoned by the word 'Polaris.'

"You'll see a lot of those and other signs and banners supporting like-minded causes," he explained. "There's so much more to be done, but major inroads have been made, thanks to many, many people working directly or behind the scenes."

We had arrived at the Avo Playhouse where we became part of an estimated one hundred and fifty other women, men, and a few teens, gathered to show solidarity in the war against human trafficking.

As we entered and made our way to our seats, Frank exchanged waves with several of the participants, and briefly introduced me to a few. "You'll have a chance to meet people during the walk," he whispered, as the event organizer welcomed us and introduced the first speaker.

I *had* done my internet homework, but listening in person to representatives from the sheriff's task force, the North County Lifeline organization, and Generate Hope made the whole sordid subject so much more real. My resolve to become a part of the crusade was strengthened immeasurably. I was really looking forward to crafting those articles which would then hopefully inform and inspire—I would become a crusader! I laughed to myself. Who was it that said 'pride goeth before a fall'?

The speakers were all good—blending actual stories with statistics—each making the case that this problem of what one called modern slavery, is *everywhere,* and thus should be the concern of all decent people. Though ethnic gangs were major players in trafficking, we were cautioned not to stereotype. The perps came in all colors, ages, sizes, economic levels, and—to my surprise—both genders. I had a lot to learn.

The walk that followed reminded me of my participation in similar events for breast cancer—without the pink shirts. Both promoted awareness and honored those victimized by circumstances outside their control. Both held out an element of hope and the walkers in each were cheerful and friendly.

It was a near perfect, sunny, early winter, southern California day—low 60s with a gentle breeze. Dress in general was casual. I was glad that I had worn new jeans and a denim jacket.

Traffic was still allowed to flow and we kept to the sidewalks, but uniformed city policemen stood at the intersections guaranteeing us safe passage.

Horns honked in support and most of the spectators along the way waved and showed us thumbs up, though at one juncture a gaggle of young Hispanics, wearing low-slung pants and bandanas, shouted out what sounded like derogatory oaths, then dissolved into laughter. They took off when a policeman approached. I was reminded again that chances were good, that on these very streets, even behind the doors of some of these modest-looking stucco homes and motels, young people were being held against their will. Used in unspeakable ways—fearful for their lives and perhaps those of family members. Isolated, praying for their hell to be over.

I shuddered at my dismal thoughts and turned my gaze toward my fellow walkers. Frank was nowhere to be found. I soon fell in step with a forty-something, tall, broad-shouldered woman with a blonde ponytail. She was carrying a large placard dominated by a portrait of a striking, dark-haired young woman emblazoned with the words "Free Sara Kruzan."

I introduced myself, told her that I was new on the scene, about my newspaper assignment, and asked about the placard.

"Nice to meet you, Erin," the woman said, shaking my hand with her free one. "My name's Paula. I'm a social worker at Tri-City Medical Center in Oceanside. As to the poster, the short version is that in 1995, Sara was given a life sentence without the chance of parole for fatally shooting her pimp, the guy that lured her away as a pre-teen from an unbelievably sick home life and before long began battering and sexually abusing her. There's so much more, but we do know that she tried to take her own life on several occasions. Not that we are advocating vigilante justice, but if there was ever a case for considering all the circumstances, and then making something at last right, this is it."

I could see the pain in Paula's eyes as she spoke. "Please tell me there's some hope for her," I implored.

"Thankfully, there is," she went on. "In 2011, Arnold Schwarzenegger, who was governor then, commuted her sentence to twenty-five years to life *with* the possibility of parole. He cited that in rendering such a harsh decision the judge had failed to consider a provision which had been adopted for just such cases as hers.

"Sara has now been in prison for eighteen years. Since a local woman started a modest letter writing campaign in 2006, the movement to free her has gone international. Thanks to media coverage many Hollywood celebrities, and even Governor Brown, have signed petitions and taken part in campaigns supporting her release. Most encouraging is that when Sara comes up for her next parole hearing the attorney general has agreed not to oppose her release. Best scenario is that she could then be credited with time served and released. If that happens think how much help she could be to other young victims and as a particularly powerful  advocate in the fight..."

"Well, let's hope, but what a tragic story. That's awful!" I exclaimed. "From what I've read, it seems that in too many cases, the traffickers can do almost anything to the victims—often with impunity—but if the victims try to physically retaliate they are jailed? What a system!" So much for a reporter's objectivity. I was livid.

"You got it. But look. In general all is not gloom and doom. On the encouraging side you heard today about Generate Hope and their new Safe Housing and Learning Center. That took a grand vision and many months of planning and hard work from a lot of people. Now, at least, a few victims are on the road to recovery, with plans to welcome many more into what could be a long-term recovery program."

"What a wonderful accomplishment," I said, "but I got so worked up when I heard some of the victim's personal stories it was hard to concentrate on the good news. Apparently things are improving as to the rate of arrests, convictions, and longer sentences being handed down. By the way do you get directly involved because of your hospital work?"

"In a way, yes," she answered, "but look, we're almost back. How about I buy you a cup of coffee after the walk breaks up? I sense I've found a kindred spirit."

"Boy, I'd love to, but I drove in with someone. How about a rain check for some time later?"

Just then Frank walked up to us. "Hi, Paula. I see you've met my latest recruit."

Paula handed me the placard and gave the copy editor a big collegial hug. "Why didn't you tell me that Frank was your ride? We go way back." Then, with a smile at me, she said to Frank, "I think you really picked a winner this time. I invited her to coffee. Of course you'd be more than welcome to join us if you can stay awhile."

"Maybe next time I'm up this way," Frank replied. "'Since Audrey died I've had Sunday suppers with her brother's family. The nephews still think I have all the answers where sports are concerned."

"Understood. And speaking of Audrey, we still miss her a lot. You doing alright?" Paula asked, with obvious genuine concern.

"Some days it's still just a matter of keeping on keeping on, but in general it's getting better. I've got my work, good friends, and Roscoe, so I can't complain. But thanks for asking. Say hi to Phil for me."

"Will do, and have a safe trip back to the big city, you two. And Erin, please give me a call soon."


"Kind of a rollercoaster day for you, I would imagine," Frank remarked as he pulled the car into traffic heading south. "At least it was for me when I first got involved."

I leaned back against the seat, feeling drained, and not just from the short walk. "How does one go back to leading an ordinary, even privileged life, after hearing the awful truth about what's going on right around us? My head is spinning and I'm questioning the direction my life is taking, Frank." Of course, I was thinking of my relationship with Mike.

"Was Audrey comfortable with your activism?" Frank's wife had died a year or so ago from pancreatic cancer. "Please forgive me if that's an insensitive question," I added.

"Not at all, though I can't promise you I won't tear up a little.

Actually it was her idea in the first place. We couldn't have kids of our own but between us we managed to become involved with young people on a regular basis: tutoring, sports, Boys & Girls Club mentoring—you name it."

The traffic had picked up considerably. An impatient driver in a red Porsche made a dangerous maneuver around us though we were going a few miles over the posted speed limit.

"Idiot!" I proclaimed, angrily. "Perhaps we should postpone this talk what with so many dingbats on the road."

"Relax, Erin. I'm fine. Slow and steady wins the race is my motto, not that this was always the case," he added. "Now where was I? Ah, yes. Of course you couldn't help but get close to some of these kids. Well, one day we noticed one of our favorites, a shy eleven-or twelve-year old, crying while she helped some of the younger children work on a poster. It seems her fourteen-year old brother had run away three days previously, after what she described as a terrible row with her mother's boyfriend, and no one had heard from him since. Could we help?"

We had turned off the interstate onto La Jolla Village Drive. "Could you? Did you?" I asked. As usual, I was hoping it came out well, but Frank's expression told me otherwise.

"We did our best, but to no avail. What we did find out from the authorities was that he had probably been duped into trusting someone friendly who turned out to be a pimp and he is now lost in the swamp of human trafficking," he explained, his voice trailing off at what was obviously still a painful memory. Then forcefully he stated, "We became advocates in the movement from then on."

"Yet look how much good came out of it," I offered in all sincerity. "I already feel a strong connection to the movement but I also know that Mike has serious misgivings. I'm really torn."

"You'll work it out. Trust your instincts; just don't be too hard on Mike. You still need both balance and love in your life or you will burn out before you even start. Well, I better get home to feed and walk Roscoe before I head over to the in-laws," Frank added, as came around and opened the passenger door for me. "See you at the paper."

The antique-looking streetlights began to turn on as I let myself into the townhouse. Somewhere in the neighborhood a dog barked, but otherwise there was an almost eerie silence, inside as well as out. Maybe we *should* get a dog or a cat as Mike had suggested—something warm and fuzzy and totally non-judgmental.

Mike wasn't at home. He and a couple of his golfing buddies had planned to play eighteen holes at the La Costa golf course in Carlsbad, a favorite since his days playing for USC.

Truth be told I was grateful that he wasn't home. There would be no need to give him an accounting of my day—at least not for the time being. I needed time to process all that I had seen and heard earlier and to give some serious thought as to what my involvement in the movement might lead to in the future.

While I heated up some leftover lasagna I checked the large calendar erase board which hung on the wall in the small kitchen alcove above my desktop PC. Much of its surface was covered by reminders from the wedding planner as to appointments with the florist, caterers, and photographers.

Crossing to the giant freshwater fish tank that formed a partial separation between the kitchen and formal dining room, I looked at the vividly-colored Boamani Rainbows and Blue Neons and mused aloud, "What do you think? Why can't I be more excited about the big day? Am I just suffering the proverbial pre-wedding cold feet, or is it something more serious?" Of course, the fish ignored me. You just swim around, look beautiful, and let someone else feed you and clean the tank—what an uncomplicated life, I thought almost enviously.

But, back to reality. A generous helping of the still-tasty lasagna and a glass of Merlot gave me a boost. Perhaps changes to the wedding plans were getting out of hand. It was high time I gave them my full attention. Maybe we were even rushing our relationship in general. We needed to slow down and give this more thought and I owed it to Mike to be more honest about my misgivings.

In addition, I felt that he was getting pressure from some of the Morgan Stanley VIPs to settle down. Family men are always preferred in the conservative world of high finance. I took another healthy swallow of the Merlot. I was also sure that he loved me, wanted to give me the moon, as he would say, and yet . . . just then the phone rang.

"Hi, honey. Just wanted to let you know that I'll be a little longer, if that's alright with you. Chet invited a few of us over to his place to wind down. You don't mind, do you? Oh, and I made a few good shots at the right time too, which translates into bucks to go in our honeymoon fund," he added, proudly.

"Congratulations. Say hello to the guys for me," I answered, almost mechanically.

"Will do, got to go. Chet's calling. Don't wait up, but here's a big kiss to keep you warm."

Mike was in his element, and I didn't begrudge him any of it, but how about at least a brief inquiry as to *my* day? Sometimes I thought our relationship was too one- sided.

My day . . . my glass of wine finished, I made myself a cup of herbal tea and took it up to our bedroom. I will *not* read any more trafficking material, I vowed. Instead I picked up the latest Nicholas Sparks novel. It might be purple prose, as some critics claimed, but at least it would have a happy ending.

# 4

*Several more days go by. Serena is starting to lose track of time. She worries about her big sister. Back at the other place Nestor had reassured her that Carla was doing fine, and that one day the two sisters would be together again, but who could trust someone who was responsible for sending her to a place like this?*

*Suddenly it came to her that Carla might have gone back to Campo looking for her. Surely grandmother would be back from the hospital by now and they could all get back to their normal lives. She must find a way to get a message to her house so they could come and get her.*

*Alicia might know how to do that. Although only thirteen, she had been moved four times in the two years since Dion convinced her father that his third-oldest daughter would have a better life in the United States. Alicia likes to brag that she is wise in the ways of the world. Perhaps she can help.*

*Later, when they are alone, the older girl ponders Serena's dilemma. "I have an idea," she whispers. "There's no way that you could smuggle a letter out to your family but maybe I can. Once a month or so, Dion lets me send a letter or card to my home, and every so often I get one back. Keeps everyone happy, he says. I have paper, envelopes, and stamps in my box."*

*Serena is not surprised. Alicia's large wooden box is full of practical items and treasured keepsakes.*

*She looks at the older girl expectantly—encouraged by what she's hearing.*

*Alicia goes on, "Write your note and make out the envelope. You do remember your Campo address?" Serena nods. "And be sure to put in a card from the motel where they take us."*

*Serena's spirit sinks again. "I don't even know the name and how would I get a card and then . . ." Her voice trails off and she lowers her eyes.*

*"Leave it to me and have faith. It will all work out. But try to be patient. Now give me a hug."*

*A few days later Dion approaches Alicia when the other two girls are out. "You'll be getting a new girl before the end of the week, so if you want to swap beds, do it now."*

*"How are we supposed to fit another person in here? We practically step on each other as it is." Alicia points out.*

*"Well, not that it's any of your business, but someone wants to give your little pet, Serena, a nice new home with him and some of his friends.*

*"Well, don't look so shocked. I've always warned you about getting too close. This is a business. How about I get you a real nice dress out of some of my profit? And then you could model it for me. Would that put a smile on that pretty face of yours?"*

*Dion's big hands are caressing Alicia's face as he speaks. Her heart is pounding, but she forces herself to smile up at him. "I'd like that," she answers.*

*When he has gone the girl realizes that she must act as quickly as possible if Serena is to get out. Alicia has been over and over her plan. As far as she has been able to tell so far about her own situation there is no chance she can escape the life that had been thrust upon her by her parents. She belongs to Dion who keeps her mostly for himself, loaning her out very judiciously. It isn't so bad and where would she go anyhow? But Serena is different. She has family who loves her.*

*With Serena's letter safe in her pocket she approaches Dion the next day when he comes to take Tara to the nearby* Budget Motel. *She knows he often stops at a nearby café before returning* to pick up the girls. In fact, he has taken her with him on more than one occasion.

"I want to mail a birthday card to my brother. How about letting me go with you to the café and I can drop it off on the way?" she asks, trying not to show her nervousness.

Dion frowns. "Didn't your brother just have a birthday a few months ago? There are too many kids in your family. I suppose this card is for a different one. Just send the one, and let them all share it, is my advice."

"You promised I could keep in touch," she says, fighting to keep her voice steady. "Besides this card is for little Pedro. He never gets anything of his own. But I still need to add a note to it. I can do that while you take Tara to the motel." Then she takes a step closer to her captor and says in the coquettish voice she knows he likes, "You will come back for me, won't you, please? I really need some fresh air and something sweet to drink."

Dion hesitates. "Are you finished in there?" he calls out to Tara who has been in the alcove dressing up to go to the motel. Then to Alicia, under his breath, "You win. I'll be back for you, but you'll owe me." He leers at her and pats her suggestively.

Truth be told, he liked showing off the beautiful young girl at the Armenian Café. He pretended to be her father and, if anyone suspected anything, they kept it to themselves. Most people in this rundown area of the city believed strongly in live and let live. His was not the only secret life in the area.


With the first part of her plan accomplished, it was time to put the second, much more risky, aspect in place. Alicia had told Serena very little, so as not to frighten her unnecessarily, but now it was time to act. Alicia had been in the same location for almost a year and so, more out of curiosity than anything else, she had explored their improvised living space and found that the back wall in the alcove was very flimsy. It hadn't taken much to pry the few sheets *of plywood apart enough to allow a slim body to wriggle through. Having done so, she had been able to walk through a basement storage area belonging to the commercial laundry which occupied the upper floors.*

*As time went on she grew bolder and found ways to spy on the actual workers and learn their habits and the layout of the plant. It became a game to her—dangerous, of course, but she began to fancy herself a detective like the ones in the comics her older brothers used to read.*

*That night after Tara had fallen asleep, Alicia, with flashlight in hand, takes Serena into the alcove, shows her the loose boards, and outlines the plan for the escape.*

*"I wish you were going too," Serena says, wistfully. "I know you can't go to your house, but you could come with me. We have room."*

*"That's sweet, but I'll be all right. Besides, who would welcome the new girls? I don't think Tara would be very good at that, do you?"*

*Serena has to smile. "But how come you have to live down here like this? Why don't you live with Dion?"*

*"Because of Marcella, his woman. She lives with him and she hates me," Alicia answers, matter-of-factly. "Sometimes to get her mad he tells her she is getting to be too old for him. He spends most of his money on her and his big car and his gambling.*

*"But there's a little left over for me," she adds, "so it's really not that bad a life. You don't know what it was like for me back home with too many people and too little money and . . ." Her voice drifts off. "Now you must try to get some sleep," she admonishes the younger girl. "You have a very busy day tomorrow."*

*But Serena lays wide awake—worrying, mostly. Alicia has told her to look at tomorrow as an adventure that will take her back, not only to her family, but to her school and her teacher, as well as the classmates she misses so much.*

*Sleep eventually does come—followed by morning, and then the usual dreary hours of another dreaded day—except that this one is to be life-changing, as Alicia calls it. It's time to follow through with their daring plan.*

*So far all is going well. Dion has gone off on business and left Tony, his raspy-voiced assistant, in charge. In mid-afternoon when he comes down the stairs to get the girls for their ride to the motel, Alicia tells him that Serena has been vomiting all morning and must, therefore, stay away from others. He goes to check the alcove and finds Serena bending over the basin, remnants of lunch clinging to her mouth and chin, hair matted, eyes red and watery. "Dion will have my head!" Tony curses. "Can't you clean her up?" he practically begs Alicia.*

*Alicia shakes her head as Serena moans and sinks down on her mattress. "What if she's contagious and passes it on to Mr. Smith? Then you'd really be in trouble!"*


*Making herself vomit had been difficult, and she really did feel a little sick, but Serena quickly puts that behind her and gets ready to make her move to escape. Alicia had given her some money, and, of most importance, a hand-drawn map showing the nearest police station.*

*She dresses quickly, puts the money and map in her jacket pocket, and goes into the alcove. The smell makes her gag, but she forces herself to concentrate on the task at hand. She pries the plywood panels apart, slips through—replaces them as best she can. Alicia has assured her that she will be able to put the wood back properly again that night. Serena fights back tears as she thinks of the older girl—her friend and protector.*

*Following Alicia's careful instructions she creeps to where she can see the factory workers and, when the whistle blows to announce a shift change, she joins the   few dozen leaving the building. As predicted many of them look to be from Mexico—several of* the women as short as she. No one pays her any attention. Most of them seem headed to a nearby municipal bus stop and she follows them there, then continues down the hill.

*You can do it, Serena tells herself.* At first she recognizes a few familiar sights, glimpsed on rides to the motel, but soon Alicia's map leads her into unfamiliar territory. Graffiti covers several abandoned buildings and broken glass and other debris litter empty lots. Another turn—wrong apparently—and she's hopelessly lost. And then a breeze blows the paper out of her hand as she turns a corner. "Oh, no!" She groans aloud.

She freezes as a familiar voice asks, "Were you looking for this, Serena?"

# 5

"Good stuff, Erin," Malcolm, my editor at *The County Voice,* said of my first few human trafficking articles. "There's been a lot of positive feedback from readers."

I now considered myself reasonably well informed, having attended a regional human trafficking conference, written some press releases, and lobbied my state representative. But I also knew I had a long way to go before I could be a truly effective spokesperson for the cause. I needed actual interaction with a victim in order to make the story more compelling for the public. Or was it something more personal? The victims own stories haunted me. I wanted, no, needed, to do something more—but what?

The answer came next day when I got a phone call from Paula, the social worker at the Tri-City Medical Center.

"Sorry to have let so much time go by before following up on our meeting in Vista, but things have been extra hectic at work lately," she explained. "But here's why I called today. When I came in to work this morning a nurse friend of mine expressed concern about a young patient who was brought into the emergency room over the weekend with appendicitis. Apparently the girl had been experiencing pain, vomiting, and running a fever for several days, so by the time she was brought in her appendix had burst. She was one sick young woman. They did an emergency laparoscopy, and she's now on a heavy antibiotic regimen."

"Poor thing. Will she be all right?" I asked.

"For now, while she's in the hospital, at least," Paula answered, "but after she leaves, I'm not so sure, and that's why I'm calling you. There's something fishy about the situation. Granted it was night and as usual they were swamped in the ER but Admitting was able to get almost no information from the guy who brought her in. I agreed to see what I could find out about the situation."

"And did you?" I interjected, when she paused.

"Well, not definitively. I talked to the patient and her so-called brother about insurance, aftercare, a possible follow-up appointment—my usual protocol. The guy was vague, at best, and bristled when I tried to include the patient. She deferred totally to him."

"So you suspect he's her pimp? Did you get a chance to speak to her alone?"

"I did briefly when he went outside to smoke, but I couldn't get through to her. She could be an illegal and afraid of deportation—the guy said she was eighteen but I doubt that very much. Anyhow I thought that you might have a better chance at getting at the truth. You're younger, and from what you told me while we were walking together, you had been through a lot yourself, in the past. What do you say?"

"I'd be glad to give it a try," I answered, thinking ahead to my schedule for the next couple of days. "But out of curiosity, why didn't you go to the police with your suspicions?"

"At this point no crime has been committed and she probably won't talk to the police anyway, so their hands would be tied. Few girls will talk to authorities—the gangs rule by intimidation. These young victims don't trust the police who too often treat them as prostitutes and thus criminals. The gangs have highly paid lawyers and the girls don't have much clout. But if you could get her to confirm our suspicions, and agree to talk to someone, we might really be able to make a meaningful intervention."

"I get the picture. How long will the hospital be able to keep her? And how can I get a chance to speak with her in private?"

"Well, the staff has her walking around already, but because hers was a medical emergency, I would guess that she should be here another two or three days. And we'll find a way to let you have time alone. Thanks, Erin. This may be the chance you wanted to become more involved with the trafficking issue."


During dinner that night Mike had spoken enthusiastically about a successful luncheon meeting which had ended with the signing of two new investors.

As we carried our dishes into the kitchen he remarked, "Speaking of lunch, why don't you meet me in town tomorrow about noon—my treat. You need a break. You've been working too hard with your regular hours for the newspaper, and now the special assignments, plus helping out at the bookstore."

He began to massage my shoulders. "See how tense you are?" he said, as I relaxed against him and let his strong hands work their magic.

After my talk with Frank about the need for balance in one's life, I had made a conscious effort to see our situation more from Mike's perspective. I was well aware of a tendency to go off the deep end when it came to my convictions.

For his part Mike agreed to rethink what I called our out-of-control wedding plans and, while he was still uneasy about my new involvement, he recognized its importance to me. Life in general was good—and our love-making was better than ever.

With that in mind, I said, "I'd love to do lunch, but I have to run up to Oceanside in the morning for a meeting. If I won't be able to get back in time, can we postpone lunch until later in the week?"

"Sure," he said. "I just asked you on impulse. Now let's see if we can find a decent movie which will end before my bedtime."

* * *

Next morning I met Paula in her office. "The girl is sleeping. The guy went to the cafeteria a few minutes ago. He wants to hang around her room much more than would seem normal. The nurse told him her patient needs rest so he should take his time. This may be our only chance because Admitting is pushing to get someone else in the other bed."

Paula opened the door to room 2003 and called softly, "Carla, the lady I spoke to you about is here."  Then to me, "Good luck. I've got to get back to work. Let me know what happens."

The girl was curled up in a fetal position, facing the wall. I pulled a chair up to the bed. "Carla, my name is Erin.  I realize you don't know me, but I'm here to help."

No response. Perhaps Carla wasn't even her real name. I continued by saying, "I don't know how long we'll have alone, so I'm just going to tell you a little about myself, and hope you will then decide to trust me."

I spoke for several minutes mostly about my growing-up years in Rhode Island and the sadness and pain of my experiences in foster care. She eventually turned toward me, but still didn't speak. When I shared that I had twice been molested— once by my foster father and the second time by a neighbor—I finally got her attention.

"Each man threatened to hurt me and get me thrown out if I told anyone so I didn't report them. I was young, and I *was* naturally afraid, but I found out later that they went on to molest the younger girls. I should have done more. I have never forgiven myself." This was not said for effect—this was a truth. I still live with my regret to this day.

Perhaps my honesty finally got through to her because she gave a little sob and tears streamed down her face.

"It's alright, honey, you can tell me." I said, instinctively reaching my arms out to her. "We suspect that the man who brought you here isn't your brother and probably is a gang member who is forcing you to work for them out of fear." Carla was nodding as I spoke. "Please let us help you," I continued. "What if I contacted the police and you were taken somewhere safe? Your supposed brother and the other gang members don't care about you. They only care that you make money for them. Am I right?"

At my mention of the police, Carla became very agitated and then said in a shaky voice, "No police, no police, Erin! They have my little sister, Serena, somewhere. I haven't seen her since we were together in Campo weeks ago—we grew up there. They promised she would be safe if I would—if I would just—do as they asked. If I didn't, I would never see her again." Her voice trailed off.

Suddenly there was noise out in the corridor. We both froze. How would her pimp react if he found her talking with a stranger? Fortunately the voices went on by. But it was obvious that it wasn't safe for either of us if I stayed.

"I can't talk to you anymore. Please go." Carla pleaded.

"I'm going, but I'll be back," I said. "We'll work this out, I promise. Your clothes are in a bag in the bottom of your bedside stand. While you were asleep I put a card I use at my job at *The County Voice* paper in the back pocket of your jeans. If somehow we lose contact, you can call me anytime, and leave a message at that number."

Before I could say more, an aide came in to help Carla walk around the corridors. While she got her ready I slipped out of the room—just in time apparently, because a tough-looking young Hispanic male, oversized pants showing a few inches of his boxers, came swaggering up the hall. We briefly made eye contact.

If only I had had more time with Carla. Perhaps I could have persuaded her to reveal enough about her situation to be able to involve the task force police. There had to be a way. By tomorrow I should have at least a tentative plan in place. I had *promised* her my help.

\*   \*   \*

It was half-time. The Lakers were hosting the Utah Jazz. We were watching the game together and, out of deference to me, Mike had turned down the sound. I had little tolerance for the constant analysis that seemed to so enthrall men. After all it was TV!

In any case my mind was on the events earlier in the day. I realized he had asked me a question. "I'm sorry, what did you say, honey?"

"I asked about your meeting," Mike said, looking at me quizzically. "You seem very distracted. Anything I can do to help?"

It was tempting to fill him in but I knew he wouldn't approve of my getting personally involved. "It needs some follow-up," was all that I said.

Next morning I could hardly wait to get on the road. I forced myself to stay in the moment. Morning commuter traffic northbound on the I-5 allowed no time for daydreaming.

About ten miles from the hospital my dashboard-mounted cellphone rang. As soon as I answered, Paula's anguished voice came through loud and clear. "She's gone, Erin. Apparently someone smuggled her out before the shift change this morning. I'll let you know when and if I get more of the details, but for now there's no need of you coming here. Hope you didn't get too far."

I pulled off at the next exit and found a McDonald's. I considered my options while drinking my second coffee of the morning. Since I was already in the vicinity, I decided to pay a visit to the sheriff's North County Human Trafficking Task Force. Maybe what little information Carla gave me plus my description of one of her captors might prove enough to get them interested in her case.

The regional human trafficking substation in Vista is housed in an unimpressive-looking building adjacent to the Superior Courthouse. It also includes a few holding cells for persons awaiting trial. I parked and, after going through the metal detector and showing my press credentials, asked if it would be possible to speak with Joe Cruz. He was the deputy who had spoken at the Human Trafficking Collaborative meeting I had attended with Frank some weeks ago.

Since I had no appointment I expected that I might have a considerable wait, but before I even had a chance to take out the material from Shared Hope International I had with me in a folder, the deputy appeared and ushered me into his office.

As I had noted before, he and Mike appeared to be about the same age and bore a strong resemblance, though he was a bigger man and appeared to be more muscular—at least in his khaki uniform.

He gestured for me to take a seat and offered to get me a cup of coffee. "Though I can't recommend it," he said, leaning back in a large, black swivel chair behind his paper-covered desk. "What can I do for you?"

There was something very disconcerting about the way he was looking at me. "Thank you for seeing me," I began. "You don't know who I am, but I heard you speak at the Avo Theatre awhile back and something has happened . . ."

He cut me off. "But I *do* know who you are, Ms. Butler. You and I have something in common. You are engaged to Miguel—excuse me—Michael Medina, and he and I grew up in the same neighborhood."

I was flustered. "But how did you know that we were engaged?"

"I always read the society columns in the San Diego *Union Tribune* first," he said, with only a hint of mockery.

I guess I expected this to be said in jest but I saw something quite different in his eyes. "I don't think Michael has mentioned knowing you but then he doesn't get up this way very often."

"'I'm sure not, but then I wouldn't blame him, coming from *his* background. 'Local Boy Makes Good in a Big Way' was one headline I remember from his USC days and he's never looked back. Now it's more apt to be Michael Medina of La Jolla and his glamorous fiancé attend a black tie event with other movers and shakers at one important venue or another."

"That's not fair," I blurted out. "He also gives scholarship money to disadvantaged kids and started a day-of-giving-back from employees of Morgan Stanley—"

"Sorry, I was out of line, and I should not have said that," he said, very abruptly. "That stuff about your fiancé got too personal. Seeing you just reminded me as to how different our lives have played out since Mike and I lived in one of Oceanside's barrios, a little envy on my part, maybe." A hint of a smile appeared briefly on his face. "After all, back then I was known as Jose Cruz, now it's just Joe Cruz."

Then he was all business again. "So what is it you wanted to speak with me about? I don't mean to be rude, but I have a very full day coming up."

What a difficult man, I was thinking, but this was not about me, so I forced myself to relate calmly and concisely the events of the past two days.

When I was finished, he said, "Now let me get this straight. You're asking us to find the pimps, rescue the girl, and hopefully get her to testify based on the sketchy information you've given us? Do you see all those pictures on the bulletin board on that wall? And that's just a fraction of our active cases."

Obviously he thought I was being incredibly naïve, but in any case, we were getting nowhere. How frustrating it all seemed; I didn't need this. I stood up and pushed back my chair. "Thank you for your time," I said, and started to walk away.

"Sit down," he said. "Please. We're on the same side. My department will do what we can. I'll have you look at some of our gang mug shots. Maybe we'll get lucky. But here, let me show you, this is just a partial list of known gangs in Southern California, so you can see what we're up against."

Amazing! It was overwhelming. No wonder it seemed that the bad guys were winning, though the passage of California's Prop 35 in 2012 which had increased penalties for human trafficking and the more recent federal anti-human trafficking legislation were promising. Still, it reminded me of the story of the little Dutch boy who stuck his finger in a hole in the dike. Could anything I do make a difference at all?


"Don't take it so hard," Deputy Cruz offered when I was unable to identify Carla's abductor from the mug shots. "It was a long shot. But we have contacts and we'll ask around—maybe get lucky. But, for you as a newcomer, I have a little advice before you go. Try not to get too emotionally involved with the victims, and be very careful when gang members are still actively involved, as they appear to be in this case. And, on a more personal note, how's Mike feeling about all this?"

"I'm tougher then you think, deputy, not some starry-eyed do-gooder socialite. But I will take your advice seriously. As to my fiancé, as you may have guessed, while he supports me he is also quite concerned for my safety.

"Thank you for your time," I said, as I stood up again to leave, and I won't forget that we *are* on the same side—and I *do* appreciate all that your task force is doing!"


Ten minutes later I was still sitting in my car in the parking lot, thinking over the unsettling talk with the deputy, but not able to get Carla out of my mind, either. I owed it to Carla to try and intercede in her and her sister's situation. There had to be a reason we had met. Just then my cellphone rang.

"Hi, honey. Am I interrupting anything?" Mike asked.

"No, what's up?

"Well, I know this is sudden, but how about us going skiing up to Mammoth for a few days, leaving the day after tomorrow? Chet and his girlfriend were going with two other couples when one had to back out because of a sick baby or something. It was a package deal with most everything pre-paid and mostly non-refundable, so we would be doing them a favor by taking over the payments. Anyhow, conditions are still perfect, and there's a winter carnival going on. Should be fun. What do you say?"

"Mike, I'm really sorry, but I can't. I'm covering two events for the paper and working at the bookstore Thursday. Maybe if I'd known ahead . . . but you've only gone skiing twice all season. Go and have a good time. You know I'm still at the novice stage. This way you will be able to ski all the black diamond trails with the others without feeling you're neglecting me."

"Well if you're sure . . . see you tonight then," he said, with obvious regret in his voice "Let's treat ourselves to ordering a pizza and eat in."

"Sounds good to me, I'm hungry already," I quickly agreed.

Later, I had trouble falling asleep, and I couldn't blame it on the pizza. Just before dawn it came to me. Mike's ski trip would give me the chance to put a plan into place—a plan that would include exploring the border town of Campo.

# 6

*Serena doesn't know whether it is the smell or the pain that first forces her to open her eyes. When she does, it is to see a strange, gray-haired man, kneeling over her applying some kind of ointment to her legs. She feels nauseous and her throat burns.*

*Gradually, as the haze clear from her eyes, she recognizes the basement hide-a-way.*

*"Don't try to get up, girlie," she hears the man caution her, then, "You shouldn't have beaten her so bad, Dion. Looks like you almost killed her."*

*"Shut up, and just fix her, you old quack!" Serena recognizes that hated voice and the events of the past few hours flood back and with them a wave of acute hopelessness.*

*What time is it? What day even? Where are the other girls? All she knows for sure is that she had never made it to the police station. And that Dion had grabbed and almost choked her after she bit him while she struggled to get away.*

*"You ungrateful little bitch," she remembers him saying. "After all I've done for you. You had a chance to go to a nice home with Mr. Smith—just do a few chores around the house and make him feel good.*

*Or did he just say them? She remembers him taking off his belt and then his ugly laugh—and then pain like she'd never felt before. She recalls trying to get away from the blows, but then falling or being pushed down, and then she felt his boots kicking her sides and her back.*

\* \* \*

*The other man was speaking again. "Her ribs will probably heal all right—young ribs are flexible—but I don't know how much damage you might have done to her kidneys. She did vomit, and you said there was blood in her urine, bad signs."*

*"Did I ask you to play doctor?" she hears Dion's voice coming from somewhere above her. "Just give her some antibiotics and painkillers. Fix her up enough to get her to San Francisco. Let them worry about it up there."*

*What did they mean? Who were "they" and why is she being sent to San Francisco, wherever that was? All she wants to do is curl up in a ball and try to make the pain stop. One minute she feels hot, then cold. She tries to be brave, for Carla, for her grandmother, for Alicia. Alicia—where was she? She begins to whimper and call out her name.*

*At that Dion drops down to his knees and looks her in the face. She notices that his right hand is bandaged. Was that where she had bitten him? She hopes his fingers will fall off!*

*"I was going to whip Alicia too. I know she helped you to escape. But I changed my mind. She's my special one. Watching me pay you back showed what would happen to her if she ever tried that again. I think she cried almost as hard as you did. Anyway, you'll never see her again. But don't worry. Pretty soon you'll have a chance to make new friends."*

*Serena didn't want to make new friends. She just wanted to go home.*

*The other man begins speaking again. "I'll give her a strong dose of the antibiotic in a shot to start her off. Then here's the bottle with a week's worth of follow-up pills. Also, give her one oxy tonight for pain, and I'd suggest two more tomorrow for pain and to knock her out for the trip."*

# 7

It was still dark when Mike came into the kitchen the next morning. "You didn't have to get up. I tried not to wake you," he said. "Is that coffee I smell?"

"I put the timer on last night," I explained, as I filled his travel mug, "and here are some roast beef sandwiches and chips to take with you."

"Thanks, you're the best," he said, as we saw the reflection of a car's headlights pulling into our driveway. "That must be Chet. Wish you were going with us."

"Next time," I promised. "Remember, absence makes the heart grow fonder, and here's a kiss to remember me by."

I'm not sure who pulled away first, but Mike smiled and said, "If that kiss lasted any longer I might have canceled the trip!"

I hadn't exactly lied to Mike when I used my work schedule as an excuse for not taking part in the ski trip—I did have obligations but I got someone else to cover the city council meeting and swapped the bookstore shift coverage—but I still felt less than good about my subterfuge. Yet how could I involve anyone else, when I had only the sketchiest plan for finding Carla, let alone helping her and her sister escape their captors?

When I let my imagination soar, I imagined Mike and me becoming a modern-day, crime-fighting duo—against human traffickers, of course. For now, I intended to take what little information I had, check it out, and ultimately present it to the criminal authorities for follow-up. I was more convinced than ever, that as far as the tragic young victims were concerned, the danger in my doing nothing outweighed all else. I would not let them down—I had crossed a line and could not go back.

That was my mind-set as I headed south and an hour or so later turned off the I-5 onto state road 94 heading southeast to the border town of Campo and a stop at their local police station. A Google search listed the town's current population at approximately 2,700—large employers included the US Department of Homeland Security Border Patrol and the San Diego County, California Probation, Juvenile Ranch Facility.

Carla grew up here in this poor desert area of scrub pines and tumbleweed—so far removed from the lush, heavily irrigated scenes, or ocean vistas, of the surrounding county area which shared the 619 zip code.

Thanks to my GPS I easily found the local sub-station. I had also learned that there was a citizen advisory group which was tasked with working closely with the authorities in matters affecting the community. I was encouraged as I approached the desk in the reception area. A strikingly attractive Hispanic woman, who looked to be in her mid-thirties, asked if she could help me.

"I'm here about a missing persons matter," I answered.

"Take a seat," she said, then dialed an internal number. After speaking quietly into her handset, she turned back to me, and said, "Someone will be out shortly."

Disembodied voices crackled through some hidden sound system, some eliciting a response from the woman. A couple of policemen came in, disappeared in back, and then went out again. I studied ads for local civic events, what appeared to be wanted posters, and also    pretended interest in brochures for the Southwest Railway Museum and the Gaskill Brothers Stone Store. After about fifteen minutes a sheriff's deputy appeared and headed straight for me.

"Morning. Guess you've met our dispatcher, Lorena. I'm Ed

Wicker."

Ed was probably in his early fifties, though his paunch and weathered face made him look older. "What can I do for you?" he asked, extending his hand and shaking mine vigorously.

"I think I may have recently seen a young girl in the North County who is from Campo and was perhaps reported missing a few months ago. She said her name is Carla and I think she's about fifteen. She also mentioned a younger sister named Serena." I explained the circumstances of our meeting in the hospital in Oceanside. "I'm certain that a pimp was involved," I concluded.

He had listened intently. "'Do you have a picture—an address—anything more for us to go on? We cover Potrero, Tecate, and Dulzura too. As you can see it's kind of desolate out here and it's hard to make a decent living. Not that much to offer the young people. All of the above adding up to more than a fair number of runaways.

"But, as you have guessed, it's quite possible that a pimp was in the mix. Sadly, as a border town, we have more than our share of human trafficking. Selling people is a *huge* money-making industry—estimated to be well over forty billion dollars annually worldwide. Unfortunately, too many people are still unaware of the magnitude of the problem, and that this county has been designated as one of the worst areas in the country." He shook his head.

"Too many people, besides being unaware, are too afraid to speak up, or even disinterested. But if you've come all the way down from the North County I'm guessing you don't fit into any of those categories."

By now our conversation had drawn the attention of the woman dispatcher and a second deputy as well. "Could the children she named be related to the Mrs. Flores who lives near the Railway Museum?" one of the women asked. "Seems I heard she had a stroke awhile back and was in a nursing home. If that no-good son of hers was left in charge who knows what might have happened to those kids."

"Could be," Ed said. "I don't remember anyone actually reporting them missing, though someone at the school might have noticed."

"And I think CPS was involved awhile back." the dispatcher added.

"And just how are you involved?" the deputy asked me. "You don't look like a private investigator," he said, with a chuckle.

"No, but I *am* involved with a county consortium against human trafficking." I also showed them my newspaper credentials. "I'm hoping we can help each other," I added.

He looked doubtful, but then suggested, "If you're willing to wait around awhile, Lorena will make a few calls when she gets a chance—see what she can find out. Why don't you come back in about an hour or so?"


"My hunch was right," Lorena said later, ushering me into a back room. "Hope you don't mind but I'm on my lunch break," she explained, as she heated up a burrito in the microwave. "I'm afraid we can't offer you anything except vending machine junk, and coffee, of course."

"I'm fine," I assured her, "but please go on."

"Well, I checked with the school and found out that neither Carla nor Serena Flores had been in class for several weeks. There had been a few attempts made to check on them, but it seems that they had a long history of sporadic attendance, so they kind of fell through the cracks. Pretty much what I was told by the welfare worker as well," she added.

"Fell through the cracks"—there was that phrase again. I had come to feel that pretty much summed up the lives of too many of those young victims. The reasons were diverse, and not all the people involved were evil—in fact many were well meaning—but it happened all too often. I owed it to Carla and Serena to check into this further.

"I can tell that you're not very happy with my assessment. You look as if you'd like to throw something, or perhaps punch someone out," she observed.

'You got me," I agreed, with a smile. "Patience is not my strong suit, and I do have a temper, but I'm working on it."

"Sisters of a different color.   Look, I have some time left in my lunch break. As I said, I made a few calls. Mrs. Flores *is* back in her home and said she would welcome a visit from you. I know you can't tell her much but at least she would know that the girls are probably alive. I'm sure she's been frantic. We'll take my car.   Yours will be safe here but, in general, I would be very careful where you leave it," she warned.

If only I had my old Volvo, I thought, not for the first time. My BMW just garnered too much unwanted attention.

"Let me give you a quick briefing on the Flores family," Lorena began, as we drove the few miles to the grandmother's house. "It certainly hasn't been easy for the woman. Apparently her husband abandoned the family early on—probably was an illegal, following the crops, and one time never returned. Anyhow, she brought up a son and daughter on her own. The daughter—Carla's mother—got into drugs and fatally overdosed when the girls were young. Their father is in prison for killing a man. Get the picture?"

"All too well," I said with a sigh. "Anything else I should know?"

"Just expect her to be less than honest when it comes to anything regarding her son, Mateo, the uncle of the two girls. He still sponges off his mother, even though he's on some kind of disability pension. As far as we can tell he spends most of his time and money gambling and doing drugs. Who knows where he is right now."

"How is the grandmother getting by since they released her

from the nursing home?"

"Well, I know that the people from her parish look in on her, and she has a few neighbors. They take care of each other, but they also cover up for their own. That's understandable, but it also makes our job harder," she explained, then added, "To answer your question further, social services and visiting nurses are also involved.

"Well, here we are," she said, as we pulled up in front of a weathered stucco house, fronted by a patch of burnt lawn, badly in need of weeding.

"Aren't you coming in?" I asked.

"No, I'm needed back at the station, and anyway Mrs. Flores doesn't like us very much since we've had to haul her son in more than a few times. And remember, no one reported those girls missing. You'll probably do better on your own. Give a call when you're ready to leave."

I saw a curtain move as I walked toward the house and stepped up on the broken slab that led to the front door. Before I could knock the door was opened by a thin, middle-aged Hispanic woman, wearing a shapeless house-dress and fluffy gray slippers. She was leaning heavily on a metal walker.

"Buenos Dias," she said, gesturing for me to enter. "My English not so good."

"Buenos Dias," I replied. "Me llama, Erin. My Spanish is not so good."

Apparently that helped to break the ice. Because at that she beamed, and led me into a cluttered, but clean, parlor. Someone had set out two glasses of some kind of fruit punch and a plate of cookies.

"Lady next door help me," she explained. Then, "Por favor," she said, pointing to an overstuffed chair and then at the refreshments.

"Muchas gracias."

After a few bites Mrs. Flores said, "They say you see my

nietas—my Carla and Serena. You help?" Her eyes were full of tears, and her voice shook with emotion.

For the next few minutes I tried to explain my connection to Carla, and at the same time, both console the obviously distraught woman, and most importantly, gain any information from her that might prove helpful in my search. Fortunately, her English comprehension was superior to her speaking skills. I recognized Carla from a framed picture of two young girls which was prominently displayed on a side table. The second girl must be Serena. Did their grandmother have any more recent ones that I could borrow to use for identification? She did, and I carefully put the photos into the folder I was carrying.

No one knew exactly how the girls had gone missing, but Mrs. Flores related a very plausible theory—obviously painful in the telling—that her son, the girl's uncle, Mateo, was an alcoholic and heroin addict, whose supplier was a petty dealer named Nestor. The latter had been to the Flores' house on numerous occasions and had interacted with the girls—all in the guise of being their uncle's friend. Mrs. Flores mistrusted him, but he occasionally brought gifts and sweets for her and the girls, and always spoke politely.

It wasn't hard to imagine that Nestor, knowing the grandmother had suffered a stroke, leaving only their addict uncle in charge, would step in and offer to help. And thus the children became trapped in the sordid world of pimping underage girls. It filled me with sadness to realize that after the events of the past few weeks I easily found this scenario totally believable.

Did the local police know about this Nestor? What story did Mateo tell his mother when she realized the girls were missing? Mrs. Flores was very vague.

She was obviously tiring. I got out my cell to call Lorena. Hopefully the police would know where to find Mateo or, better yet, Nestor, and lean on them for some answers as to Serena's whereabouts. I looked again at the picture of the young Flores sisters. When the authorities caught their traffickers would they be allowed to use torture when they were interrogated? It seemed only right to me, although I feared that only happened in the movies!

Suddenly Mrs. Flores struggled to her feet and began to murmur in Spanish. She pushed the walker to a hallway chest of drawers and began to rummage through a basket of what looked like an accumulation of mostly junk mail.

"Here, Senora," she said triumphantly, holding out an envelope addressed to her Campo address. Inside the envelope there was a visitor's postcard from The Budget Motel in downtown San Diego, also a note from Serena containing a short message addressed to Mrs. Flores, written half in Spanish and half in English. In essence it said that she was all right, but scared, missed her and Carla a lot, and had a plan for getting back home soon. Obviously she hadn't made it back. The envelope had been canceled in a way that made it impossible to read the date. Mrs. Flores said, "You take," and handed it to me. I had to turn away—such were the questions and pain in the older woman's eyes. But at least now I had a card with an address and the photographs too. And there was still a chance that Carla would get in touch. For now that would have to be enough to keep me going. I had received all kinds of choices in my life. What were theirs?

Before I left, I gave Mrs. Flores my *County Voice* business card. We promised to let each other know if there was any new information as to the girls' whereabouts.


Back at the substation, Sheriff Wicker confirmed Lorena's belief that little would come out of a search for Nestor. "We shut down a prostitution ring at a local hotel not long ago, but he managed to get out of the sting—probably just blended into the population south of the border. As for Uncle Mateo, he's in detox yet again. Worthless piece of . . ." Lorena gave him a look and winked at me.

"But as we promised we can give you the names of some detectives in the main San Diego headquarters who might be able to help. The address on Serena's card shows that the motel is in their territory."

He shook my hand. "I had you pegged wrong," he admitted. "Just be careful," he added as he walked me to the door. "Those trafficking people are a nasty bunch. And let us know what's going on," he called after me.

On the way to the downtown precinct I stopped at a Kinko's to make several copies of the pictures. I put my newspaper phone number at the bottom. It couldn't hurt to blanket the area where Serena apparently had been taken, in the hopes that some good citizen would recognize her, and come forward with a little information. I intended to add a citizens' police tip line when I obtained it.

I parked the car in the precinct visitor's lot and went directly to the reception desk.

# 8

*Serena drifts in and out of consciousness. She is barely aware that at some point she is carried into a vehicle and that there are many others on board. Troubled sleep overtakes her again. At intervals the vehicle—an old SUV of some kind, she will learn later—stops for gas, for food, to use the restroom. The journey and the muddled dreams seem to go on forever, but finally, day two or three maybe, she regains full consciousness, and pulls herself upright in one corner of the back seat.*

*"Well, it's about time you woke up," says the girl sitting next to her. "You hogged more than your share of the seat," she criticizes, adding a scowl, "but I guess you got beat up pretty bad." The scowl turns to a look of concern. "I know how that goes." And with that she smiles and points to her mouth, revealing missing teeth.*

*"My name is Wanda—my street name, that is, and I'm fourteen. What's yours and how old are you?"*

*Serena isn't feeling very friendly, and the torrent of words and the residual grogginess doesn't help, but the girl seems sincere. "I'm Serena, and that's my only name. I'm almost eleven," she answers.*

*"Glad to meet you, Serena. Gosh, you're still a baby. Did you run away from home? And who beat you—your pimp or a john? They told me that we're going to be sister wives. Have you heard anything about who'll run us in San Francisco? Or where our track will be?"*

*Sister wives, run us, track—what was she talking about?*

*"Don't look like that. I am speaking English you know? What kind of a pimp did you work for anyhow?"*

*A mean, horrible one, Serena wants to say—or maybe two. Nestor had taken Carla away.*

*"Ah, I get it," Wanda says. "You're a pretty, young thing. Bet you only go to motel rooms with the johns who make a re-ser-va-tion!" Wanda laughs, as she draws out the word.  Serena nods in affirmation.*

*"I always wanted to go to a motel, but who would ask for an old, black, kinky-haired girl like me?" She sounds wistful.*

*Since Serena's memories of her times with strange men in mo-tel rooms are anything but pleasant, she finds it a little odd that Wanda would be envious.*

*She has noticed that there are several other girls in the SUV, and a woman who sat across from the driver might be the one who gave her the pills, but no one has made an attempt to join their conversation. She turns back to Wanda. "Are we all going to the same place?" she asks.*

*"Nah, just you and me," her seatmate answers. "I've been up here before, but never in a house, or with this pimp. I grew up in Oakland—practically next door—but the gang had me down in Oxnard last."*

*Serena is perplexed. "Who are they, and why don't you call your family and have them come get you?"*

*"They is the gang who own us, silly, and I don't go home be-cause I don't like it there much, and anyhow they don't want me," she says, defiantly—but Serena notes that Wanda's  chin trembles and her eyes look  sad as she says that.*

*"In any case, we'll have our answers soon," Wanda continues. She points out the window. "We just turned off 101 onto Van Ness. We'll be in the Mission district soon. San Francisco's not so bad. East Palo Alto is the worst," she states, knowingly. "And be careful not to wear all red or all blue because the Bloods and the Crips hate each other."*

*Serena is feeling emotionally overwhelmed and, now that the Oxy had worn off, physically exhausted as well.*

*"There I go again, scaring you half to death!" Wanda pats her hand. "I promise to have your back. And come to me if you have any questions. Our pimp doesn't really want us to get along. He'll have favorites and give them presents and punish other girls who don't bring in enough money. He wants us to snitch on each other. All that makes it easier to keep us in line."*

*Before Serena can respond, the driver shouts out, "Mission Street coming up. Wanda and Serena, this is where you get out. Grab your things. Angel will meet you."*

*Serena puts on her backpack and follows Wanda to the front of the car. All eyes are on them now. Angel? She had known ordinary family men named Angel before in Campo. Maybe this Angel would be kinder than Dion, at least—maybe even see that she didn't belong here in this life and let her go home.*

# 9

My trip to Campo had been very enlightening but now I reminded myself that I needed to obtain the citizen's police tip line number for my posters before leaving the precinct. Ever since I had become aware of the huge problem of human trafficking the issue was dominating my life. I had given myself a mission to find the two young sisters. How could I turn my back on them? Prioritize, Erin, I reminded myself as I walked into the downtown San Diego police station.

"Anything I can do for you, miss?" the officer at the reception desk asked, as he gave me one of those aren't-you-in-the-wrong-neighborhood looks.

Did my cowl-necked teal cashmere and tailored black slacks really make me stand out? I had deliberately left my good watch and better jewelry at home.

"Would anyone from the human trafficking division be available?" I asked, handing him my list of contacts and my business card.

"Let me check," he answered. "Take a seat."

Three police facilities in two days, I mused. What was my life becoming? There was a general hubbub as people, many on their own, or accompanied by officers, came and went. Many of the civilians appeared to look scruffy and beaten down—most with lowered heads, avoiding eye contact. Except for two young men who openly leered at me and smacked their lips before sharing a lewd-sounding laugh. Pimps, maybe?

After about ten minutes a trim, dark-skinned young woman dressed in beige slacks and a tweed jacket came toward me and shook my hand firmly. "'Erin Butler, I'm J.C. Williams. Why don't you follow me?" As we walked through a long corridor, she explained, "By the way, for your information, there are three of us who comprise the human trafficking task force. We cover the whole of southern San Diego County, dealing with forced labor, domestic servitude, sex trafficking issues and other forms of modern-day slavery."

Was that a subtle way to tell me that they were really too busy to become involved with my request, I wondered? She ushered me into a medium-sized room separated into three cubicles with each cubicle containing a desk and two chairs. A chalkboard dominated one wall and numerous mug shots and wanted posters adorned another. A large metal file cabinet and a coffee maker completed the picture.

A giant of a man in wrinkled black slacks and a white shirt with the cuffs rolled up and red tie askew came out from behind one of the desks. His gray crew cut, deeply tanned face and furrowed forehead gave him a menacing look, but there was a twinkle in his intensely blue eyes. I guessed him to be anywhere from his mid-forties to fifty.

"Stan Kukesh." My hand was swallowed by the one he extended. "Ed Wicker called and said you might be dropping by. You've met Detective Williams." He nodded in her direction. "The third member of our team, Agent Gomez, is out trying to catch the perps. I understand you are hoping we can help you rescue two sisters from the local scumbags?"

I wasn't sure I liked his mocking tone, but he *was* the expert, and Carla and Serena's welfare was all that mattered. "I'm not trying to tell you how to do your job," I said, "but I do have information that puts the younger sister in this neighborhood, at the Budget Motel, in fact. At *ten years old* she has been sold at least twice into sexual slavery," I added, for emphasis. I thought I saw the woman detective wince. Before they could reply I took out my Kinko's posters and pointed to Serena. "I'm hoping that you can find out if anyone at the motel or in this area in general has seen her lately."

Detective Kukesh looked briefly at the picture. "We throw a scare at the motel now and then, have even made a few arrests. But there is a difference between making an arrest and moving forward to a trial—it's almost impossible to get the victims to testify. Furthermore, we can't just go bursting into the rooms without probable cause. Invasion of privacy, you know.

"Anyway, why don't you leave a couple of those posters, we'll circulate them, and let you know if we turn up anything. It's obvious that you are a very caring person, and we do try to work closely with the public, but in cases like this it's usually best to leave it up to the authorities. I say that, in good part, because it's a matter of your safety," he said, pointedly.

Talk about feeling patronized! But I wasn't going to give up that easily. For now, it was obvious I was not going to get any more help here. "Well, thank you for your time," I said, turning to leave.

"I'll see you out," Detective Williams interjected, as I headed for the door.

"I can see that this has been frustrating for you," she said, as we headed along the corridor. "My partner is really one of the good guys. He even has daughters the age of the young victims you've described. Human trafficking is such a huge problem. This kind of duty takes its toll and we're spread really, really thin. But we do care. Don't give up on this and I'll do what I can and give you a call."

We were back at the main entrance. She gave my arm a squeeze. I felt an impulse to give her a hug, but settled for a sincere thank you. She headed back to her department and I went out to my car.

I was encouraged by her response, but it was obvious that my quest could hardly be a top priority for their unit when the problem was so all-pervasive. What had I really hoped to accomplish? My precinct stop was a start, but I still had the rest of the posters, and my mission had not changed. I pulled the car out of the parking lot and headed in the direction of the Budget Motel.

What a sordid neighborhood! Given my background, I could have ended up someplace like this, I thought, not for the first time. No one starts out to end up like this, a place of broken dreams, as it were. Vacant, trash-filled lots and abandoned buildings dominated, and several sorry-looking structures with "Rooms for Rent" signs in the windows coexisted with a handful of pubs and diners which still showed signs of life. The few pedestrians either walked quickly, avoiding eye contact with those openly panhandling, or slouched along seemingly aimless. Some even appeared to be talking to themselves or to an unseen audience.

Despite her own pain and situation I remembered that Carla had been more concerned for her little sister. And this is where that sweet little innocent girl is being kept! I was so angry that I wasn't paying enough attention to the road and nearly drove into a group of young men crossing against the lights at an intersection. For that indiscretion I got the middle finger salute from several, and at least two pounded on my hood and shouted obscenities. One even started to chase after the car as I slowly pulled away.

My heart was still pounding as, a few blocks further on, I pulled into the motel. It was not much to look at, three stories of flaking tan stucco with outside staircases, but at least there would be other people around in case I had been followed. I parked near the entrance and entered the lobby, carrying a few posters.

The lobby, such as it was, consisted of a small, open space containing a couch and two chairs covered in a faded red print.

Some fake greenery adorned corner tables. The clerk, a balding, older Caucasian man of indeterminate age, sat behind a low counter, reading a newspaper. He barely looked up when I approached.

I held one of the posters out. "I was hoping you could help me with a missing person's case," I began. "We have reason to believe that, on occasion recently, the younger girl may have been forced to spend some time here against her will."

Now he was paying attention. I had noticed that he was wearing a wedding band and that his lapel badge read "R.J. Billings." He began to shake his head, but before he could speak, I said, "I'm not accusing you of anything, Mr. Billings. I'm sure you're just doing your job. Do you have children? Maybe even grandchildren?"

"What does that have to do with anything?" he answered, but I noted that he licked his lips and lowered his voice as he spoke. "I never saw the kid. I can't be expected to remember every guest, and I only work part-time, anyway." Now, his tone was plaintive. "Look, lady, I've got work to do. Leave a poster and I'll show it around."

The phone rang and a couple came in and went to a nearby elevator. The man wore a suit. The girl, heavily made-up, was dressed provocatively; hard to guess her  age, but my antenna was up. I wasn't going to find out anymore from the clerk, but I was more convinced than ever that I was on the right track. Serena had been pimped here.

Back in the parking lot I got out a few posters and, according to the clerk at the hardware store, a roll of the strongest tape available. Thus armed, I began to attach the posters to utility poles and fences in the surrounding blocks, vying with graffiti and torn announcements of events long past. The man who answered the door at a tiny Salvation Army drop-in center also agreed to show the picture to his clientele.

A handful of people passed me as I went about my work.

Some gave me a quizzical look and a few stopped to check out the poster, but I wasn't aware of the trouble I was stirring up until I decided to move my car so that I could cover a wider area. As I drove slowly back along the route I had taken from the police station, I noticed that several of the posters I had first put up were missing or hanging in tatters!

Another few yards, and further down the block, I saw the thieves in action. Hard to tell, but from that distance, at least a couple of them resembled those young men I had encountered earlier. I thought of going to the police, but what could I say? Agent Kukesh had discouraged me from getting personally involved. Were they just out to annoy me, or was it more? In any case, this was my only chance to get a possible lead on Serena's whereabouts. Surely someone who read the poster would want to be a Good Samaritan and give me or the police a call. With that in mind, I got angry again.

I pulled up along the curb in front of a vacant building. I'd be damned if I'd let them intimidate me that easily! Two could play at their game. I began to put up replacements, totally focused, so that I actually jumped when I heard, "You better watch your back, lady. Don't turn around. Just get in your car and go back where you belong."

"Stop messin' in our business, or else," another accented Hispanic voice said threateningly.

My courage evaporated, or perhaps reason took over. For now I was no match for them. As calmly as I could, I did as they ordered, and headed for the freeway that would take me north and home.


My day had started out early with such promise. Now at twilight, I was bone-tired, famished, and very discouraged. Somewhere on I-5 northbound, I added paranoia to my woes. Was it my imagination, or had a big, black Lincoln Town Car been following me the whole way? In the next few miles I made several abrupt lane changes, gave it plenty of chances to pass, but, though the car occasionally fell behind a few lengths, it was still within sight as I took the La Jolla cut-off. Now I *was* frightened. I decided to turn into a heavily built-up, well-lit neighborhood, a few streets before my own. The black car slowed, but went on by. Apparently, I had let my imagination run wild, or had I?

I stayed for several minutes parked in front of a house that had several cars in its driveway. Finally, I timidly continued on, ready to drive to the local police station if I saw the same car with the strange grill and high-powered headlights again, but there were no other sightings. I garaged the BMW, and entered our townhouse without incident. Ours was a 'smart' condo so a few selected interior lights were already turned on. I checked all the doors and made sure that the security system was re-armed.

Mike would be calling soon. How much of the day's events should I relate? If I am totally honest and tell him everything, he'll insist on cutting his trip short. And when I tell him that I've been less than straightforward about my plans, he'll be upset, maybe even insist I drop all my involvement with the girls. Unthinkable, and yet at this point, I just wished he would walk through the door, take me in his arms, and tell me everything was going to turn out for the best.

Of course, just then the phone rang. I was still struggling with what I would say, but had no clue as to how to even begin. Nevertheless, I slowly picked up the phone.

I was saved by a poor connection on his end and the background noise from the other patrons at the pub where Mike and his skiing buddies were celebrating a day of perfect spring skiing. He accepted the sanitized version of my activities.

"Wish you were here," he said, as we closed our conversation. "Love you much," he added, with conviction.

"Miss you, and I love you, too," I managed to get in, before the connection was broken.

\*　　\*　　\*

Next morning at the newspaper, my editor Malcolm and I met to discuss my upcoming assignments. I filled him in on my deepening involvement with actual victims of underage sexual trafficking, concluding with my attempt to involve the public by putting up posters with contact numbers for the San Diego police and *The County Voice*. As I talked, I could feel myself getting angry again. "I wish I'd had a photographer with me to take some mug shots of those miserable excuses for human beings!"

Apparently my voice had carried further than I had intended. A couple of the other staff people stopped what they were doing to gawk.

"I'm not quite sure that would have been the way to go," Malcolm said, "but let's take our discussion into my office." Once settled, he continued. "How many more of those human trafficking articles had you planned?"

"That's what I wanted to discuss with you," I began. "Of course you have the final say, but when you encouraged me to bring this subject to our readers, we never did discuss an ending date. I hope it's not soon, because I think I have some excellent material which shouldn't go to waste."

Malcolm was hard to read this morning. Something was bothering him. Usually he was more than ready for staff to come up with ideas. But then he said, "Sorry, I'm a little preoccupied. Go ahead and tell me what you had in mind."

"Okay. I've been thinking that so far I've filled my articles with statistics, postings of conferences, names of pertinent organizations and the like—informative and important, but definitely somewhat mundane. The steak, as they say in the news business. Now I want to go for the sizzle." I paused.

"I'm listening," he said, leaning back in his chair with his hands resting on the back of his head.

"'Well, here goes. Why don't I do an expanded series of hard-hitting personal pieces—put a face on the subject, as it were. Maybe you could even run the articles on the front page. I want to draw the readers in and shake them up, and what better way to do that than by writing about Serena and Carla's story? Make it sing, as you might say." I was getting excited again in anticipation.

"As usual, I admire your passion, Erin, but I'm very doubtful that we would be able to give you any more space, let alone front page coverage. To be blunt, our numbers are down and our expenses are up. We small weeklies don't have the luxury of encouraging writing such as you are proposing. Coverage of local events is our bread and butter; it's what the advertisers want."

It wasn't hard for me to see that this was difficult for Malcolm, but I'm sure I looked thoroughly deflated. "Tell you what," he said. "Why don't you put some of your thoughts down on paper? I'm not making any promises, but I'll see what I can do."

Mike wasn't due back for another thirty-six hours so I decided to stay at the paper and get started. I sat down at my laptop.


*Picture this,* I began. *You are a ten-year-old girl named Serena— long, dark hair and eyes that sparkle—living happily in a small, southern California town, with your big sister and your grandmother, or abuela, as you called her. You are kind of shy, but you like school, your teacher, and most of your fourth grade classmates.*

*You and your fourteen-year-old sister, Carla—in your opinion, a girl as beautiful as a movie star—share a bedroom. She teases you about the bedraggled yellow Easter Bunny you still take with you to bed, but she also reads to you, and helps you with your homework. She is your protector. And you love her fiercely.*

*Only three years ago you made your first communion in a white chiffon dress with lace trim that your abuela had scrimped and saved for. It is wrapped in special paper and packed away along with a circlet of tiny flowers and a pair of lace gloves for the day when you hope to pass it on to your own daughter. But that will, in all probability, never happen, because several months ago, when your grandmother suffered a stroke and was hospitalized, a man named Nestor, known by you girls as a family friend, interceded, and removed you from your home. He turned out to be a gang member/pimp and within days, you two had been subjected to emotional, sexual, and other forms of abuse, hard to imagine, even by the most jaded. But it gets worse.*

*Your columnist has learned that since they were originally kidnapped, the sisters have been separated; sold to different gangs in other parts of the county! Carla was last seen in Vista and Serena in downtown San Diego. Yes, you read that right: sold, just as any expendable commodity such as the drugs and illegal guns these gangs deal in. For, hard as it is to believe, these pimps brag that they are business men; competing in the same markets, but, when it is to their advantage, also cooperating with each other.*

*We here at the paper have a two-fold reason for stepping up our coverage of human trafficking in San Diego County. One is to personalize the issue and the other is to enlist your help. You see, unfortunately, at this point, neither we nor the police, nor that distraught grandmother, know where these girls are. We're publishing their pictures in hopes that someone, somewhere, will have seen them recently, or have heard something that might prove helpful. Your responses to the numbers you will see at the end of this article will be kept totally confidential. Please help!*

# 10

*Serena watches the SUV's tail lights until they are out of sight. It is early evening now. The air is chilly and damp. The SUV has left the two girls on a sidewalk on Mission Street in what appears to be a crowded, lower-class neighborhood of eateries, pawn shops, discount stores and shabby apartments above the stores. A neon sign blinks "Rooms".*

*"Ladies, over here." They turn and look toward the alley where a Hispanic man of thirty or so is beckoning to them. He doesn't look menacing, though he does have a long scar across one cheek. "Come on, don't be afraid. I'm Angel and I'm going to take you up the back way to your new home."*

*The alleyway reeks of some kind of cooking and urine, there is an overflowing trash dumpster against a wall, and the outside staircase is rickety. The girls wrinkle their noses and share a conspiratorial glance, but Angel climbs ahead, buds in his ears, rapping to some music only he can hear.*

*When they get to the third, and uppermost landing, he takes out a key and opens a door into what looks like a pantry area. "All of the girls are out working. It will give you a chance to settle in before you meet your new sister wives."*

*Angel leads them through a small kitchen into a cramped, but neat, bedroom, containing bunk beds and two cots, plus open shelving and four cube-type partitions   like those seen in a preschool.*

*"There's one cot, an open top bunk, and two empty storage areas. You work it out. Oh, and you all share the one bathroom, and you're expected to keep it clean," Angel tells them, "but you*

*notice there are two extra mirrors in the bedroom so you can primp all you want. I like my ladies to look fine. I'm going out to relieve my homie now. Get yourself something to eat."*

*The girls hear the door being locked from the outside. "Well, we might as well settle in," says Wanda. "Do you mind if I take the cot? Heights make me nervous."*

*"I wanted the upper bunk anyway," Serena answers.*

*"Well, what do you think?" Wanda asks. "Was your place down south better than this?"*

*Serena looks around the bedroom more carefully. It's cramped, and there is only one small window covered by a torn shade, but there is a clean-looking pillow and a blue spread on each bed, and a few colorful prints—including one of Mary holding the baby Jesus—on the walls. This is a big step up compared to her previous dingy basement quarters.*

*"This is much better," she has to agree.*

*"For me too," Wanda says. "Let's see a smile. That's better. Now how about finding something to eat? I'm starved!"*

*A search of the cupboards proves disappointing—the refrigerator even more so. "Guess Angel must bring take-out in a lot. Looks like it's going to be either dry cereal or soup if we can find a pot and a can opener," Wanda observes.*

*Their search pays off and soon they are eagerly devouring bowls of chicken noodle soup*

*"Where do you think Angel's going?" Serena asks between mouthfuls.*

*"You really don't know much about the life, do you?" Wanda answers. "He's going to check up on his girls—make sure they're really hustling. He'll probably mostly sit in his car somewhere he can see most of them, listening to Nelly or Master P on his iPod and drinking coffee or Red Bull. I'll be out there tomorrow," she adds, casually.*

*Serena can't tell if her new friend is sad or just resigned. She can't be happy about it, can she? As for herself, she still feels some residual pain from the beating and a continuing sense of dread as to the future.*

*After they have eaten and cleaned up they explore the rest of the apartment—Serena afraid that any minute Angel will return and they will be in trouble.*

*In the living room they find that in addition to a broken-down, overstuffed couch and big black leather recliner, there is a monitor and an old combination VCR/DVD player, but no regular TV. No sign of magazines or books, either. There is one more room, but the door is shut. "Must be Angel's pad for him and his favorite," Wanda whispers, though she and Serena are alone.*

*The girls retreat into their bedroom. "Might as well try to get some sleep," the older girl advises. "The others won't be back until at least two, I would guess. Goodnight Serena," she says quietly.*

*Serena is grateful for the kind words even as she resolves anew to fight against her current situation. She must be tough. She tries to give in to sleep, but despite her earlier exhaustion, she finds it hard to do. Sirens—police, fire, ambulances—loud laughter and cursing, blaring music, intrude.*

*Sometime in the middle of the night, Serena hears as if in a dream, girlish voices, arguing, laughing, perhaps one even crying, as they come into the apartment. Someone turns on a light.*

*Wanda sits up. Serena peaks over the side.*

*"Oops, sorry," says a pale, lanky, blonde, her cheeks streaked with mascara. "Guess Angel forgot to tell us we were getting company. I'm Ariel and this is Simone," she continues, pointing to a chunky, dark-haired girl who mumbles something without raising her head. "You'll meet Tina later when Angel gets through talking to her. She tends to be lazy," Ariel adds, yawning deeply. "We'll get your names tomorrow. Now we gotta crash."*

*Soon there are sounds of rhythmic breathing and gentle snoring. The door opens and closes quickly and for a few minutes a noise between hiccupping and sobbing is added to the mix. Serena has trouble getting back to sleep.*

*She hugs her yellow bunny—miraculously still with her—and tries to quiet her thoughts. Fear of the unknown with Angel fills her with dread, but imagining her home, so far away, is also painful. She is glad she has a top bunk—her own little hideaway. For the first time in quite a while she lets her tears fall freely, not because of bodily pain, but as a release; a well-deserved pity party, as Carla would say.*

# 11

"I'd knock if you had a door." Frank poked his face around the partition and saw me hard at work on the office computer. "Don't tell me that you found last night's school board meeting that fascinating?"

"Something much more important," I answered, gesturing to the extra chair. "Actually, I swapped assignments with Nell. You're just the person I hoped to see. How long has it been since you introduced me to the tawdry world of human trafficking?"

"I sense more to that question than meets the eye. What have you been up to?"

So I filled him in fully on the events of the past few days—marveling in the telling at just what a turn my life had taken.

"And now I want to take some of that and put the stark reality into the kind of features that will make our readers sit up and take notice. Malcolm wasn't too supportive, actually, but he has agreed to run at least my first attempt; front page with byline, even. Let me make you a copy right now. I'd like to hear what you think."

"I'll be glad to take a look at it, but I have to admit I'm concerned that you might have gone too far yesterday. Sounds to me as if you may have run into some really nasty characters—did you tell Mike?"

"Well, not all of it," I admitted. "He's on a ski trip so we only spoke by phone." The elation I had experienced as I pitched my feature idea and actually wrote the copy was evaporating. Why couldn't someone just give me a compliment or some credit? Or were they right and I was foolishly minimizing the danger? No doubt I was also feeling some guilt that I had been less than forthcoming with Mike.

Meanwhile Frank was reading Serena's story. "I like it. I like it a lot," he said appreciatively. "I'm sure that Malcolm will, too. That won't be the last, right?"

"It's hard for me to tell. I have a lot more material, but Malcolm can't commit, because he's worried about the paper's bottom line."

"Understandable. In tough economic times the ad revenue goes down and therefore the publisher's not happy. More feature articles mean less space for ads. But don't look so glum. Keep the faith. I'll look forward to seeing this on the front page next week.

"Now I'm off. I get to cover three sporting events in the next two days," he said, as he got up to leave. "Just a thought—I'm sure society would be a lot better off if those sleazy gang members had spent time perfecting their jump shot or learning to hit a curve instead of practicing the pimp-walk and listening to rap and hip-hop."

For the time being I put aside thoughts of the two sisters. My main job at the paper was to cover civic events so I spent the next hour writing from my notes, then stopped next door at Nick's for a slice of pizza with fresh tomatoes and extra cheese, before heading on to my shift at the bookstore.

More than once I had heard the Reader's Roost called a sanctuary. I thoroughly concurred. There was something so comforting about the stacks of colorful books, the comfortable seating scattered throughout, and the dedicated, book-loving staff who seem like family. In addition to buying books, many customers took part in discussion groups or writing seminars, and the book signings were often well-attended.

"Do you have a 'staff recommendation' for me yet?" My coworker, Pam, asked, as I settled in.

"Sorry, not yet," I said. Not only had I not gotten around to that monthly assignment but I hadn't even begun to read a new book! Still, one more sign that my involvement in sexual trafficking had begun to take over in my day-to-day living. I really needed to work on restoring some balance in my life! And I certainly owed it to my fiancé, and yet . . .

That evening when Mike called I told him honestly how much I was looking forward to his return the next evening. He seemed pleased and even concluded his end of the conversation with a few steamy suggestions as to how I could prove it to him! That night my dream was, for the first time in several weeks, not a disturbing one.

Next morning my cell rang as I was getting ready to cover the mayor's weekly prayer-breakfast meeting with the city council. I knew that at the end of the meal, there would be an attempt to answer complaints of lack of transparency in government, and then a question-and-answer period available to members of the media and the public-at-large. These could actually be quite entertaining, as well as occasionally informative, so I had come to look forward to this type of assignment. I took one last swallow of coffee and answered the call as I grabbed my suit jacket and press pass from the hall closet.

"Erin, this is Detective Williams from the San Diego police station. About that matter we were speaking of recently, I'm afraid I have bad news."

She was speaking in a tone that suggested she didn't want to be overheard.

"Go on," I encouraged, with a sinking heart. What could have happened?

"Well I was able to speak with a part-time desk clerk at the motel—the contact I had mentioned to you—and she remembered Serena after I showed her the picture you left with us. It seemed that a certain man had reserved a room on several occasions and tried to pass off the young girl as his granddaughter. She remarked that he was very attentive to her and that, though she seemed subdued, there were never any noticeable bruises nor did the young girl seem overly afraid. Then the visits abruptly ended. My contact doesn't approve of the sex trade and she admitted feeling somewhat protective of Serena, but she *is* related to several gang members—they are sadly generational in nature—so she kind of looks the other way and goes about her business."

"Is that the bad news you mentioned, or is there more?" I asked.

"I'm afraid there's more," she continued. "The main bad news is that sometime in the last week or so Serena's pimp apparently sold her to someone up north—L.A. perhaps or even into the San Francisco area. Apparently she had run away but was found. After beating her as an example to his other girls, he judged her to be too much trouble to keep, so. . ."

"You okay?" Detective Williams asked in response to the moan I couldn't hold back.

"Guess I was naïve to think we'd find and rescue her," I answered, holding back my tears.

"I'm really sorry, too, Erin. I was hoping we could pull off a rescue. I don't know what you plan to do now, but I have to warn you that my contact was aware that a   pretty Caucasian woman put up posters and that some members of the Alley Locos, and their homies, the Devious Hoodlums gang, were not amused. You were trying to mess with their bottom line. I don't know that they would go out of their way to retaliate, but I do hope you'll keep a low profile for the time being. Well, got to go." She paused, and then said, "I'll keep in touch."

I imagine I thanked her but I couldn't swear to it. How ironic that she had used the phrase "bottom line!" First Malcolm, then the officer—referring to bottom lines in newspapers and also in pimping! The rest of the morning passed in kind of a haze, though I was able to ask the mayor a coherent question or two. The words "keep a low profile" kept going through my mind.

It was early that evening when I heard a car pull up. I went to the front door, waved to Chet as he dropped off Mike and his ski equipment, and opened the garage door so the gear could be stowed. We kissed long and hard. "Tough ride," he said, emphatically, while turning his head side-to-side and rolling his shoulders.

I knew he always wore sunscreen when he skied but Mike had still managed to pick up that healthy outdoor glow which to me made him appear more handsome than ever.

I began to give him a neck rub. "Hmm, that feels good, lady. You should get those hands insured. It's tempting to go for the whole body massage, but I think I need to shower first. I know that my natural body odor is a turn-on, but . . ."

"Get out of here," I said, shaking my head. "It doesn't sound as if you stopped for a real meal. I'll have a light supper for you when you're ready."

I'm not sure if the thought of resuming our sexual teasing or the promise of food was the main incentive, but Mike finished his shower in record time.

"You do smell very nice, in a manly way, of course," I said, as I got a whiff of cologne. "Let's eat."


After we finished our gourmet-deli soup and focaccia bread we took our glasses of Chardonnay into the den. Mike had fleshed out his account of the ski trip during the meal. "Now it's your turn," he said. "What happened in the last few days that you were going to tell me about?"

"Well, I'll get more specific in a minute," I said, "but first I have something exciting to show you." I handed him a copy of my upcoming feature article. "This is going to run on the front page in next week's edition along with my byline!" I couldn't help but smile at the thought.

Mike read it carefully, looking up at me quizzically a few times.

"It's certainly well done, but just how did you get involved in this case? It reads as if you have personal knowledge and an emotional stake here. This does not sound like, or read like, just straight reporting."

I owed him an explanation, so I went back to the beginning and fleshed out what little I had told him on the phone. I started with my brief hospital visit with Carla and my subsequent disappointment when I found out that she had been signed out early, apparently by her pimp. Then it was on to Campo and the rest.

"Let me get this straight," he said, with a frown. "You're saying that you impulsively decided to drive all the way to Campo to find out more about this Carla and her younger sister? And, based on what you learned there, you made up the posters and drove to the San Diego County precinct hoping somehow to join with them in bringing about their rescue? Have I got that right?" He had pulled away from me as he spoke.

"Well, essentially yes, but you make it seem. . ."

"Erin, I really don't get it. It sounds as if you have managed to get yourself in the middle of a nearly impossible situation, and a potentially dangerous one at that, and kept it from me as well. And you don't expect me to be upset? Incredible!"

It was obvious that he was angry now—and hurt. He yawned rather theatrically and stood up. "I've had a long day. I'm going up to bed now. Are you coming?"

"You go on. I think I'll stay down for a while."

"Suit yourself," he muttered.

I sat there as night descended, but I didn't turn on a light. I kept going over the events of the past few days. Mike's reaction, though not exactly unexpected, was disappointing, but it forced me to acknowledge that I too had begun to fear that I might be getting into real danger. Messing around with a gang member's girls—in their eyes, their property—could not be allowed. They might be sleazy, ignorant, law breakers in the eyes of most people, but in their world it was a matter of commerce, and by their code they had a right to defend that in any way they saw fit. By having the article published and enlisting the public's involvement, I might well be putting myself at risk for physical retaliation. Would they ever resort to beating me up to prove a point as they sometimes did to their girls? *That* was frightening!

Thus, it seemed to me I was at a crossroads. Pull the article, and go back behind the scenes in the fight against human trafficking, or continue forward with my heart. In the end, the answer for me had to be, that while I would exercise caution, there could be no turning back. Doing nothing was not an option. I *had* to do something that would make a real difference.

Coming to that conclusion brought me some peace of mind, but could I get Mike to see it that way? And what would happen to us if he couldn't?

By tacit agreement neither of us brought up the touchy subject in the next few days. Our lives went on more or less as usual. We even managed to be congenial while dining out one evening with two other couples from Morgan Stanley and, on another occasion, attending a repertory theatre production benefitting a local homeless shelter.

Our few hours at home together, while lacking a certain closeness, were not unpleasant. But there was no more wedding talk. We kept our conversations neutral—safe.

And then my feature was published. Amy called to gush. Paula from the Tri-City Medical Center, and others, weighed in, praising my activism in support of the innocent victim. But, best of all, the number of copies sold on the newsstands was way up, and in addition, many readers took the time to post favorable e-mails. They *had* been paying attention. My message had been heard!

Of course Malcolm was pleased, especially when advertisers would learn about the increased readership—more copies being sold meant more potential customers. Now, if only the tip line would do well. The detectives had warned me not to expect too much. Chances were good that not much valuable information would be forthcoming, but they promised to keep me up to date.

A few days later the receptionist at *The County Voice* buzzed me. "Erin, there's a call for you on line two. The guy said he wanted to speak to you personally. He wouldn't give his name."

"Erin Butler?" The voice was not familiar. I said I was her and he continued. "I read about the girls. I think I know the older one." He hesitated, and his voice was so low I could hardly hear him. Should I say something or wait him out? I didn't want to lose the connection.

Finally, I said, "I'm listening."

"This isn't easy for me and I'm not proud of myself, but when I said I knew her I meant as a prostitute. But I didn't know she was so young. Believe me, I would never have . . ." His voice trailed off again.

"I do believe you," I said. "I'm not here to judge. I just want to find her. Can you help? Do you know where she is?"

"Not really, ma'am. We've only met four or five times in Oceanside where I'm stationed at Camp Pendleton. Those girls hang out regularly at a few spots along Pacific Coast Highway, at various times, mostly at night. The pimps stay out of sight but they keep an eye on their girls and pick them up at some point, I guess. Rosy—as she called herself—never talked about that part, and I didn't really want to know."

"You're sure that Rosy and the older girl shown in the picture are one and the same?" I asked.

"Ninety-nine percent," he answered. "A couple of times she let me buy her ice cream and we talked about families. What she told me was right out of your article, except for the kidnapping and gang stuff." Then he cleared his throat several times. "I wasn't going to call. As a Marine squad leader I'm supposed to set high standards so if it got out that I was acting against military regulations it would have a serious effect on my career." He sounded somewhat remorseful.

*Now* he was worried about his reputation! However I'd promised not to be judgmental, so . . . "But, you did call," I said, with as much encouragement as I could muster. "Please tell me anything you can about her whereabouts. Your involvement will never come out."

"The last time we were together—early last week—she seemed frightened. Apparently there had been rumors that she and two others were to be sent to a gang out of L.A. in the near future; apparently, sometimes they swap the girls around. Rosy, excuse me, Carla, doesn't belong in that world, ma'am," he said, vehemently.

None of them do, I wanted to shout. And you johns  as users are a big part of the problem.

He continued, "I never hurt her—some of the men do—but, well you  know we have needs, and the prostitutes come around, wearing those clothes and . . . I hope you find her and take her someplace safe. I really do. But be careful, I hear these guys are some pretty ugly dudes."

I had more questions but he had hung up. At least I had reason to believe that Carla was still alive, and I tried not to think further about the warning. I felt drained but also a sense of urgency, one of the sisters already having been moved and the other fearing that she, too, will be relocated.

I put in a call to Deputy Cruz at his Human Trafficking Task Force headquarters in Vista. Those officers knew the local gangs. There must be informants who could find out if my anonymous caller was on to something. I was informed that he was out in the field. I left a message stressing how urgent it was.

Now, all I could do was wait and hope. Oh, Carla, if only I could promise you that help was on the way!

The continued positive response to my featured article was gratifying, but so far my main immediate objective had not been achieved; no Carla, no Serena. Perhaps Stan Kukesh and J.C. Williams were having some success with the quest to locate Serena. I dialed the number for Kukesh given to me by the detectives in San Diego handling her case.

"Detective Kukesh here. I imagine you're calling about Serena."

# 12

"Psst. Serena, are you awake?"

Serena leans over the side of the bunk. Wanda is standing beside her cot, looking up.

"Come on down," she whispers.

Neither girl speaks again until they are in the kitchen. "The rest of them will probably sleep for hours," Wanda says. "This life really messes up your inner clock, but right now mine is saying, "Give me breakfast!""

There is still no milk in the refrigerator so the girls settle for cinnamon oatmeal in individual packets mixed with hot tap water.

The street outside has begun to come alive again. They look out the window to see delivery trucks going by and merchants across the way raising their metal theft-protection outer doors. A bearded older man is sweeping the sidewalk in front of a diner.

"Do you think they have donuts?" Wanda asks. Serena shrugs. "I'd die for a big, fat, frosted one with colored sprinkles on it," the older girl says with a dreamy look in her eyes.

Maybe Wanda can run away with her, thinks Serena. Her abuela Flores would make them donuts called churros. They'd sit around the table in Campo with Carla and drink mugs of the special Mexican coffee just like the grown-ups. And none of them would ever again have to let strange, cruel men do bad things to them. They would be free forever!

"A penny for your thoughts?" asks Wanda. Serena startles—so real has been her vision of family.

"Have you ever tried to run away?" Serena asks, in a low voice.

*Wanda seems to be weighing her words carefully. "Are you just curious or are you actually giving it some thought? Didn't your last pimp beat the crap out of you for trying that?"*

*"Just curious," Serena answers—not quite sure why she's not being totally honest.*

*"Well, to tell the truth, I have twice," Wanda confides. "Once I was found by a homeboy and he and the other gang members decided to make an example out of me. No need to give you the details. I'll just say that I couldn't be put out on the track for a while. Some men really prefer brown sugar, but my messed-up mouth was a turn-off. My main man was not pleased!" she said, with a self-deprecating laugh.*

*Serena felt a chill. Her own beating was so recent. "You actually tried it again?" she asked, her heart going out to her brave friend. At the same time she felt her own resolve falter.*

*"That one was a little different," Wanda begins. "One night a john went all psycho on me and I thought it was all over. I managed to get away from him and run to Snake's car. I was shaking and crying, but instead of taking my side he had a fit—hollering and yelling. Gave me a coke and said I had fifteen minutes to get back out there. That happened in Oxnard about thirty miles from where my mother lived, so when he nodded off from all the pot he was smoking, I just sneaked out and hitched rides home."*

*"But it didn't work out."*

*"It sure didn't," Wanda confides. "Of course, good old mom had to take me in at first. I was only thirteen and CPS had been asking about me when they came to check on my younger half-brother and sister. But she was the same drunk, still blaming me somehow, because my father ran off and left her to raise me alone. You sure you want to hear more?"*

*Once again, Serena nods in the affirmative. "Okay," Wanda agrees. "Well, in the months I'd been gone yet another strange man had settled in to sponge off my mother and her welfare check. Uncle Bill, as I was told to call him, didn't drink as much as* mom, but he made up for it by shooting up. He enjoyed ordering her and the kids around and before long suggested that he and I should have sex together. After all, I was a prostitute, he pointed out.

"When he began to force himself on me I made the mistake of telling Mom. Of course she sided with him. I left before she could throw me out..."

"And then?" Serena asks—fascinated in spite of herself.

"The police picked me up first; asked me why I wasn't in school. When they checked on me they found I was listed as a truant runaway so they put me in temporary lock-up for two days while they sorted it out. Then, since mom claimed she couldn't handle me, it was on to a group home in Santa Rosa."

"But at least you were safe there, weren't you?"

"Enough of the scary stories for now, Serena. I'll finish that part some other time. You'll find I don't always do what's best for me, but I try. I want better for you."

The door to the second bedroom opens and Angel emerges, bare chest showing off his well-developed pecs and several tattoos which include an American flag and a star with a broken point. "You like, ladies?" he asks, with an insolent grin.

He is followed by a J-Lo look-a-like of about eighteen. Her long, black hair is tousled, and she is wearing a pale-green camisole and tap pants. She barely looks at the girls before reaching up to give Angel a long kiss, her curvaceous body pressed against his. He breaks away first. "Say hello to my girlfriend, Mariana, and introduce yourselves."

The girls do as he asks. At her boyfriend's urging, Mariana says, "Welcome," but then goes back to admiring her professionally-done nails.

Seemingly satisfied with that exchange Angel says, "Sorry there is so little to eat, but we'll fix that later. Wanda will be working," he says dismissively, "but Serena will come with us to help pick out groceries—and we need to get her some new clothes, too."

*Mariana mumbles something in Spanish before flouncing off.* "Can you believe she's jealous of you, my chica linda," Angel says to Serena, a smug look on his face.

*Serena can't help but be flattered by the compliment, but she remembers Wanda's words of caution about the divide-and-conquer techniques used by the gang members.*

# 13

I listened to Detective Kukesh from the downtown San Diego precinct admit that Serena could be most anywhere. "I'm sorry, Erin. At least for now, all we know is that she's been moved. We have received a few calls since your article was published, but none has panned out..."

"I know this may sound naïve," I interrupted, "but couldn't you find some reason to press charges against the gang or gangs in your area that probably were pimping Serena herself, or at least others like her? You *know* they are involved in trafficking and quite possibly buying and selling drugs as well."

"That's a fair question, and occasionally we *have* arrested a few members, but arresting them is the easy part. It's when we get to trial that the case against them too often falls apart. Unfortunately, the system is heavily weighted in their favor. In the case of trafficking, especially, we need one or more preferably credible witnesses, who can stand up to the high-powered defense lawyers the gangs employ. But, as you can imagine, the young victims who have been living that sick life, sometimes for years, are easily demoralized and discredited. Believe me, we would like nothing better than to see every gang member in prison."

"Sounds hopeless," I said, slumping in my chair.

"Not quite. Look at it this way. Awareness of the whole problem of human trafficking is up. More people like you are getting involved at some level. You know—we in law enforcement are only human. We get discouraged, angry, suffer burnout, you name it. But we never give up and neither should you."

"Thanks for the pep talk," I said, thinking how first impressions weren't always accurate. He was all right.

"I'm just practicing my morale-builder speech for tomorrow's roll call." The flippant tone was back. "Anyhow, Erin, keep up your good work, but don't take unnecessary chances. Word gets around. Even some gang members read newspapers, and they really know how to hold grudges and retaliate."

It was difficult to concentrate on the minutia of my more routine activities at the newspaper while I waited for my call from the sheriff's department in Vista. I even resorted to stopping by the cubicle shared by Muriel, the society editor, and Barbara, the woman who doubled as food and music critic.

"I was so impressed, Erin," Muriel exclaimed, when she saw me. "I wanted to cry when I read about the sisters."

Not to be outdone, Barbara stated, emphatically, "I actually did!"

They were nice women, but while I appreciated the applause for my writing ability, it wasn't helping to find the girls.

After all the waiting, Deputy Cruz's return call was a letdown. He was polite enough and even seemed glad that I was still involved with the county Human Task Force, but as to finding Carla—that was another story.

"According to the tip you got, at least she was still in this area recently. We'll send out some feelers as to which local gang might be planning to move the merchandise, as they like to call the girls," he explained.

I wondered if I would ever get used to hearing such callous talk.

He went on. "We can even round up a few of the members and threaten them with jail. But without a strong witness their lawyers will have them out before we can even get the DA to prosecute. If either of us is able to find your Carla, maybe she'll be the one brave enough to bring them down, what with the other charges we can pin on them. We do win a few. I have your number if anything comes up. Remember me to Mike. Oh, and Erin, I was impressed by your latest newspaper article."

Call concluded, I knew I should finish writing up my notes from the recent Rotary Club luncheon, but my heart wasn't in it.

Carla, Carla, Carla, I began to chant under my breath.

A broad frame filled my cubicle entrance. 'Talking to yourself again. Not a good sign," Frank observed, shaking his head at me.

I filled him in on my conversations with the police.

"Sounds as if you've had a brutal day," he remarked. "I can't stay to discuss this further, but here's an off the top of my head suggestion to at least temporarily lift your spirits. Why don't you call Mike, have him come home early, order take-out, and then sit close while you watch a mindless movie?"

"You are *such* a romantic," I said.  No sense letting on that the temperature at our house was still a little chilly. "Actually this is my night at the bookstore and Mike plays poker with the guys. I'll be fine, but thanks for stopping by. You always make me feel better."


Once again the Reader's Roost lived up to its reputation as a haven for customers and staff alike. I fielded customer questions, unpacked merchandise, and even found time to write a recommendation for a slim volume of poems that so expressed the angst I was feeling as the result of my situation with Michael. And then, to top it off, I got an upbeat call from Amy.

She began with a compliment for the newspaper article, explaining, "I've been away, but Yolanda saved a copy for me behind the counter at the restaurant. Actually, I think she bought a dozen copies and put them near the coat rack, so customers could see how far her former employee has risen. To Tony and

Yolanda, you will always be the waitress who made good."

Dear Amy, I thought, always building up others. That does it. No matter what comes up I *will* find time to get down to the Bella Italiano in the next week. As if she had read my mind, she added, "My main reason for calling is to invite you to my apartment for lunch either this Wednesday or Sunday. And we can drop into the restaurant while you're down here. I know it's sudden, but I have some news I can't wait to share."

She sounded so happy.

"I'll work it out," I answered, "but can't you give me a hint as to what's going on?"

"You know me. I'm tempted, but I really want to tell you in person, so no hints."

"Then Sunday it is," I said, knowing that I had no newspaper assignments over the weekend, and that Mike would be playing golf.

Meanwhile, I knew that the police would not call unless they had some concrete news to report, but I still found myself staring at the telephone, willing it to ring. There *were* a number of calls and messages that came to me directly from the general public. Most were well-meaning but way off the mark as to the young sisters I was seeking. A few were obviously from the cranks I had been warned about. A handful—the most poignant—were from parents who had also lost a child to the sex trade. . .some, many years before.

At home, Mike and I, in an unspoken agreement, skirted the issue—don't ask, don't tell, worked for a while, but at what cost to our relationship?

On Sunday I made the familiar drive south to the apartment I had once shared with Amy. "Welcome," she said, when I arrived. "No need for a tour, though I have made a few changes since you were here last."

"I like what you've done," I said, with sincerity. "The new window treatment and the mirrors make the apartment look so much bigger, and that multicolored throw on the divan is perfect."

"It does look nice, doesn't it? Tim thinks so, too."

"Wait a minute. Isn't that the name of the bartender they hired awhile back at the Bella Italiano?"

"Oh, him. He's still there. Nice enough guy, but a little bit macho for my taste. In any case it's not him. He's never seen my place."

"Alright, you know I'm dying to ask. Who is this mysterious Tim and does he have anything to do with your newfound urge to decorate?" I asked, marveling, as always, at the warmth of her smile. "Out with it!"

"Oh, Erin, I'm in love. Hopelessly in love like a heroine from one of those dopey romance novels we used to make fun of. And he seems to feel the same way about me. Isn't that amazing! But look at the time. I asked you to lunch. You must be famished." When I started to protest, she added, "I promise to tell all while we eat."

Amy put out a platter of ham and salami slices, a variety of cheeses along with romaine lettuce and some garnishes, and with a big loaf of asiago bread, we built our own sandwiches. "Iced tea or wine?" She asked.

'Tea will be fine—driving, you know," I answered. The food was excellent. I ate with gusto. I realized that I'd had so much on my mind lately that my appetite had suffered. I noticed that Amy, on the other hand, went particularly easy on the bread, butter and mayo. She did look as if she had lost a few pounds. Should I say anything? She had never dwelt on it, but I knew slimming down was a goal of hers.

"That was *so* good," I said, as I shook off a tea refill. "And, by the way, you look marvelous. Could being in love have anything to do with the added glow? Come on, you said you would tell all."

"Well you know I never envied your career or your beautiful

house and other stuff—I've always been glad for you—but what I did wish I had was the love you and Mike share. I wanted to be part of a couple like you are. So if that was envy, I guess I was guilty."

Before I could respond, she said, "But that is all in the past. I know it must seem too sudden to you but I've actually known Tim for almost a year now. Remember when I was having neck and shoulder pain after a few weeks of waitressing and I went to a chiropractor on Eighth Avenue?"

"Vaguely, but wasn't the practitioner an old guy with warts whose dentures slipped? You can't be saying . . ."

"Heck, no, I was never *that* desperate for a serious relationship. Anyhow, he retired shortly, urging us patients to give the new fellow who was taking over his practice a chance." She stopped to sip some tea.

"And? You've managed to keep your romance from me all these months and I've never even got to meet him!"

"Well it was strictly patient and doctor at first, though I did think he was good looking, and noticed he wasn't wearing a wedding ring. On the other hand, his assistant *was* young and attractive." Her voice trailed off.

"So who made the first move?" I prompted. "And has he taken you to meet his family yet?"

"In a way *he* did, and yes, in answer to your question. Actually it was sort of both. It turned out that his pretty assistant, Megan, was one of his three sisters. We've actually become good friends."

"This just keeps getting better and better," I commented. "You're not going to tell me that you were both denying your true feelings because, somehow under the circumstances, you thought it would be unethical for you to date?"

"Not really. He never made a move on me when I was getting some physical adjustments and, on a personal level, we're both unencumbered adults. It turned out that we're also a little shy and have some issues with rejection. So, Megan stepped in and played cupid. And we've been dating ever since," she finished with a satisfied grin.

"Good for you both—you seem *so* happy, and that's enough for me. Have you made any long-term plans?"

"Well, I went with him to a convention in Las Vegas last week. We were quite compatible as first-time roommates—had a perfect chance to talk seriously about a future together. It turns out that his family has been pushing him to settle down—he's thirty-two—and think we make a great couple. Oh, Erin, they've been wonderful to me! It's a big, close Irish family, an older brother and his wife and the three sisters—one married with two kids—and Mr. and Mrs. Doyle are the best."

Having someone totally in love with you, together with a big, loving family, now I was envious. I could never have the latter, but there was still hope for Mike and me. Amy was looking at me, quizzically. I stammered, "I'm sorry, I missed what you just said."

"I said, how about double dating one of these days? Of course, I'd love you to meet Tim, and vice versa. Not that we're planning a wedding quite yet, but he has spent a few nights here and we are talking about getting engaged, probably on my birthday. Speaking of future plans, how are yours coming along? I'm still your first choice to be maid of honor, aren't I?"

"I think I will have some more of that iced tea, after all," I said, stalling before answering. "We've put our plans on hold for a variety of reasons," I began. "Of course our busy schedules, for one, and we began to question our need for such an elaborate celebration and it just . . ." I was losing it. "Amy, it's all falling to pieces," I wailed. And then I told her everything.

Before I was finished, we were both crying.—clinging to each other for comfort as we had in the past as young girls.

*    *    *

Mike had had a good day on the golf course. I could always tell. Not that he was temperamental about that or anything else, but he was much more talkative if things had gone well. With some prompting on my part he reconstructed a good part of his day— the holes he had parred, the one he had eagled, and a few that he had bogied—finishing with a particularly satisfying putt on the final hole to win the match for him and his partner. As usual there had been some good-sized bets wagered but, unlike in the past, he didn't suggest putting his share of the winnings into our honeymoon account.

"And how was your day with Amy?" he asked. "You've hardly mentioned her lately since you've been so busy with other things," he commented, in a light but judgmental tone, I thought. However, I refused to rise to the bait. I would concentrate on Amy's joy.

"She's in love," I said, and went on to flesh out what I had learned. I knew that Mike was fond of my best friend and appreciated the special bond we shared. "We spoke about getting together soon. I promised I'd get back to her. How does your schedule look?"

When he paused, I could see his thought process—'What would her guy and I find to talk about?' Not that he was a snob: he'd even told me that he had gone to a chiropractor to relieve some of the effects of old football injuries—but now that he was in the world of high finance?

His tone was soft. "I'm sure we can work it out. Tell me more about him—Tim, you said? What does he like to do in his spare time? Does he play any particular sport?"

"I'm afraid we didn't get into much of that. After lunch we went over to the Bella Italiano and you know how those reunions go! I was even hostess for a few minutes to give Yolanda a break. So back to your question about Tim: Amy did say that he was handy as a fixer-upper—worked a lot on the old family home in Del Mar, and that some of the Padres and Chargers who live locally come to him, in their off-seasons, for adjustments."

I called Amy back with the two dates Mike had free. She chose Friday night and mentioned a famous restaurant up the coast in Del Mar. "And Erin, Tim is adamant that this is our treat. I know how generous Mike can be but Tim needs to do this."

"Understood," I said, "Mike won't make a scene but it *will* be hard for him not to pick up the check. Oh, and speaking of scenes, I'm counting on you not to mention the one I had in your kitchen the other day."

"What scene?" she said firmly, then added "I'm really excited about Friday."

I was also looking forward to getting together but not just for the chance to be with friends. The dining room on the patio of the Pacifica Del Mar restaurant had a well-earned reputation as a Southern California treat. It perched high atop the town's plaza with a stunning view of the ocean. Added to that, was an eclectic menu of excellent food and outstanding service, making it easily one of the most memorable dining experiences in the whole county. For all they offered, one did pay a price, but I vowed not to dwell on that. Tim had grown up in the area and this was his choice.

On Friday as we were getting ready, Michael remarked, "I like your hair like that," as he lightly touched one of the tendrils that I had freed from my chignon. "But then I always like your hair."

Such compliments used to be routine—lately, not so much. But I couldn't really blame him. Somehow I had changed from being an easy-going, loving fiancée, to an uptight, worried companion.

"I'm glad," I said, leaning briefly against his shoulder. "By the way, you look great yourself." If not exactly a make-up session, I thought it was a start.

We decided to take the BMW for the short drive north on the Pacific Coast Highway to Del Mar. We were in no hurry and Michael settled into a middle lane going just above the posted speed limit. I relaxed as we passed familiar landmarks. Lulled by the comfortable ride I was startled when I heard him exclaim loudly, "Idiot!" as he sped up.

"What's going on, Mike?" I asked, jolted out of my reverie.

"Oh, just some impatient driver, or some yahoo wanting to drag with our car. Whatever his intent he came up so close behind me I thought he was going to crawl up my bumper."

I felt a cold chill and looked in my side mirror. It *couldn't* be, my rational brain was telling me, but there was a black Lincoln just behind us. There had been no sign of it on the winding roads leading from our home to the main freeway.

Mike was speaking, as he continued to check the rearview mirror. "'You don't see many of those big old cars these days. Well, our exit is next. He's had his fun."

I prayed that Mike was right, but no such luck. "Well, I'll be damned. The jerk is still right with us. I have half a mind to pull over and see what happens."

"Amy and Tim will be waiting for us."

"You're right," he agreed, as we passed the famous Del Mar racetrack and fairgrounds. As we pulled into valet parking the offending car went on by.

Our hosts met us on the lower level. Handshakes and hugs ensued, the men sizing each other up, while Amy and I admired one another's outfits.

"We've got a table reserved upstairs on the patio," Tim said, catching the eye of a hostess. Our sea-view seating was perfect, setting the stage for a very satisfying evening ahead.

"Ah, this is the life," Mike said, as he sipped his margarita, and looked around with a smile.

"Amen," Tim chimed in. Amy smiled and high-fived Mike.

I forced a smile and murmured in agreement but my heart wasn't in it. I was still shaken by the incident with the tailgating car.

While waiting for our food to be served, Mike and Tim discovered they shared a mutual love of surfing, though neither had done much lately as their careers and other activities had intruded. And, though shop talk was discouraged, Tim suggested that Mike stop by his office anytime to see if a few chiropractic sessions would help alleviate the back pain he had been experiencing lately after playing a round or two of golf. Mike, in turn, agreed to look over the financial side of Tim's business plan and his goal of the practice becoming part of a future wellness center.

And then our plates arrived and we all concentrated on savoring our choices. The men had both gone for traditional steaks, but also with the imaginative side dishes the Pacifica was known for. My barbecued sugar-spiced salmon was mouth-watering. Amy had played it safe and chose roasted chicken. "You're sure you don't want to try something different, honey?" Tim had asked.

"No, I'm fine," she said, "but it does come with corn leek bread pudding—want to try some?"

I understood where she was coming from. Given our background we had never eaten in high-end restaurants. I had been afraid to take a risk and it had taken months after I met Mike before I stopped ordering the cheapest entrée on the menu.

After coffee and shared desserts we headed back to our respective homes.

A few hours had passed since our arrival. Surely anyone who had been following us would have given up by now. And yet, I found myself tensing every time another car's headlights came up behind us.

"I can't believe how late it is," Mike said, as we drove into our garage. "But I really enjoyed the evening."

"It *was* nice," I agreed. Nice and normal, I said under my breath, hoping that would continue to be the case; hoping, but not really believing. It was really up to me—up to me and Carla. And when I find her, what then?

# 14

*Word gets out quickly that Serena has been singled out to go on errands with Angel and Mariana. Reactions range from disbelief to overt jealousy. Wanda defends her friend and reminds the others that, for everyone's sake, they should stick together.*

*"I can't believe you fell for that crap," she scolds them. "I was there. He's just trying to tick Mariana off—show her that he calls all the shots. Get over it. Now, let's finish getting ready for work. Oh, and if you want something special to eat, tell Serena. Maybe he'll let her pick some things out and we'll all win."*

*There is silence, until Ariel says, "Wanda is right." Then she turns to Serena who had come quietly in during Wanda's lecture. "If he lets you choose I would love some fresh fruit."*

*"And ice cream," Simone pipes up.*

*"How about a big chocolate cream pie," Tina adds. "Let's make a list. We can dream, can't we?"*

*After the girls have been picked up, Angel comes into the bedroom where Serena waits nervously. She has put on the best outfit she owns—a pink polka-dot dress over navy-blue tights. He looks her up and down. "This isn't San Diego, chica. You don't even have a jacket. Guess I'll have to spend some real cash on you before I get any back, but it will be worth it. There are a number of high-class gentlemen waiting to meet you," he tells her, as if sharing a wonderful secret. "Now, let's see what's keeping Mariana and get out of here."*

*It turns out that Angel keeps his car in a mechanic friend's large garage about a block away. When they reach their destination, Angel points to a shiny, older vintage, white Cadillac. "Get in," he says, "while I settle with my man, Charlie."*

*Mariana gets in the passenger seat, Serena in back, almost swallowed up by the huge interior. She marvels at the black and white shag carpeting and matching zebra-print interior lining. Small mirrors are set in the headliner and in some of the cup holders are tiny sprays of silk flowers.*

*"Don't think I don't know what you're up to," Mariana says, without turning her head. "Pretending you're some poor little girl who doesn't know what's going on just so Angel will feel sorry for you and treat you special."*

*Serena doesn't know what to say. "I'm sorry if . . ." she falters.*

*The older girl turns to face the back seat and Serena notices that she is wiping tears from her eyes. "I think you're so beautiful," Serena blurts out. "I'm sorry if I make you sad."*

*Mariana looks totally puzzled, and then she smiles. "I'm not really angry with you. I just get sick of Angel always trying to make me jealous. I know he loves me. The rest of you are just part of his business. But be glad you're with him," she goes on, after checking to be sure they aren't being overheard.*

*"He'll take good care of you as long as you do what he asks. Some of the others you could have ended up with are just plain cruel. They are mean to their girls just to prove what tough guys they are. But here comes Angel now." She smiles, and says, "I'm glad we had this little talk."*


*Later, at the mall when Serena is modeling clothes for Angel's approval, she almost forgets the purpose of her new wardrobe.*

*"Well, what do you think?" Angel asks—obviously pleased with his choices.*

*"They are beautiful," Serena answers, then hesitates. "But don't you think they are a little young for me? I am almost eleven." She looks to Mariana for backing.*

*Angel sighs. "Those men I told you about, like little girls. That's* why I took you off Dion's hands. It's just play-acting for you," he says, soothingly. He lowers his voice so the saleslady can't over-hear. "Now pick out something for Wanda and we're finished here."

Lunch is at a buffet chain restaurant on the premises, but to Serena it rivals any previous dining experience she's ever had.

"Be sure you save room for a big bowl of ice cream with chocolate syrup," Angel advises.

"Or a cone," Mariana suggests.

Serena gets the latter. While she licks the cone she sneaks a look at the other diners—ordinary people going about their ordi-nary lives. She is aware that anyone looking at the three of them would notice how much they resemble each other. Why can't I be in a regular family? She wishes desperately, and the ache in her heart is back. Her grandmother? Carla? Would she ever see them again? She turns her face away. She will not let the others see her cry. Her spirits lift again when they get to the grocery store. De-spite some grumbling from Angel he lets the two girls buy almost everything on their wish list. Mariana reminds him that it is to his advantage to keep his workers healthy. He counters that they bet-ter meet the quota that he has set for each of them, after all, he has expenses.

Back at the apartment, Angel goes off to work on business, as he calls it. Serena helps Mariana put their purchases away. She can't wait for the girls to see all the food. Angel has told her that starting tomorrow she will be expected to earn her keep. She doesn't want to think about what that means. For tonight she is content for Mariana to give her a manicure and pedicure. Later they watch a Disney animated feature. She has no way of knowing how long it will be before she gets to enjoy anything that pleasant again.

*   *   *

*Next day after Angel drops the other girls off he takes Serena to a mid-level hotel near Union Square. He uses the in-house lobby phone and then escorts her to the fourth floor and a room next to a stairwell. "Mr. X will call me when he's finished and someone will be back for you. Make me proud," he adds, gently stroking her cheek. "Mr. X is an important man. If he likes you it will mean repeat business and that's a good thing."*

*"Come in, child," the small Asian man beckons as he speaks, "and take off your coat so I can see you better." Under her new coat Serena is wearing skimpy navy-blue shorts and a flared floral-print top which exposes a wide band of bare skin between the two pieces.*

*"You are lovely," he says, or at least Serena thinks that is what he says—his accent makes it hard to tell. "Don't be afraid. I can tell we are going to have a fine time together. I have a business meeting later, but if I like you, I can arrange for you to stay longer next time."*

*Mr. X begins to caress her bare flesh. She can smell alcohol on his breath. He sees her eying the several small, opened bottles on one of the bedside tables. He gives a half bow and says, "Forgive my bad manners. Would you like something to drink before we begin?"*

*She says yes, and he gets her a can of Sprite from the under–counter refrigerator. "Later, you might like some fruit or yogurt. For now let's get you undressed so I can see what I paid for."*

*When they get to her panties he tells her to keep them on—Daddy's Little Girl, they read. He grins sloppily, showing tobacco-stained teeth. "Ah, yes. Just how little are you?" he asks. "Seven? Eight?"*

*Serena just nods, hoping that the john doesn't make an issue of it. She hates to lie but she knows that it is her petite size that makes her valuable to Angel.*

\*   \*   \*

*Jose, Angel's business partner, brings her back to the apartment and locks her in. She looks wistfully down to the bustling street below. Even if she could open the paint-stuck window and scream for help, who would pay any attention to her? She decides to take a shower—a long, hot shower to scrub away the ugly smells that her afternoon with Mr. X have left on her body.*

*Even after the shower she feels strangely disoriented—unable to remember all that went on in that hotel room. Could she have just blocked out the details, or was there something else happening? She had been told that some johns, as well as pimps, gave the girls drugs.*

*She gets into her buttercup-yellow sweat suit, eats a bowl of Cocoa Puffs, then climbs up to her bunk, clutching her tattered bunny, and falls asleep in minutes.*

# 15

"What else can I get you?" I asked Mike next morning as I poured him a cup of coffee.

"Just juice and toast, please," he answered. "That was *some* meal last night, but I think I overate."

"Tell me about it," I groaned in remembrance, choosing only some mixed fruit to go with my toast and coffee.

We were seated in our breakfast nook, Mike reading the sports page of the San Diego Union Tribune while I went through some flyers and coupons.

"Oh, by the way," I said. "Did you see that our Homeowners Association is putting on a program at the clubhouse this Thursday night called 'How to Protect Your Unit Against Burglary'?"

"No, but I think we have a good handle on that already, don't you?"

"I've certainly read enough articles on the subject and we do have a good alarm system, but what gets me is that the fellow they've chosen to present the program is an ex-con . . ."

"Who used to burgle for a living," he finished. "And they pay those speakers and that pisses you off, right?"

I ignored the comment. "And I read a piece where a former car thief offered tips on protecting our cars from someone like him, and what about the hackers who are hired by government agencies to show them how to stay one step ahead!"

"I thought you were all for giving people second chances. After all, they paid their debt to society."

He's purposely ignoring my point, I thought. "Second chances are good, I agree, but some of them probably broke the law numerous times before they got caught, and then got only a slap on the wrist. And, now that they are out of prison, and supposedly going straight, because they saw the light or got religion or whatever, they are rewarded. And what about their victims—the people they once terrorized?" Of course, I was thinking mainly of those responsible for human trafficking. I knew my voice was becoming shrill, the more I tried to defend my views, but I couldn't help it.

"You know Erin, you can't obsess over every example of social injustice," Mike said, calmly. "As I've told you before, I thought that helping to promote the cause of those hoping to stop trafficking would prove to be rewarding enough for you. Obviously it is not. For your sake—for our sake—you have *got* to stop obsessing. I'm sorry that those two little prostitutes have vanished, but you did what you could. Now let it go!"

"What did you call them?"

"I didn't call them anything, since I don't remember their names, but your article called them sisters, as I recall. I could have said the sisters, but I just called them the little prostitutes because that is what they are," he said, matter-of-factly. "Why are you looking at me that way? What does it matter?"

I wanted to cry out in sorrow and frustration. How could the man I loved be so misguided—make such a cruel assessment of the plight of those exploited children?

I tried to explain as calmly as I could. "It matters a lot. That word, prostitute, which continues to carry such a stigma, doesn't apply here. Sometime in the nineties, UNICEF adopted the terminology, 'commercially sexually exploited child or youth,' and that perfectly describes children like Carla and Serena."

"Semantics, Erin. They get paid to have sex with men—multiples of men, right? You're making a big deal out of nothing here."

"Am I? You're saying, if we were talking about some of those young girls I met at your office Christmas party, and, in the past, had been abducted or somehow coerced into working for pimps, they would now be stigmatized forever as hos?"

"Of course not! Now you're just being vulgar." He reached for my hand.

"Don't touch me!" I said, my voice rising in anger as I pulled my hand back. I got up and left the table, afraid to say anything more. Afraid, also, that the gulf between us might be too deep to bridge, but not willing to accept that what we had might be lost forever.

Mike looked stunned or perhaps it was just anger I saw in his eyes? To be honest, a part of me wished he might also be sad. In any case, I feared it might be awhile before either of us swallowed our pride and tried to make up. Unfortunately, for the time being, we might just live as strangers sharing a house.


I remember reading once about a married couple who, at the time, had been sharing a home for thirty, or maybe it was even forty, years, had physically separated the home into his and her sections. Neither would sell out to the other, or leave the premises, or let go of the animosity that had caused the rift in the first place. Supposedly, they never spoke or otherwise interacted, though they could see and hear each other from certain rooms!

Not that the situation between Mike and myself was that impossible—we spoke politely and even ate some meals together—but let's just say I hadn't felt this sad and lonely in a very long time. So, to compensate, I filled my weekly planner with one activity after another.

Monday, I answered a backload of e-mails, ate lunch with other *County Voice* staff members, and took a Hatha Yoga class. Tuesday, I made calls to potential donors for a Polaris project annual fundraiser, went to a Pilates class, and had a hair trim and manicure. Wednesday, I covered the mayor's wife's charity luncheon benefit for the local Boys & Girls Clubs, and then worked that evening at the bookstore. Thursday, I took clothes to the cleaners, and then had my routine six-month dental cleaning.

After that last appointment, I swung by the newspaper to start work on my second byline feature—this one focusing on Carla. And that's when I decided to check, once again, my voice mail. As soon as I did there was the voice I had been hoping and praying to hear since that day in Tri-Cities Medical Center: "Erin, it's me, Carla. I need to talk with you. It's very important. I'll call again tomorrow about this same time."

That meant she was still in the vicinity—or did it? I *couldn't* lose her again. That evening I settled in with a copy of a highly recommended staff pick from the Reader's Roost. It had previously grabbed my attention from the opening paragraph, but when I returned to it this time, my mind kept wandering back to Carla. Finding her, up until the call, had been a hypothetical. Had she been able or willing to make her situation known to the police, she would have done so, and I would have heard from them. Now she might actually be counting on me to save her from the nightmare she had been thrust into. What next for her and how best to deal with the Serena situation? As ever, her sister's whereabouts would no doubt be Carla's main concern.

"I didn't expect you in today," said Barbara, when I arrived at the paper late the next morning.

"I left some of my notes here, and I'm also behind on answering e-mails, so thought I'd get caught up."

"Well, as you can see there's nothing going on, so you'll have plenty of peace and quiet. Oh, and Erin, I just got an idea. Since you're here, would it be possible for you to lock up this afternoon?" I nodded. "That way I could stop by the mall and get my makeup done at the Estée Lauder counter before I meet Rick for lunch," she said. "I had agreed to stay until one, so I'll owe you."

"No problem," I said, wincing at my use of that all-pervasive cliché.

"You're a doll. Oh, and be sure to reset the alarm code," she added, as she grabbed her purse and hurried off, her stiletto heels clicking down the hallway.

Ah, romance. It seemed to be everywhere, except in my own home, I thought, with a twinge of self-pity!

At eight minutes past two, my phone rang. "Collect call for Erin from Carla, do you accept?"

I could hear that familiar voice in the background saying, "Erin, it's me. Please say yes."

"Yes, I'll accept," I said, willing myself to remain calm.

Carla, her voice low and breathless as if she had been running, explained. "I'm calling from a phone booth and I don't have much time."

"Understood," I acknowledged. "I'm so glad you reached me. Where *are* you?"

"Still in Oceanside but I think I won't be for long. I know this is sudden, and I know it's a lot to ask, but can you come and get me? You said at the hospital that I should get away from the pimps who brought me in and that you and that other nice lady would help me. Do you remember?"

"I remember very well, and that offer still holds, but have you any idea how we can actually get you away from them? I understand that they watch you all quite closely and aren't at all afraid to harm anyone who tries to get in their way. Is it possible for you to get to the police? They . . ."

"I can't—you don't understand! They say they know where my grandmother lives, and where another gang is keeping Serena, and that they will hurt them badly if I ever go to the authorities." Her voice was trembling. "If you won't . . ."

"It's alright, honey," I said, "I'm sorry I upset you. Let's think about how to go about this."

"Here's what I had in mind," she continued in a halting voice. "Some nights a few of us girls are dropped off near the cheaper hotels—especially those that have convention rooms—so there are always a few out-of-town johns looking for action. Lately, Emilio is the guy who watches us and sees that we work hard enough," she explained, in a monotone.

Work hard enough! I actually tightened up, but I spoke slowly. "Emilio, is he that pimp I saw in the hospital?" I asked, as I remembered the swaggering punk I had seen walking down the corridor.

"That's him. Anyhow," she went on, "when he's on duty keeping track of his girls he likes to have one of us get him something to eat. It's almost always me. He stays in a car a few blocks away, keeping watch, and collecting our trick money and listening to hip-hop on his headphones. I thought maybe you could meet me at Angelo's Burger on Pacific Coast Highway near the Rodehouse Inn. We could get away in your car before he realizes I'm not coming back with his order."

"Of course I'll meet you." It just might work, I thought. I had no better idea.

Carla continued. "The reason I'm calling about this now is because two nights ago when I brought him his coffee, Emilio said he was going to miss me. He told me that soon some of us are going to be sent to another gang in L.A. It turns out the Oceanside Los Posole gang plans to go big time and expand their prostitution business into the ritzy hotels where the johns with lots of money stay. So they will need a stable of high-class girls, maybe even take over an escort service."

"So they are going to sell you girls to another gang?" I still could not wrap my mind around the fact that such transactions were going on in communities all over the country, let alone in the beautiful San Diego area.

"It's just business for them—Emilio told me that we younger girls didn't fit in with their new plans, so it's off to the big city. He made it sound like we were going on a grand adventure." Then her tone changed again. Desperation took over and I heard her wail, "Erin, I don't want to go to L.A.!"

"We won't let them take you, honey," I said, with more conviction then I felt. "Keep your spirits up, and just to be on the safe side, here is my cell phone number. Make sure you memorize it and I'll see you tonight."

I wrote down the directions to Angelo's after agreeing to meet Carla there the next night. I had so many questions, but it was obviously not safe for her to talk longer. She had begged me not to speak to the police. I would probably have to involve them, with her permission once she was safe, but for now I needed to honor her wishes. Could her plausible, but rather naïve, plan really work? I was about to find out.

I sat at the desk, staring at the phone long after Carla broke the connection. She's just one girl out of hundreds—thousands. Why *do* you care so much, the pragmatists would ask, understandably. You *mustn't* care so much, Mike had warned, as well as had Deputy Cruz. But I did care.

I had tried to be totally honest with myself. Admittedly, there would be an ego boost if I ended up as a rescuer, but that was not my main motivation. Fate, or whatever you want to call it, had brought Carla and me together once before. Pure evil, as I had come to think of the traffickers, had snatched her away. Now I had another chance to make it right.

I'm not particularly religious, but somehow the phrase "she has a beautiful soul" came to mind when I thought of Carla. That lovely young woman with the fighting spirit, torn from her normal life, never giving up hope that she will find and rescue her little sister and return her home.

"I'm spending the evening with Amy," I told Mike later; not as far from the truth as it might seem, because I *was* going to take Carla to my friend's apartment after we made our getaway. "There's leftover curry and mixed veggies in the fridge."

"Drive safe," he said, barely looking up from his copy of *Golf Digest.*

# 16

*At some point while it is still dark outside, Serena awakens to the sound of more than one girl crying, and Angel saying angrily, "You lazy slut, see what you made me do!"*

*She decides to pretend she has heard nothing but her heart goes out to whoever has been punished. All the girls have been nice to her, especially since she was able to get Angel to buy some of their favorite foods.*

*"And stop your whimpering. I barely touched you. Next time I'll show you what a real beating is!" the angry male voice continues.*

*Serena pulls the covers over her head. To her surprise the next thing she hears is Wanda's voice calling to her to wake up. "Come on, sleepyhead. We're having a house meeting. You don't need to get dressed."*

*"Come in, come in," Angel says, pointing to one of the over-stuffed pillows that make up most of the seating. "Now as I was saying, last night was a disappointment, and I was forced to physically punish some of you, which you know I hate to do, but when someone seems to be slacking off, it sets a bad example. However, this morning when I added up all your take and threw in Mr. X's generous contribution"—he nods at Serena—"it actually turns out that our business did pretty well these past few days, so . . ." He pauses dramatically. "I've decided to give everyone the night off."*

*Ariel and Tina begin to clap. Simone even gives him a kiss on the cheek. After Angel has gone off somewhere with Mariana, and the others are doing each other's hair and nails, Serena finds out that he had used a straightened coat hanger to raise welts on their thighs and buttocks as punishment, and yet they act as if he's this great guy!*

*She doesn't get it, and says so. She's even more perplexed when they defend his actions as better than other pimps, and the occasional punishment as proof that he really cares for them.*

*"After all," Ariel says, "he has a lot of expenses—the rent and food, and our clothes and his car."*

*"Not to mention the doctor and the dentist," Tina chimes in.*

*Ariel adds, "And when we're in PMS mood . . . think what it must be like for him putting up with six bitches—or five, I guess. You haven't started yet, have you?"*

*But Serena isn't ready to let it go. "But this life is not right, not normal!" she states, her voice shaking with frustration. "They can't watch you all the time. Couldn't you find a policeman who could help you get away? I know some of you don't want to go home but there must be some place that would take you in so you could go to school, and . . ."*

*Serena's words unleash a torrent of responses. In the next few minutes she hears horror stories of policemen who rape, of being thrown in what they call baby-jail, of being put in a group home where the other girls steal their clothes and some of the staff treat them shabbily and label them scummy hookers!*

*"Angel warns us about the straights who promise us a better life, but just want to use us to help relieve their conscience 'cos they have so much that we never will," Ariel comments. "He calls them the 'holy do-gooders.'"*

*"We don't mean to dump on you, girl, but you just don't know much about the real world—about our world anyhow," says Tina, firmly. "Just because you have a good family somewhere who want you doesn't give you the right to judge us," she adds, lifting her chin defiantly.*

*Wanda weighs in. "I'm sure Serena wasn't judging us," she says in her calm way. "Let's pick out a video. And is there any more ice cream left?"*

*They settle on yet another viewing of "The Princess Bride" and apportion out the remaining ice cream.*

*The three other girls regale Wanda and Serena with their remembrances of a day the previous year when Angel took them to a Carl's Jr. Restaurant near Union Square and let them buy anything they wanted. Apparently he had won some bet with another pimp from the same gang as to whose girls would bring in the most money by soliciting at a major truck terminal outside the city.*

*While speaking dreamily of the ice cream concoctions—vanilla with chocolate syrup and whipped cream on a brownie for Tina and Ariel, and a banana split with three scoops for Simone—they all agreed that they were glad that servicing truckers was not their regular beat. "Sometimes they get cranky if you wake them up and then they ask too many questions about our lives," Simone says.*

*One by one the girls fall asleep, all except Serena. Her sister wives had painted a grim picture of their options in the straight world. She knew that they had dismissed much that was obviously bad about being in "the life." But they had agreed that it was different for her. She came from a good family—a family that loved her and that she could one day return to. But was that still the case?*

*Once she had been so sure that, if only she could return to Campo, all would be right again. Carla would have found her way back, her grandmother would have regained her health, and Uncle Mateo would hopefully be jailed for a long time. That had been her fantasy, the dream that had kept her going—but what if none of it was true anymore? What if? What if?*

# 17

The sun was just setting as I headed north on I-5, a red ball scorching the horizon before it disappeared into the Pacific Ocean—a mesmerizing sight I never tired of viewing. This stretch of coast, though not as ruggedly beautiful as it is to the far north, offers much to admire. Ocean views are interspersed with properties, big and small, belonging to the inhabitants of the disparate towns—Del Mar, Encinitas, Carlsbad—each with its own unique charm.

At the same time I had learned that many of these towns were hiding dark secrets of illegal drug dealing and the selling of young women for sex. And the gangs were gradually extending their reach up and down the coast. How could this continue to happen? Why weren't we all up in arms against these creeps?

Though it was yet another balmy Southern California evening, I felt an involuntary shiver as I thought of what lay ahead. The saying "right makes might" came to mind. I sure hoped that would be the case tonight.

After making a few false turns I arrived at Angelo's in Oceanside, well before the window of time Carla had given me. This was, after all, fast food, and the in-store customers didn't tend to stay long. I was hoping that by ordering a complete grilled chicken meal, and bringing along a copy of *Glamour Magazine*, I could stay as long as it took, without calling undue attention to myself. I had parked my car close to the well-lit entrance so that Carla and I could make a quick getaway; I blanched at the phrase. Obviously, I had seen too many mob movies! I didn't think Emilio knew my car, but I was still uneasy.

Shortly after nine, I refilled my coffee cup and began to check out my magazine article on the latest hair and makeup tips, while maintaining my surveillance of the door. A family of six straggled in and I saw Carla duck in behind them. She was in in her working girl uniform—short-shorts of a shiny material, a revealing halter top and some kind of fancy ballet flats—though, in general, she really didn't stand out from what I had observed being worn by some in her age group.

I got up from my booth, leaving everything, and  made my way quickly to her side. "Let's go, honey," I said, taking her by the arm and guiding her back the way she had entered. Once in the parking lot I had just pressed the open button on the car remote when I heard Carla's anguished, "Oh, no!"

I looked up to see Emilio pimp-walking across the parking lot heading straight for her. "I decided I wanted some onion rings instead of fries," he explained, "but how come.  . ." And then he noticed me.

"Hurry! Get in the car," I urged her, but it was too late. To my horror, I found myself in a tug-of-war with Emilio over Carla as the prize. Of course it was an unfair contest, but I refused to just give up, so I began to scream *help*, over and over. Surely some other customers or restaurant workers would come to the scene? Hopefully, one of the police cars that frequently cruised the neighborhood would pass by.

Carla slipped from my grasp and I could hear her begging Emilio not to hurt me. I was only vaguely aware of the blow to my head that followed, but the next thing I knew I was falling forward and hitting the pavement hard—both  knees, also my hands and an elbow being  skinned for sure. My ears were ringing and I felt bleeding when I touched the side of my head. I managed to get part-way up, swinging wildly at Emilio's smirking face as he leaned over me and hissed, "Stay away from her, bitch. She's *my puta!*" And then they were gone.

Now, a few people came forward, asking if I was okay, where

it hurt, suggesting I go to the hospital, giving advice: "Don't get in your car yet, he may be watching," and, "You shouldn't mess with them, lady, next time it will be worse."

I didn't cry. I knew there would be plenty of time for that. Perhaps I was in shock, but I didn't feel faint or disoriented. I also knew that injuries always hurt worse some hours or even a day or two later—the infamous DOMS effect, well known to athletes. But the hardest truth to deal with, was that losing Carla would be by far the most painful and long-lasting of my injuries.

With my limited Spanish I fended off suggestions that the police and an ambulance should be called, and assured them that I would return directly to my casa where my esposo was waiting. I let them help me into the car, said many gracias and pulled out of the parking lot, eager to get back on the I-5.

I was anxious to put as many miles as possible between myself and the restaurant, as fast as I could. But, as I became more and more aware of the extent of my injuries, I wondered if I should have sought medical attention after all. My knees throbbed and the shredded skin on my palms made it difficult to hold the wheel properly. With a free hand, using some Kleenex tissues, I dabbed at the blood still trickling from my scalp wound. I drove especially cautiously—willing myself to be extra vigilant. It was a stark difference between the drive I had made earlier and the one now taking me home.

As I drove south, the landscape pitch black now except for the clusters of lights glimpsed on the outskirts of towns, I pondered the past day and a half. Had I been fooling myself from the beginning? How could our plan have gone so horribly wrong! And what will be Mike's reaction? I had made it seem to the onlookers as if I couldn't wait to get back home to my husband who would bind my wounds and otherwise take good care of me. But chances were very high that would not be the case. I had lied to Mike again, and now had actually paid a physical price for my obsession, as he called it. If I ever needed understanding and a heavy dose of tenderness, it was now. Yet I knew, deep down, that I had crossed a sacred line of trust, and probably forced Mike into taking a stand we both might forever regret.

The next morning the house was quiet—eerily so. In the guest bedroom, where I had spent the night, I leaned over and checked the clock on the stand nearest me. Mike had left for work hours before, as usual, but this morning *nothing* was as usual. It was nearly eight, so obviously I had managed to get a few hours of sleep—a minor miracle after the painful scene that had taken place when I returned the previous night from Oceanside.

The memory of sitting in the car for a few minutes after pulling into the garage, trying desperately, hopelessly, to come up with just the right words to say to Mike, was still vivid. Efforts to make me presentable had been equally futile. One look in the rearview mirror confirmed that I would undoubtedly suffer a shiner, and my skirt wasn't long enough to cover the damage done to my knees.

Everything about my lower body had stiffened during the drive home so I was hobbling as I walked into the condo. I kept thinking, if I was lucky, Mike would have already gone to sleep; if not, maybe I could at least spend a few minutes in the downstairs bathroom making a few repairs to my bruised body before we came face-to-face, but neither scenario came true.

Instead, there he was, holding the door open for me. I can only imagine what went through his mind when he saw me standing there in total dishevelment. But there was nothing uncertain about his reaction after I confessed *everything*. The scene that followed wasn't pretty, and I'll admit that I even resorted to an attempt at pleading, but in the end there remained only the impossible choice he gave me: stop *all* involvement with the anti-human trafficking movement, or it's over between us.

My fiancé, the man I thought I knew and loved, had given me an ultimatum—an ultimatum that in good conscience I could not honor. I had taken to heart the admonition that, if one was aware of a problem, there was a real danger in doing nothing. Now, I could *not* stay—I had to leave.

The unit I had booked at a mid-priced motel in Ocean Beach included a kitchenette and free Wi-Fi. To tide me over, I packed only a few personal belongings, plus items related to my newspaper job and some non-perishables. This arrangement, paying a week in advance, would do for now.

When I had called Amy, late the night before, to tell her of the debacle at Angelo's and my subsequent break-up with Michael, she had urged me to come and stay with her—tempting, but I felt I needed some time alone.

I had a fair sum of money in my personal checking account, and my regular, if modest, salaries from my part-time jobs. Fortunately I had almost eight months paid up on my leased BMW. In the past I had started over from almost nothing and I could do it once more if I had to. I'd be all right. But what about Carla? We were back to square one. I had probably even made her situation worse! Now, she would certainly be quickly moved, undoubtedly beaten as well, and any chance of a reunion with her sister was even slimmer.

I left Mike a brief note on the kitchen counter and, at the last minute, added the modest engagement ring I had chosen some months ago.

Once out of the garage I forced myself not to look back. Ironically, it was a particularly beautiful morning as I wended my way up La Jolla Village Drive onto I-5 going south, past the eclectic beach towns—Pacific, then Mission—until I reached the I-8 cut-off into Ocean Beach, seven miles northwest of downtown San Diego.

Painful as it had been to cover my bruised legs, I wore slacks and, before entering the motel, I checked that the pancake makeup and dark glasses I wore were doing their job. A floppy-brimmed hat completed the look. Maybe the clerk would think I was someone famous wanting privacy for a few days! Or, maybe just an author traveling incognito, while gathering material for a book or exposé?

I had arranged to park my car out of sight around the back, away from any entrances—money to the desk clerk given to him under the table, of course. Hopefully, the Oceanside gang would leave me alone now that they had Carla again, but one couldn't be too careful. I intended to stay put for at least a few days.

But as time went by, I decided that maybe holing up in a motel—alone, hurting, jumpy, and sad—wasn't really such a good idea. After I had twice applied antibacterial ointment on my knees and palms, watched more daytime TV than I had in the previous year, and read two more chapters of Jane Austen's *Sense and Sensibility*, it still wasn't even dark. It was going to be a *very* long night!

Other than an apple and a chunk of medium cheddar, I hadn't had anything to eat since the chicken sandwich the night before. How I longed for two big slices of pizza with the works, or an order of jumbo shrimp with lobster sauce, and a large side of sticky rice. I settled however, for using the in-room microwave and heating up some ramen noodles and a second cup of instant coffee.

I had avoided looking in the mirror other than when I first arrived. Now a second inspection confirmed that, without any Hollywood magic needed, I would make a great extra in one of those popular zombie movies! And my hair . . . I desperately needed a shower, but the sting from the spray drove me out almost immediately. Now I really was feeling sorry for myself!

Keeping a journal had never been a part of my daily routine, though I knew that many therapists and their patients considered it to be a valuable tool in their work. Such introspection wasn't for me. I had a lot of compassion for others going through tough times, but as far as I was concerned, I had always been more of a 'suck it up, get on with it, never let them see you cry' kind of a person. "That's your defense system talking, Erin," I had been told more than once, back in my foster care days. Maybe it was time I took their advice and put at least some of my feelings down on paper. So far, this certainly had qualified as one of the true low points in my life.

So I got out a blank reporter's notebook and for the next few hours filled page after page—pausing only to turn on some lights and heat up my coffee. I don't know what a professional therapist might make of the content, and I might never even read my words again, but I do know that the sense of letting go was real and freeing. Now, I could deal with Carla's situation and my future with the human trafficking movement with a much clearer head. And, as to my possible future relationship with Mike? Cliché or not, I hummed Doris Day's "Que Sera Sera," and meant it—what will be, will be!


Fatigue had finally caught up with me. I remember starting to watch a sitcom rerun at seven, and, next thing I knew, the familiar lilting strains of Beethoven's *Fleur de Lise* on my cell phone broke into my dream-filled sleep. I groped for my cell, noting that it was now eight-twenty.

"Erin, it's me, Carla. I'm calling from a phone near a women's restroom at The Carlsbad Premium Outlets. Do you know where they are? And can you come for me?"

Maybe this was a dream—or a trap? The thought that the gang might force Carla to betray me to save herself crossed my mind, but I quickly dismissed it as paranoia.

Amazing! She had been able to accurately recall my cell number. "I can be there in twenty-five minutes, honey," I said. "I know there is a Starbucks in the Outlet, find it, and I'll meet you there."

"I did see it," she answered, "but please hurry. This whole place closes at nine. Oh, and Erin, the pimps will be looking for me by now, but not down here. I'll tell you all about it when I see you. But are you okay? I'm so sorry about the other . . ."

I cut her off. "I've got to get on the road. Stay safe." Of course I was nervous because of the recent confrontation with Emilio, but I was familiar with the Carlsbad Outlets, knew that they were well-lit, had surveillance video throughout, and were heavily patrolled by hired security, as well as local police. That ugly parking lot scene should not be repeated. Carla and I had been given another chance.

Thirty-five minutes later, and after we exchanged a long, tight hug, Carla was safely in the BMW and we were on our way back to the motel in Ocean Beach—avoiding the freeway, and instead, taking local surface streets. Also, and as a precaution, a generally circuitous route as well. Since my eyes were fastened to the rearview mirror, and my heart skipping a beat every time a dark-colored car came into view, by tacit agreement, we exchanged only a few words. There would be plenty of time for talk later.

# 18

*Serena is beginning to lose track of time and that scares her. Oh, there is a calendar in the kitchen, but what difference does it make if it's Tuesday or Friday, the beginning of a new month, or the end? All the days are pretty much the same. She still longs to find Carla, and to somehow get back with her to their grandmother's house in Campo, but it gets harder and harder to believe that this will happen soon.*

*So far there has been no punishment from Angel for not bringing in enough money. Twice a week she is taken to a hotel to see Mr. X—Angel had told her proudly that he was the owner of one of the biggest restaurants in Chinatown. She still finds him to be as repugnant as ever, though she uses the term gross. He pays to have her stay with him for several hours, and apparently pays well—though, of course, she never sees the money herself.*

*The other girls think she is lucky because she doesn't have to go from john to john, most often outside, even in bad weather. Lucky is not a word she would use to describe her life.*

*Angel tells her that what she does is a kind of acting. She gets to wear different outfits and pretend she is a princess, or Barbie, or a nurse, or even a baby, complete with diaper and pacifier. You are the star of my movie, the johns say, showing her on their cells in dozens of embarrassing poses. Her abuela would cry and call her names if she ever saw them. Then that devout woman would most likely pray for Serena's soul to the Virgin Mary.*

*In the beginning Serena prayed, too. A few times Angel even took her and his girlfriend Mariana to Mass at Saint Peters Catholic Mission Church. He acted so proud of his bonita chicas. When they entered, he gave them some coins so they could light votive candles. What would he say if he could hear her special prayer to God? It was always the same. "Please let me get away from here so I can go back home."*

*Her body is sore most of the time, and no amount of scrubbing gets rid of the male smell she has come to hate. She rarely smiles and interacts with the other girls less and less.*

*Even Wanda scolds her. "You used to be fun, now you're turning into a grump," and Angel warns her that she'd better change her mood before the customers begin to complain.*

*Getting away is never far from her mind, but the enormity of being on her own in such a big city is overwhelming. She has considered trying once more to reach the police. Surely they would help her, but recent events have convinced her that such help is definitely not a sure thing. Simone, and a new girl named Charity, both are now in juvenile detention, charged with prostitution.*

*Each had been asked to have sex by men who claimed not to be policemen—the question all the girls are trained to ask, before they discuss money. Then the men said they wanted to go to a motel. Thirteen-year old Charity didn't know how much to charge for that, so asked if she could check with her pimp, Diego, who was running the girls that day. He told her one hundred and fifty dollars, at which point the man showed his badge and arrested both her and Diego who was sitting in a nearby car. Diego, of course, was out on bail the next day, but the two girls remained in juvenile detention for what would be an indefinite time, waiting for their cases to be heard.*

*Angel related this story apparently to show how stupid Charity was to involve the pimp. Serena saw it differently. How unfair that the girls who were forced to work for the pimps were punished in that way. The second thing she came away with was that the police should not be trusted. Who could she turn to?*

*So the days passed in numbing succession. First Simone, then*

*Charity returned—though not directly. Charity had originally been returned to her alcoholic mother whose latest boyfriend didn't work, of course, and resented sharing their combined welfare benefits with yet another child. It was no contest when he asked the mother to choose between him and her oldest child.*

*Simone—a ward of the state since early childhood—had run away yet again from the group home where the court system had sent her. She had called Angel—all contrite—to come get her. He welcomed her back, told her she had made the right choice. That only he understood her and now she was home. They even had a welcome-home party complete with ice cream and a DVD; no one worked that night. If anyone noticed that Serena wasn't taking part, they didn't mention it. They were having too much fun!*

*Life, for Serena, might have gone on in a similar manner for an untold amount of time if it weren't for two unexpected events. The first was that Angel announced the upcoming arrival of two new sister wives. "Expenses are up," he says. "We got to get more revenue." The girls looked up expectantly. "That means that you will have to double up on your sleeping arrangements." He looks straight at Serena. "You've got plenty of room for one of them to share your little upper-bunk hideaway, right?" Then back to the group, "I expect you all to make them feel welcome."*

*The second incident turns out to be more of a problem for her. "Mr. X has a friend—we'll call him Mr. Chang—who would like to spend some time with you," Angel says to Serena a few days later. "I don't have to tell you how important it is to make him very happy."*

*Mr. Chang is a big man—speaks better English then Mr. X, and is younger by a few years. After they have got acquainted, as he calls it, and he has zipped up his trousers, he gets a hairbrush out of a men's toiletry case. She thinks he wants to brush her hair, as has often been the case with the other johns. Instead, he grabs a* chair, sits on it, and in one quick motion lays her across his lap. With each blow on her bare skin he groans, "Bad girl."

She won't be able to sit comfortably for a week, but she tells no one. However, in her own mind she has come   to a decision. Whatever it takes, she must get out of this life.

She gets her chance when Mr. X, during one of their regular sessions, adds opiates to his alcohol consumption. This time he has with him a silver flask from which he drinks generously. He grins stupidly at her—and as usual asks if she wants to swap her cola for a stronger drink from the mini-bar—then he takes two pills from a small bottle and pops them into  his mouth. "'These not for you," he says.

Next he lies down on the bed and pats the covers beside him, his signal that he wants to cuddle. Serena settles in beside him, clutching her yellow bunny—her security blanket. Soon he appears to be falling asleep, but she notices before long he begins making strange, gasping sounds, and his skin turns grey. She watches him anxiously until his normal color returns, and he begins to snore.

That was frightening. She considers calling the desk to report the incident until she realizes that this is her chance to get away. She almost feels sorry for Mr. X. In his own way, he has been good to her, even bought her a huge yellow Easter Bunny when he saw her tattered one, but she doesn't  want to play dress-up, or star in his or anyone else's movies, ever again.

Now is the time, she thinks, while he is snoring, to run away from this horrid life forever. Fortunately she has her windbreaker with her, but nothing else of a practical nature. But then she notices the wallet and, looking around to be sure Mr. X is still asleep, reaches in and takes out a few bills.  It will only be later that she will count the money and find herself richer by almost seventy dollars. She stuffs the bills and two small packages of chips in her jacket pocket and slips quietly out of the room, down the staircase and out the back way.

# 19

Back at the motel I drove the car around the side and we slipped quietly into my unit. Carla's shorts were covered by the pearl-grey sweater-jacket I had thought to bring along, her bare colt-ish legs ending in beaded pink ballerinas. There were mascara smudges under her eyes, traces of heavy makeup on her cheeks, and her long, dark hair was tangled and in need of shampooing. How could this child-woman bring out such callousness in the gang members who trafficked her, and what kind of men were the johns, who used her so willingly, while overlooking her ob-vious vulnerability? Did they have any consciences? I wondered.

Even the young john in his sporty Mazda Miata who dropped her off in Carlsbad at the Outlets, had apparently done so more out of a sense of excitement that he could outsmart the gang members, then with any sense of decency. He had already made her earn the money he had paid her.

No, I would never be able to understand or justify their ac-tions, because what I saw when I looked at Carla was a deeply wounded young teen, crying out for some TLC. And, after she had washed her hair and taken a long, herbal-infused bubble bath, I wrapped her in one of the fluffy oversized towels I had brought from home. Then, following deep conditioning and blow drying, I brushed her hair until its original shine started to return, all the while assuring her that she was safe now.

To add to the relaxing ambiance I lit some scented candles. I also kept my movements slow and my voice as soothing as pos-sible, since I had noticed that she startled easily when she heard night sounds from outside—especially those coming from the other motel units.

I knew that perhaps on one level I was deliberately postponing the inevitable conversation about Serena and the need to let the police know that Carla was with me. However, I also sincerely believed that initially, pampering her physically, would help her to emotionally handle distressing news.

I was given a reprieve when, soon after I  supplied her with a pale-green cotton jersey sleep-set, she lay down on the second double bed and soon fell fast asleep. As I watched her chest rise and fall rhythmically and the weariness leave her face, the newly-found affection I felt for her almost took my breath away

I'd heard new mothers liken the feeling they had for their baby as that of a lioness protecting her cub, but surely that was not my case. My biological clock was a long way from ticking, and Carla was certainly no baby.

Perhaps my strong emotion had something to do with the fact I had grown up in the foster care system with no siblings of my own. While it was true there had been times I had lived  with children younger than myself, even taken care of them, it had been more of an assigned chore, a distant kind of caring.

No, I decided, it had more to do with Carla herself, and not just because of her tragic situation—more likely because of her quest. This very strong, resilient, undoubtedly wise beyond her years, young woman had touched my heart because of these traits. Over the years I had been told more than once that I possessed many of these same positive qualities. Previously, I had just lacked the mission, and now I had it—a mission to protect Carla, the younger sister I never had.

I pondered this as lay in bed waiting for sleep to arrive. There were so many hurdles to overcome, but I felt that I was ready.

\*   \*   \*

Still a creature of habit, I woke up before seven. Carla was used to working well into the night, sleeping into the early afternoon. Changing that would be just one of the many adjustments she would have to make as she eased back into the normal world, but for now I let her sleep. While I waited for her to stir, I read some from the Austen novel, jotted down a few sentences in my journal, and ate some crackers and the cheese left over from the night before.

I also spoke with Amy, talking softly with the bathroom door closed, checked my messages—all work related, none from Mike—and contemplated calling Deputy Cruz, but decided to wait until I could involve Carla. But this *would* probably be a good time to check in with the police in Campo. My call was put through directly to Deputy Wicker. "Erin, what's up? I hope you have some good news for us."

"Actually I do. I have Carla Flores here with me. It's a long story, but she managed to get away from a gang in Oceanside." I didn't mention that I had ended up badly bruised and in a lot of pain because of my tussle with her pimp.

"That *is* good news. But, how about Serena, the younger girl?"

"I'm afraid I lost track of her in San Diego." I went on to fill him in on my misadventures with the posters, the gang members, and my interaction with the detectives at the Broadway precinct. "Detective Williams," I continued, "checked with one of her sources at the hotel where we know she had been seen and was told that Serena and a few other girls, kept by a pimp named Dion, had been sold to a gang somewhere up north."

"That's too bad. It sounds as if you got yourself in a tight spot after you left here. Glad you're all right. Speaking of lowlife, Nestor's back in town. We don't think he's dealing girls, but he's got to be up to something. We're keeping an eye on him."

I'd like to do more that keep an eye on him, I thought, and it wouldn't be pretty!

I sighed. "Do you know the current whereabouts of Mateo, and also how I could get word to Carla's grandmother?"

"As far as I know the uncle is still in court-mandated rehab, but I'll let you speak with Lorena. She keeps in touch with Mrs. Flores. Good to talk with you, Erin. Take care of yourself."

"Not such good news," Lorena said, getting on the phone. "Mrs. Flores is back in the nursing home after suffering a series of mini strokes, or TIAs, as they call them."

"I'm so sorry to hear that. Does she know where she is? Can she talk?" I asked.

"It's hard to tell, but in any case, she's very weak. Would you like me to tell her about Carla? At least it's partial good news— might lift her spirits. I can go visit her for a few minutes tomorrow."

"That would be great, Lorena. Thanks. And please let me know what you find out about her condition."

How sad for that poor woman. I had no doubt that the plight of her granddaughters had a lot to do with her ongoing medical problems. In some ways I envy those people who can be comfortable with chalking such unfairness up to fate, or God's plan, or evil or . . . but in my case, I just get angry when bad things happen to good people, and the sources of their grief keep getting away with it. For now, turning the other cheek was not an option for me!

Pep talk given to myself, I prepared to share the bad news with Carla, who was just waking up as I walked back into the bedroom. "Erin, I really *am* here with you!" she said, with a broad smile. "I had such crazy dreams, I wasn't sure you and this room were real. Can I give you a hug?"

"Anytime," I said, with conviction. Our mutual hug was very satisfying, Carla hanging on as if she didn't want it to end. A hug—such a simple thing, but so lacking in the world she had just come from. No need to ruin her good mood quite yet.

But the decision was taken out of my hands when she pulled back and her chin began to quiver. "If only Serena could be here with us, Erin. Did you find out anything? Where she might be? Emilio said they would hurt her if I didn't do what they asked. Maybe I shouldn't have run away!" she moaned.

She was actually shaking now as the enormity of yesterday's defection hit home.

"Carla, you *must* believe me. Serena is not in any increased danger because you left. I can't tell you where she is just now. I just don't know and I don't believe that Emilio knows either. He just threatens to hurt family members to keep you girls in line. Remember, she is valuable to them. They want her to stay healthy. They have an investment in her."

I handed her a tissue. "And, on the good side, I have met some very fine people, especially in the police department, who are working hard to find her. And they will, honey," I said.

She didn't look totally convinced, but she did stop sniffling. Suddenly, she said wistfully, "Erin, I wish you were my big sister."

Had she read my mind? I managed to reply, "You *are* special to me, too. For now we could play 'let's pretend'? Will that work?" Erin, I cautioned myself. Be careful, for both your sakes.

"I guess that will have to do," she answered, with a sigh.

"Now, you must be hungry," I said, deliberately bringing us back to the mundane. "I know I am. Let me find you something of mine to wear, and then we'll go out for a bite to eat, and do a little clothes shopping for you after that."

"Really?" she asked, excitement at the prospect temporarily chasing away her gloomy mood.

"Really," I answered, so pleased to be able to bring some happiness into her life, however fleeting it might turn out to be.

Then I saw a frown begin to replace her smile. "What if they. . ." she began.

"The gang won't be looking for you down here," I interjected. "But we'll only go where there are a lot of other people, just to be on the safe side."

Finding something that would both fit Carla and not look too old for her was not that easy to do, especially since I had left many clothes back at the condo.

We finally settled on a pair of black stretch yoga pants and a rose-colored, raglan-sleeved, cotton knit top. Her own shoes would work well.

She asked me to put her hair in a ponytail like mine, and agreed to put on just a tiny amount of mascara and lip gloss. She was a knockout, but now an age-appropriate one.

I had to remind her to buckle up when we got into the BMW. Apparently neither the girls' safety nor California law was of concern to the gang members.

Carla settled back against the metallic-grey leather—if not totally relaxed, at least determined to have a good time for my sake. "Can you tell me where we're going," she asked, as I took the Friars Road exit off of I-5, "or is it a surprise?"

"We are going to San Diego's outdoor Fashion Valley Mall, but I'm going to keep our lunch destination a secret until we get there."

We chatted a little, Carla bringing up the fact that the group of girls run by Emilio and the other gang members had no chance to really become friends and that she missed her class-mates a lot. "But not as much as I miss Serena," she said, on the verge of tears again. I could find no soothing words that would be adequate. At this point, there was little I could do to address such grief, so I just squeezed her hand and let her compose her-self in her own time.

After a few minutes she straightened up and said, "I really wish you would let me pay for my clothes."

That was the second time she had offered to pay for her clothes with the money she had kept from her last two tricks in

Oceanside. No matter how much she wanted to help pay for her keep, as she put it, for me that money was tainted.

And working for the pimps, no matter how coerced, in order to have money for nice clothes and such was not any idea I wanted to encourage. Strong as she was, Carla didn't realize that some of the brain-washing indulged in by the pimps against the enemy—the straight world—had rubbed off on her.

"You keep your money for now, but I promise I'll think of some way you can help me out," I countered.


A few minutes later we pulled into the gigantic parking area which surrounds the over two hundred or more stores in the mall. I hoped I hadn't miscalculated. After all, growing up poor in small-town, rural Campo, more than likely meant that Carla had probably never even been to *any* mall, let alone one of such size. It might prove to be a little intimidating for her.

As usual, I had to drive a considerable distance to find a parking spot. "Help me remember what entrance we're near. I've misplaced the car more than once in places like this."

"If you have some paper, how about writing down our location here, and then the names of the stores when we first get inside," she suggested, matter-of-factly.

"Good idea," I answered, impressed by her common sense. "I'll do that."

We entered near the Neiman Marcus store. Other big anchor stores included Macy's, Bloomingdale's, and Nordstrom's—all high-end. There were so many smaller venues that one almost needed a map to find one's way around—a shopaholic's paradise. Understandably, Carla was entranced. She expressed interest in almost every store we passed, but we had limited time and were on a mission to build a wardrobe for her—after we ate, that is.

"Well, here we are," I announced as we approached the famous Cheesecake Factory Restaurant, two hundred items on the menu including sandwiches, soups, and salads—but most of the crowd that filled the vast interior were dining on a huge slice of their signature dessert. By design, the restaurant showcased a wide variety of whole cheesecakes in glass cases just inside the entrance. Trying to decide easily keeps the patrons busy so that the wait for a table goes by quickly.

"We've got to choose," I said, after several minutes had passed.

"How can I?" Carla asked, with a groan. "Everything looks *so* good!"

"How about if you pick two that look especially appealing and we'll share both?" I suggested. "I'm really bad at choosing, anyhow."

After more deliberation she settled on Chocolate Chip Cookie Dough and Banana Cream. Forty-five minutes later we pushed our plates back—not a crumb left—and continued on our way. I already felt the headachy beginnings of a sugar rush, but it was worth it. My young companion had been thrilled. Healthy eating could come later.

I knew that the Wet Seal store would be a good fit for Carla. They cater to teens and juniors and offer great prices. For starters she picked out three colorful casual tops and two pairs of shorts on a five for twenty-dollar mix-and-match sale. The jeans were another story. There was a huge selection of colors, patterns, and fabrics, but most were deliberately torn, which they called 'distressed'. I could tell that Carla liked some of them, but she looked to me for advice.

This was going to be harder than I thought. Obviously, from the looks of the large selection and my observation of the other shoppers her age, those jeans were very much in style. On the other hand I was thinking of the future when she might need more conservative clothes. For starters, I intended to ask the owners of my bookstore if she could help out when I worked my shifts, and then, later on, there were the police who would want to talk with her, and no doubt, other people in authority.

We compromised on a pair of two-button slim-cut jeans—no shredding. The new tops paired nicely along with the jeans.

Then it was on to more mainstream Old Navy where we were both pleased with her choices of a pair of grey roll-up capris, a floral flutter-sleeved dress, and a white denim jacket—all at great low prices. She even asked the clerks to include the clothes hangers. They were having a half-off sale on two pair of shoes so she got canvas slip-ons and dress-up sandals. Underwear, two sleep sets, and a bathing suit completed our purchases.

Last stop in the mall was at Claire's where, for a tiny sum, Carla was able to pick up several pieces of costume jewelry and hair accessories. Walking back to the car, we high-fived—bargain hunter partners, at least for the day.


Back at the motel, though tired, we both agreed that a fashion show was in order. My bank account had taken a hit, but it was well worth it. Then Carla carefully folded and put her clothes away. After a simple supper of soup and a salad she asked, "Can I have a bath like I did last night?"

"With bubbles and candles—the whole works?" I asked.

She nodded.

"Sounds good to me, but before you start, we need to talk about some important things."

# 20

*It is late afternoon and Serena has no real plan. The idea of spending the night in some strange place, perhaps even outdoors, is frightening—but turning back is more so.*

*Then she has an idea. St. Peters Church is not that far. All her life she has been told that a place of worship is a sanctuary for everyone. Surely, someone inside will be able to help her find her way home. She remembers that the elderly Father had smiled kindly at her when she took communion just last week.*

*The familiar Spanish style façade is welcoming but Serena almost changes her mind about entering. There are no cars to be seen—no signs of life at all. The door is not locked, however, so she enters the handsome nave and calls out "Hello?" in a quivering voice. Far down the long aisle, below the altar, she notes that some votive candles are lit, and considers making a donation and a final plea to be delivered from her current wretched life.*

*Just then a young priest, dressed in traditional black with the Roman collar, comes out from a side room. He looks surprised to see Serena. "Are you looking for someone, little lady?" he asks.*

*"Not really," she answers, "but I'm hoping you can help me get home." She notices for the first time a plump, grey-haired Latina arranging flowers in front of a side altar.*

*"And where is that?" the priest continues.*

*"I live with my sister and grandmother in Campo."*

*"I'm afraid I've never heard of it. Is that in Mexico?"*

*"No, but it is in California near the border."*

*The priest looked perplexed. "And how is it that you are so far from home?"*

*When she doesn't respond, he goes on. "Perhaps you were visiting relatives around here and got lost?" he suggests.*

*By then the woman has joined them. "My name is Mrs. Morales," she says. "There's no need to be afraid. We want to help you."*

*They seem nice. Serena considers telling them about Angel, but she knows that he and other gang members consider St. Peters to be their church. Word would certainly get back to someone who would want her returned! And surely this time she would be punished severely. She doesn't know what to do or say.*

*There is a long pause and then the priest says to Serena, "I need to speak with Mrs. Morales for a minute. Stay right here and we'll be right back."*

*As soon as they are out of sight, Serena creeps close enough to overhear one side of a phone conversation—apparently one with some kind of agency dealing with missing children. "No, we don't know. She won't give us any information," she hears the priest say. "Poor little thing seems afraid of something. How long do you think it will be before someone gets here?"*

*Serena will never find out. She is out the door before the others even realize she is gone. This has not worked out well. They haven't helped her, just wanted to turn her over to some agency. Her housemates had warned her repeatedly that little good ever came of that.*

*She has not thought ahead, but now her immediate objective is to put as much distance between her and the 1200 block of Florida Street as she can, before it is totally dark—but where should she head next?*

*One day Angel had taken her and several other girls on an outing to Fisherman's Wharf. That had been early on, when she was doing all she could to stay in his good graces, but she has to admit that she remembers that day fondly. Surely, in such a bustling at-*

mosphere full of shops and food and tourists, she can find somewhere to hide, or better yet, someone to ask for help who won't turn her in to the authorities.

Serena had listened closely when Tina, who had grown up in neighboring Oakland, regaled the other girls with her many solo adventures riding BART, the muni busses and the cable cars. Her stories included tips on how to avoid paying the full fare and how to blend in to avoid being recognized as the truant she usually was.

She walks for several blocks, staying in the shadows, startling at sirens and the sounds of barking dogs, until she comes to a school. By the looks of the playground it is for preschoolers. Of course, at this time of the day it is closed, but a covered back entryway offers some protection from the chill, and the chances are slim that it will be patrolled.

She decides to eat one of the packets of chips and makes a welcome discovery when she discovers a rolled up pair of her plaid tights in the same windbreaker pocket. They will look fine with her white sneakers. Using her bunny as a makeshift pillow, she makes herself as small as possible, and settles down on the ground for the night.

The sun comes up early, but it is hunger that first wakes Serena. She wishes she had a watch. It will be the first thing I will buy when I get to Fisherman's Wharf, she vows. Cautiously, she edges out of the schoolyard, and begins a search for food. Several blocks later she comes to a neighborhood bakery—opens at 5:00 AM, the sign says.

The wonderful smells make her want to rush in, but she knows she has to be patient. There are several cars in the parking lot—a few with the driver remaining behind the wheel. Unfortunately, one of them belongs to the local police. She keeps out of sight until the cruiser leaves.

*When it is her turn at the counter she is careful to order two of everything, hoping that they will believe that a parent waits in the car. "I'll have one coffee and one hot chocolate, please," she says, "and two of those big ones there," she adds, pointing to the bear claws.*

*"That will be five-dollars and forty-nine cents," the clerk tells her, "and the cream and sugar are over there."*

*Serena's knowledge of money is meager, so she hands over a twenty and hopes that she will be given the right change.*

*Fortunately, she has been supplied with a cardboard carry-tray, but still it is awkward to handle the very hot beverages. At the counter, she adds milk to each, and then throws a handful of sugar packets, powdered creamers, and napkins into the bag with the donuts.*

*No one pays any attention to her as she goes on her way past a strip mall, bars on the front doors—none open at this early hour. She is tempted to just sit down and eat on a concrete bench, half-hidden by a divider planter, but a sign warns that the complex is patrolled by a security company. Finally, she comes to a small, wooded park and sits down on a wooden bench placed in front of a statue. There she eats the best meal ever, she decides.*

*The second bear claw is saved for later. Soon, she is once more in a heavily populated area and there, before her, is a Greyhound bus station. She remembers seeing many of those huge buses pass as she and Wanda made the long trip by van to join Angel's household.*

*She gets an idea. Why not use her money and go back to San Diego County? From there she would find a way to get to Campo. Hopefully, Carla would be back by now, and her grandmother too, though she can't shake the feeling that the older woman might be dead.*

*Since she is always aware that a child alone might be the object of undue attention, Serena notices a shabbily dressed older Hispanic couple hanging back near the ticket counter, and gets an idea. When it is her turn, she says to the clerk, "My grandparents don't speak such good English. They need to get to San Diego for a funeral day after tomorrow. Can you tell me which bus goes there, and how much it will cost?"*

*The uniformed clerk shakes her head. "I need to know more, hon. For example, what time do they want to leave and where do they want to get off? I'm kind of busy, as you can see, so why don't you take this schedule, get some answers and then come back."*

*While the clerk is busy, Serena walks rapidly away and sits down to study the material she has received. It doesn't take her long to realize she probably doesn't have enough money for the trip, the list of destinations is so long, and the names of the towns so foreign to her as to be useless. In addition, there would probably be all kinds of questions asked if she tried to travel alone. She has to come up with another plan.*

*Then she notices a stack of free tourist maps of the city in a rack advertising harbor tours, museums, restaurants, hotels and the like.*

*She discovers that her meandering walk has already taken her to Market Street which will eventually lead her into the heart of The Embarcadero and then on to Fisherman's Wharf. Hiding from Angel and the others remains her main concern but who says she can't enjoy celebrating her freedom in such an interesting place? She even giggles a little as she thinks of Mr. X waking up to find her gone and then drunkenly trying to explain her absence when a gang member comes to pick her up.*

*Everything is wondrous to this young girl from a tiny, rural, southern California border town. School is out for the year in many places, so children are everywhere, with parents or in groups. Serena has no trouble blending in. The day is warm and sunny, deceptively so, since early summer days in San Francisco can suddenly turn chilly and damp—though she doesn't know that yet.*

*One block leads to another. Soon she is at Fisherman's Wharf. She ties her windbreaker around her waist and wanders first through the crowded seafood stalls.*

*She watches in fascination as burly men wearing white aprons cut, grill, and wait on customers—all the while shouting out that each has the best crabs and seafood available. It is very crowded and the customers have to elbow their way in to make a purchase. Prices aren't cheap, and Serena wouldn't know what to choose anyhow, but the smells remind her that she hasn't had anything to eat for some time.*

*For now, she decides just to buy a drink to go with the second bear claw. With a bottle of grape soda in hand, she strolls along until she gets to Pier 41. There she sits on a bench in front of the Blue and Gold Ferry signs. The pastry is slightly stale, but it satisfies her hunger—though when she makes the mistake of using the flattened paper bag as a plate, an aggressive sea gull almost makes off with part of it. The gulls are everywhere, and their harsh cries and quarrelsome natures can be intimidating, but Serena enjoys watching their antics, and even picks out one of the smaller ones to throw some crumbs to.*

*A young couple, with a toddler in a stroller, sit down on the other end of the bench. Perhaps they are waiting for friends or family members to arrive back from a harbor tour. A large 'ARRIVALS' sign is nearby and people mill about looking out to sea. Many more people are lined up behind a rope barrier, apparently waiting to board the handsome two-story ferry which Serena can see in the distance. She watches entranced, as it grows larger and larger as it nears the dock. Now she can see and hear the people who line the railing of the upper deck. Everybody seems to be in a festive mood and she longs to take a tour.*

*A discarded brochure she has picked up shows beautiful ocean views and famous San Francisco landmarks, but she knows such treats are not for her. She must guard her money carefully.*

With a sigh she gets up from the bench and begins to meander back toward the numerous shops, concession stands, and other attractions that line the boardwalk between Pier 41 and Pier 39. Some stores even place merchandise outside to entice people to come in. Serena spots some watches and sunglasses on a table bearing a homemade sign with original prices crossed out but now just marked 'SALE.'

Several other people have been attracted by the potential bargains. Serena stands back until a tiny Asian woman, holding the hand of a girl about six or seven, inquires as to the price of a watch. The teenage clerk looks toward a very stocky, older, bearded man who has been standing just inside the door. "Ten dollars," he says, nodding to the boy.

"Too much," the woman complains, and turns away.

Serena has her eye on one with a pink strap and jewels on the side of the dial, but ten dollars?

A skinny man, wearing cargo shorts and a T-shirt from a music festival, remarks that he has seen similar watches and glasses at another location for less than eight dollars. He also starts to leave, but stops when the shop owner comes out and offers to sell him a watch for seven dollars and fifty cents, all the while grumbling that he is losing money on the deal.

The Asian mother has returned to the counter and, while she is making her purchase, Serena picks up the watch she has coveted and begins to count out the price she has heard the woman agree to. "Ten dollars," says the teenager.

The woman looks at him in disgust. "You should be ashamed of yourself—trying to take advantage of a little girl!" she scolds.

So Serena gets her dream watch for a good price. She thanks the woman, then immediately joins a family group walking by, before she can be asked any questions. For a brief minute she had been tempted to share her story with the woman, but during the day she has noticed members of the San Francisco police patrolling the area, many on bicycles. The experience at the church is *still fresh in her mind. She's not ready to take a chance.*

*Nearby there is a store that sells suitcases, backpacks, and purses of various sizes. Serena reasons that not only would a backpack be practical, but wearing one will help her blend in with other children—especially those who belong to groups.  In front of one is a large cardboard box marked 'AS IS.' She has seen boxes like that in Campo at the Salvation Army Thrift Store. Many items in her grandmother's house came from boxes like this.*

*Sure enough, she spots a small beige canvas backpack with a red logo advertising a national soccer team which should do nicely. It is slightly soiled, but the zippers on the separate sections work perfectly. And the three-dollar price is a steal, she reasons. And, for two dollars more, she gets a baseball style cap with the faintest of stains on the underside of the visor.  She puts the free brochures and the three-for-a-dollar postcards she had purchased earlier into one section of the bag, and makes a ponytail to poke jauntily from under the cap.*

*She can't remember when she has been so pleased with herself. Now it is time to get some real food into her stomach.*


*The yeasty smell coming from the famous Boudin's Restaurant is incredible. In one of her brochures she has read that having one of their clam chowder sourdough bread bowls is a must, but once again, cost gets in the way.*

*So she chooses instead a hot dog from an Annie's Hot Dogs and Pretzels sidewalk cart. The young red-haired, freckled-faced vendor is wearing khaki shorts and cap, and a white T-shirt sporting her employer's name.*

*"Do you want a cold drink to go with that?" she asks, as Serena squeezes mustard and ketchup on her dog.*

*"No, thanks," Serena answers, holding up the bottle of grape soda. "There's still some left in this one."*

*"A few swallows, maybe. Why don't you throw that out and I'll*

*give you a fresh one. And how about a pretzel?" the older girl asks. "I only have two old ones left but you can have them for free. Another batch will be ready in a few minutes."*

*Serena can't believe her good fortune.*

*The stand is about to get busy, but the vendor still takes the time to offer some advice. "Tell your parents, or whoever you're with, that they shouldn't leave you alone for such a long time, honey. Unfortunately there are some not–so-nice people around who might hurt a young girl like you." Then she turns to her next customer and asks, "What can I get you?"*

*The girl's advice really affects Serena. She has been reminded of just how alone she is. And of how hard it is to tell just who is good and who might wish her harm. Her throat feels tight, and as a result, she ends up throwing away the last few bites of the hotdog, but puts the pretzels  away in her backpack for later.*

*Now, as the afternoon comes to a close, it is definitely time to plan ahead and look around for a place where she can spend the night. Oh, how she wishes that her friend Wanda was with her! They could make this journey into an adventure.*

*She stops to use one of the free restrooms in the area, and it occurs to her, that just maybe she could hide overnight in one of the stalls after closing time. While there are others open to the public in various locations like this one, and on both floors of the buildings that house the many specialty shops and restaurants at Pier 39, she fears that someone from a clean-up crew or security detail could discover her easily.*

*A mother at the next sink washes her daughters' hands. The younger of the two wriggles down and whines, "Hurry up, Mommy. You promised we could see the big fish."*

*The older one chimes in. "I want to see them feed the sharks and dolphins."*

*"'Let's go find your dad and your brother and see what they*

*want to do," the woman says soothingly, as they head for the exit.*

*Serena fondly remembers watching undersea adventure films on the Discovery Channel with her grandmother. This would be her chance to see some of those curious creatures up close. Hopefully there might even be a few of Carla's favorites, the dolphins. Perhaps she might even be one of the lucky ones chosen to help the attendants at feeding time.*

*Her hopes are dashed, however, when she arrives at the aquarium entrance to find that admission isn't really free. The ticket taker explains that a coupon or cash is needed. "Sorry, kid," he says, not unkindly, "but we gotta go by the rules."*

*As Serena stands outside, trying to decide what to do next, she hears a woman standing close to her say, "Let's go, Dave. Lacy's fussy and Todd's fallen asleep. I need to get them to bed. Why don't you see if that young girl and her family could use our coupons?"*

*And that's how Serena gets to spend a magical hour gazing into the giant tanks at the sharks, and eels, and rays, but disappointingly, no dolphins.*

*However, now she is tired when she leaves, and no closer to finding a place to stay the night. She remembers the mother's words, "I need to get them to bed," and lets herself picture what it would be like to be part of their family, and she can't help but feel sad. Then she reminds herself that she has her own family, and that one day soon, now that she's away from the pimps, they will be together again . . . if she can only stay strong.*

*The answer to a temporary sleeping arrangement is found in another of her brochures—this one for the Pier 39 Marina. With a little luck, she reasons, she may be able to sneak aboard one of the smaller craft available as a day rental.*

*Someone checking a certain security camera about nine that evening might have noticed a young girl wearing a cap and a* beige backpack slip away from a family group and head to an adjacent dock.

Most all of the smaller boats have tied-down blue tarps on them but, tiny as she is, she has no trouble slipping beneath one. It is pitch dark so she just feels around until she finds a bench of sorts—low to the deck—and settles down for the night. It is cold, but her windbreaker and tights help. Her backpack makes a fair pillow.

She thinks of big sister Carla who keeps a scrapbook which includes magazine cutouts of people, places, and things. She has labeled it 'MY WISH LIST.' Several pictures are of ships and exotic locales.

Serena had seen several big vessels like those in Carla's scrapbook docked in another part of the marina. How Carla would love this place! Maybe someday they could come back together. Better yet, maybe someday they could go on a long ocean cruise together!

These are her thoughts as the gentle bobbing of the boat lulls her into a dreamless sleep.

# 21

I hated to spoil Carla's mood—to bring her back down —she was so fragile, but there were important things that had to be addressed. I'd like nothing better than to do a repeat of the bubble bath, hair brushing, and massage-giving routine of the previous night, but I had some major concerns about her future, and I also owed her an accounting of my efforts to find Serena.

She had been living a very unhealthy lifestyle for months. This needed to be addressed first, so I began, "Carla, you know that your safety is my number one priority, but I'm also concerned about your health. For example, I wouldn't be surprised if you were a little anemic. You seem rather frail and you mentioned that your hands are always cold. I suspect that you haven't been able to eat right. And there could be other things going on." I was deliberately vague about 'the other' things that I was worried about. Carla didn't respond.

"Have you had a physical lately?" I prompted.

"Not really," she answered, then, avoiding my eyes, she admitted, "Emilio did have us give him urine samples every so often. And some man would come by and check a girl out if she'd been beaten up but I don't know if he was a doctor or not."

I tried to stay noncommittal so I wouldn't upset her more than she already was. "Anyhow," I continued, "what would you say to going in for a check-up with my doctor in the next day or two? She could run some tests and prescribe medication or vitamins, if she thought you needed them. I think you would really like her."

"If that's what you want me to do," Carla said, with resignation in her voice. She looked down at her hands and fiddled with one of the rings she had bought at Claire's earlier in the day.

I kept on talking, retracing most of my actions on her behalf since we met at the Tri-Cities Medical Center, including my visit to the police and her grandmother in Compo. I described my subsequent attempt to find Serena, including the taping up of posters of the two sisters, and the encounter with the San Diego gang members that followed. I ended with my recent conversation with Ed Wicker of the Campo police and his dispatcher's offer to visit Mrs. Flores in the nursing home.

Carla asked a few questions, but for the most part she just listened intently, eyes brimming with tears, at times.

"Would you like to speak with Lorena, the dispatcher, yourself?" I asked. "Both she and Deputy Wicker care a great deal about your family. I'm sure she would be glad to speak with you in person."

"I'd like that," she said, then added, "Thank you so much for trying to make things right, Erin."

"You're more than welcome, honey, but there is one more thing we should discuss. I really need to let a certain policeman know you're safe with me. He is very involved with trying to stop the kind of thing that happened to you. From our previous conversations I imagine he would very much like to meet with you, and see what you would be able to contribute to their investigation."

"No police!" she interrupted. "Someone like me can't trust them. You don't understand. They arrest us or turn us over to social services. Or they call us vile names and ask us for favors because they think we're dirt. Please don't make me see him." She was shaking.

"I won't *make* you do anything, Carla," I answered, taken aback by her outburst. In our conversations, Deputy Cruz, and the San Diego police as well, had made a good argument that testimony by an underage victim would go a long way in building a court case against these gang members, but for now, Carla's feelings had to come first.

It was almost eleven, and I longed to go to sleep, but it was obvious that Carla was still on her street time.

"Erin, after we get ready for bed could we just talk for a while? I have so many questions swirling around in my head that I don't think I could fall asleep yet."

"Well, sure," I said, stifling a yawn. "Anything in particular you have in mind?"

"Well, I listened to all the things you say you tried to do for me and Serena, and also I'll never forget how Emilio shoved you down and hurt you when we met at Angelo's that night. I used to pray that someone like you would come and rescue me. So I guess my biggest question is, who are you, and why did you come to visit me in the hospital that day? I'll believe it if you tell me you actually are an angel, but . . ."

"I can assure you, I am no angel—big sister in training suits me fine," I said, feeling that unfamiliar sibling affection again. "But I will give you a little of the back-story, as they say in journalism." And so I did, starting with my newspaper assignment to inform our readers about the problem of human trafficking, which led to the anti-trafficking walk in Vista, followed by a meeting sponsored by the North County Collaborative.

"I had already gone on the internet and downloaded material on the subject. I met the Paula you know from the hospital on the walk, and afterward, listened to the program speakers. They really opened my eyes. I learned so much, in fact, I almost drove my fiancé crazy talking about the problem, especially as it pertained to young girls like you and Serena and the gangs."

"I didn't know anything about those horrible men," she said sorrowfully, chin trembling. "If I did, maybe I could have done something more to try to save Serena!"

I crossed to the other bed and held her in my arms. I felt so inadequate. Would she ever get over feeling that she had let her little sister down? We *have* to get Serena back, I vowed.

"You mentioned a fiancé?" she questioned, "Where is he now . . . and why are you living in a motel?"

"Briefly, we had agreed that things between us were perhaps moving a little too fast, so a trial separation might be a good thing. Later on I can fill you in more." I kept my response short on purpose. No need to discuss Mike and his negative feelings about my involvement with the movement.

"But back to Serena, you mustn't blame yourself," I pleaded. "There was nothing you could have done to stop those evil men. Too many people still don't know about human trafficking and what role the gangs play. But things *are* improving.

"More recently, many, many good people and organizations have been working with the police and the courts to educate the public and help shut those gangs down. There are also safe-haven houses now for girls like you. They offer school classes and job training in addition to counseling. And from what I understand the staff is very caring."

"You sound like a TV commercial," she said, "and I sure hope that things *are* getting better. But I already have my best part. You found me to save," she said, quietly, almost in a whisper.

"Actually, I think it was the other way around. I wanted to do more than just write articles and attend rallies. Paula met you in the hospital and thought I might be able to help you in some way, and here we are," I said, giving her hand a squeeze, "having a sleepover."

"Hmm," she murmured, a playful grin replacing her worried frown. "Then if this is a sleepover, can we make popcorn and have hot chocolate, too?" she asked.

Ah, youth, I thought. Her future still looked bleak, but I was committed to easing it, however and whenever I could. If food and drink would help, sleep would have to wait.

"Yummy, yummy in your tummy," Carla said, sing-song fashion. "We used to say that in my pre-school," she explained—draining the last of her hot chocolate. "*Now* what shall we talk about?"

"This is your party. You choose," I suggested.

"Well, maybe you could tell me more about when you were younger, and I could tell you things,"—she hesitated and chewed her lip—"just things you might want to know about me," she finished weakly.

I had a sense that Carla wanted to talk about her life on the track, to confess what she had done, to somehow justify it, and it broke my heart.

I had read enough to know that this was a common reaction. Since society judged girls and women like her as among the lowest of the low, that's how they came to see themselves; even those who were abducted at a young age and forced into virtual slavery! But I would have to tread carefully here. So I would go first.

Thus for the next hour or more, propped up by pillows on our adjoining beds, we swapped stories. She seemed to get the biggest kick out of the ones I told where I—usually with Amy's help—played some trick on a house-parent or a truant officer or a teacher. Actually, my current twenty-six-year-old responsible self, was somewhat embarrassed, even sorry for those people who, in the main, had only been doing their jobs. Of course, that excluded the occasional perverts and abusers.

Finally, she turned the conversation to her. "But you never did any *really* bad things, like dirty, bad things with men. No one ever gave you money to . . ." Her voice became somewhat shrill.

I hoped the vague noises I could hear from the adjacent motel unit didn't mean someone was overhearing  our conversation.  Anonymity was a major consideration for each of us. Paranoia on my part also intruded.

"Carla, you did nothing wrong! Those men were wrong. The

pimps were wrong. You and the others aren't at fault. Didn't you say you, and sometimes your families, were threatened? And you said that often times there were beatings if a girl didn't bring in enough money? You and the others are good girls. Can't you see that?"

She shook her head. "People don't call good girls prostitutes or hos or worse, Erin. Good girls don't talk dirty. They don't steal from each other or tell lies to get someone else in trouble. They don't get arrested, or . . ."

"Stop!" I broke in. "I will not have you saying such things about Miss Carla Victoria Flores, who, by the way, I have chosen to be my younger sister," I said, indignantly.

Carla was looking at me as if I had gone crazy. Then her chin went up, and she said haughtily, "You forgot Florencia."

By mutual agreement, shortly after that, Carla and I decided to call it a night. It appeared to me that she fell asleep almost instantly. But I had too much on my mind to just let go. Our evening's conversation had been most revealing. It was obvious that I would have to be much more persuasive if I was going to get her to cooperate with the police. But it was her dislike and mistrust of men in general, understandable as it was, that disturbed me the most. It was important that in the future she have positive interactions with some mature, healthy, caring men.

And, she also needed some meaningful activity to fill in her time at least until she could see the wisdom of entering someplace like a safe house for young women in difficulty. I could try to supply both, and had already set a plan in motion.

Today, I thought that we would drop in to *The County Voice* where she would meet Frank and Malcolm and see where I worked. If she was agreeable, I was going to ask for her input into a follow-up article to my original, which had featured her and Serena. I had been notified earlier that my doctor could fit her in later in the day, and finally, Dave and Judy, the owners of the book store, had readily agreed that she could accompany me during my shift.  Well, it was a start.

Amy's fiancé, Tim, and, of course, Mike, naturally made the list of acceptable men. Though, when she would get a chance to meet the latter, I hadn't a clue. I hadn't received a cell phone message from Mike yet. Was his pride still getting in the way, or was it something more ominous? And what about my feelings? My self-righteous anger had abated, leaving me more confused than ever.

# 22

Why were those babies screeching like that? True, there was a chill in the air, but it was that eerie sound that raises goose bumps on Serena's arms as she struggles to wake up from her improvised bed on the deck of the boat.

Carefully she peeks out from beneath the tarp, relieved to see that it is only seagulls wheeling about overhead, squalling in their distinctive way.

The sky is a streaky combination of purples and grays as she carefully makes her way to the main dock without seeing another soul. Yet, early as it is, there are pockets of activity along Pier 39.

The remaining few boats belonging to local fishermen were offloading their catches and restaurant bakers were filling the air with their tantalizing aromas. Night crews were getting ready to go home, passing the torch to the first-shift personnel. Soon, hundreds and hundreds of day trippers will descend on this famous area.

Serena has no firm, long term plans yet, but thanks to her many brochures, she has a wish list for the next few days, at least. Within easy walking distance is Ghirardelli Square, and the store of the same name which, they claim, has some of the best chocolate candy and ice cream in the world. In the same area is Marina Green: seventy-four grassy acres and a pedestrian walkway, a nearby harbor, and great views of the Golden Gate Bridge.

But before she ventures away from her present location she has things to do and places to see. And, as always, blending in remains a prime objective. She must keep up appearances. With that in mind she finds an unoccupied, open restroom and, before she can lose her nerve, gives her hair a perfunctory wash in the sink, using liquid hand soap as shampoo. The rinse that follows is cut short when she hears approaching voices and hides in one of the stalls until the voices fade away.

She is finally able to finish up, and fortunately the sun is breaking through the clouds, but long hair doesn't dry that quickly. That gives her an idea. If she can ever find a pair of scissors, she will give herself a cut. That will also make her less recognizable because she is afraid that Angel or one of the others is still looking for her.

Now to find something to eat and she knows just the place. They were closing when she happened to spot Trish's the previous night, but now she sees a short line forming in front of one of the Pier's must-try attractions. They sell only one kind of tiny, melt-in-your-mouth donuts. Serena watches in awe as the bakers mix, knead, and send the dough down the conveyer belt to be dusted with cinnamon and sugar and put into paper bags for the customers.

"What will it be, honey?" the elderly clerk asks, when it is her turn.

"Just one," Serena answers, holding out a dollar bill.

"Give the kid a couple more, and I'll pay for them," says the man next in line. "Looks as if she needs them more than I do," he adds, patting his ample belly.

Serena hesitates. She remembers her grandmother's words— "We don't take charity"—but the events of the past few days have convinced her that she will need all the help she can get from here on in. Someday, she vows to be the one who does nice, unexpected things for other people.

"Thank you very much, mister," she says, politely.

As she walks away she hears one woman say, "That was very nice of you."

"At least she wasn't begging," a teenager chimes in.

As Serena walks toward the old marina to watch the dozens of *sea lions entertain, she spots a cart selling a variety of drinks. A small, hot coffee is the least expensive and goes perfectly with the donuts. After she has added plenty of sugar and creamer it tastes almost as good as the Mexican version she had been allowed to have on special occasions back in Campo.*

*Once again such thoughts intrude to put a real damper on her good mood. Hopefully, the seals will cheer her up, and for a while they do, as she joins the crowds of little kids and adults giggling and clapping at the antics of these creatures. From floating platforms the big, fat-bellied males, and slightly smaller females, bask in the sun, fighting each other for prime spots, sliding off into the water, and hoisting themselves back up, all the while making those strange, distinctive barking sounds.*

*Serena spends a good part of the morning this way, watching the sea lions, drinking her coffee, and eating two of the donuts, carefully adding the third to yesterday's pretzels in her backpack.*

*When she has seen enough of the sea lions, she continues strolling along the Embarcadero, heading towards the Marina Green, extolled in another of her brochures. She pauses to enjoy the free outdoor performances by various jugglers, aerial artists, clowns, musicians and magicians scattered throughout, some on specific schedules, others at random. Serena spends time at several. Her favorite is a young man who juggles while on a unicycle. She puts a precious dollar in his upturned top hat and gets a big smile in return.*

*Show over, she meanders toward the Marina Green, joining the many others who plan to spend an afternoon in that beautiful location. Evening will come too soon, and as darkness falls she will need to find shelter—but for now, life is good.*

*There is so much to see and do. Serena can do little to be more than a spectator, but she concludes that being a spectator in such a fabled environment is pretty special. For a few minutes, she watches a group of men and boys play flag football, before moving closer to the bay where several people glide along in kayaks. Closer to shore, a dozen or more men and women swim long laps, their bathing caps bobbing up and down.*

*Trim, young women push strollers, and joggers of all sizes, shapes, and ages take advantage of the many pathways. While watching them, she indulges in a pretend game of I wish I could join you, or you, or you. Maybe she'd join the joggers. She had been the fastest runner in her PE class. Or should she join the swimmers? Her instructor at the Y said she was a little fish. Of course, if one of the mothers would let her, she could be the best mother's helper ever.*

*With her daydreams indulged, she climbs a small hill and there, kites in a myriad of colors and types, soar and dip, sometimes pulling their handlers along as the strength of the breeze dictates. Serena has never seen such a colorful display in the skies before.*

*There are many picnickers seated on blankets on the grassy area. Insulated containers and coolers abound, but she notices that several families are carrying at least some of their food in plastic Safeway bags. So she retraces her steps and enters that nearby neighborhood grocery store to choose something for her own lunch.*

*Back on the green she takes a thin, cheap, souvenir towel from her backpack, spreads it out, and settles down to enjoy  her half-sandwich and orange soda.*

*After today's food purchases, and the towel, plus a tee and short-set and a couple of panties she bought at a discount stall the previous day, she is down to approximately forty dollars. She has been an excellent observer and a quick learner and it hasn't taken her long to understand how to bargain, or even how to get some things for free. But she realizes that she will need to be even more careful with the funds she has remaining.*

*Thanks to Angel and his cheap ways she knows there are all sorts of bargains in the Mission district. Especially at the Salvation Army store, where he sometimes took the girls to pick out used clothing, and also where she might obtain free meals, but the need to stay safe and blend in remains problematic.*

# 23

"Rise and shine, sleepy head," I called out next morning at eight. All I could see of Carla was one arm hanging out from a mound of bedcovers. "We have places to go and people to see," I continued. No response. Getting her back on some sort of a schedule seemed like a wise move, though I was certainly willing to cut her some slack.

"I'll let you stay in the shower as long as you want," I wheedled, as I pulled at her covers. I wasn't sure she had heard me, but soon a sleepy face emerged, nearly covered by a tangle of dark brown hair.

"Go away, you cruel person," she groaned, then, with a grin added, "Did you really mean it about the shower?"

After a long shower and blow-dry, Carla was ready for her favorite at-home breakfast of orange juice followed by Cheerios and a banana. Then, after making our beds and cleaning up the kitchen area, we helped each other pick out our clothes for the day. Since I had filled her in on the busy day ahead, we each chose wrinkle-resistant slacks and short-sleeved print blouses.

"Erin, will you do my hair like yours?" Carla asked, admiring my rather severe French twist. Her minimal makeup and conservative new clothes would do fine for a day of meetings and work, but I still wanted her to look like a normal teenager of barely fifteen.

"Tell you what," I said, as I took out the pins. "How about a thin braid circlet to hold our hair off our faces, and then we let the rest go free?"

That style suited us both and we were finally ready to face

the outside world.

First stop was at *The County Voice*. Carla was excited to see where I worked, and looked forward to getting behind the scenes of a real newspaper. I feared that she was in for a disappointment. Very little actually went on at that location.

But I needn't have worried. Fortunately, my colleagues, Muriel and Barbara, were on site, and glad to have a fresh recruit to impress.

Malcolm, as editor, welcomed her. She asked such insightful questions that he ended up giving her a publicity pass, allowing her to attend local events for free, and suggested that someday she apply for a student internship.

Frank welcomed her into his cubicle, the walls of which were covered with signed pictures from players from every pro sport imaginable. When he found out that she had played some softball in school, and that her favorite major league team was the San Diego Padres—though she had never been to the park—he offered to take her to one of their games the following week.

If either of the latter guessed her true identity, they kept it to themselves. I had just introduced her as a young friend. Finally, after most everyone else had left the building, I took her into my little makeshift office.

"And this is where you write up your notes and things," she declared; underwhelmed, I'm sure, though I had tried to warn her not to expect much. Her eyes did light up when she saw a picture of me and Mike taken at some gala last year. "That must be your fiancé. I didn't know he was Hispanic. You're such a beautiful couple!"

Such a beautiful, or perfect, or lucky, or . . . couple. *Everyone* said that. Had we fallen for such a superficial assessment ourselves? I realized, as I let myself ask that question, despite what had happened recently, I still refused to believe our relationship was over. We couldn't have been so wrong. Our love couldn't have been superficial, but could I live with our differences?

Could he?

Carla was looking at me expectantly. "You promised to tell me more about you and Mike and stuff like that. Also, when do I get to meet him? I really want him to like me, Erin. Do you think he will?"

"Oh, he will definitely like you, honey, but right now we need to go next door for some excellent pizza, stop at my doctor's office, and then go on to my bookstore job."

The physician's assistant took a nervous Carla into an examining room, but when they reemerged Carla seemed much more relaxed. The lab results wouldn't be back for a few days but nothing negative showed up in the physical exam. A daily multivitamin with iron and some wholesome food was all that was prescribed.


At about the same time I was pondering my future with him, Mike got a totally unexpected call. "Sorry to get you at work, Mike, but I didn't have your number at home—unlisted, right? Anyhow, this is Joe Cruz. Do you have a minute?"

"Yes, I can make time, but are you sure you don't want my—want Erin? She mentioned meeting you at one of those human trafficking seminars, or something."

"No, this is a more personal matter, but speaking of your fiancé, she's quite a woman—but I'm sure I don't have to tell you that.

"I'm afraid we got off to a rough start. I had her figured as one of those bored society wives but she's proven me wrong. And I'm not the only one who thinks so. As you know we have a San Diego consortium made up of law enforcement and some very dedicated civilians. I've heard favorable reports about her from my colleagues. Her involvement in trying to combat sexual trafficking is real and few can match her passion."

"Yes, she certainly has the courage of her convictions, alright," Mike agreed. He was somewhat taken aback to hear the deputy extoll Erin's passion—the very passion that he had used against her. In truth, he missed her a lot. But it wasn't just pride that was keeping him from calling her.

When you loved someone deeply you set yourself up to be devastated if something serious happened to them. He was worried that Erin's trafficking involvement might end badly—and it almost had. He could still see her ravaged, beautiful face after her altercation with the pimp. So he had chosen to give her an ultimatum, which unfortunately, ended up driving her away.

"Mike, are you still there?" Joe broke in on his reverie.

"Still here, but now I'm curious," Mike interjected, uncomfortable with the way the conversation had gone so far. "What is it you wanted to speak to me about?"

"Well, in case you haven't given it any thought lately, we graduated fifteen years ago this month from Oceanside High. So I was in the Value Plus with my wife the other day, picking up a few groceries, and Renata Lopez—she was Garcia when she was in our homeroom—came up to me and said she was planning to put together a reunion and begged me to be on a committee. Elena accepted for me—she likes things like that—so what could I say? Calling alumni is now part of my job."

"Do you have a date yet? I'm not much for ..."

"I know. I haven't seen you at any of our previous reunions. Look, Mike, I know we haven't had much in common since you broke away from the old neighborhood, but I have another, more serious, reason for hoping you'll consider renewing some old ties.

"You may have heard that the gang problem in Oceanside and its contiguous towns is worse than ever—and it's still generational. Some of the older guys are aging out of the rough stuff or are so into drugs themselves that they are useless at intimidation. So they are enlisting younger and younger kids to be the enforcers. Some of these gangster wannabes are only ten or eleven. Everyone knows the juveniles will just get a slap on the wrist if they are caught. Those stupid kids even consider it a badge of honor to be sent to juvey."

"Some things never change," Mike said. "I don't know how you can keep trying to shovel . . ."

"Shit against the tide," Joe finished. "Look, Mike. I'm anything but perfect, as you well know, but I can't just stand by and let those sleazebags win. Now, they've added human trafficking to selling illegal drugs and guns. They're nothing but a bunch of thugs, and that includes some of our own relatives."

"'So you had to remind me. I sense a little blackmail here. So where do you see me fitting in?"

"Some of us are putting together a program of intervention, you might call it. And we need successful guys like you, especially from the old neighborhoods, to be mentors and to set up alternatives to the lure of the gang life. And, of course, there would be fundraising and recruitment opportunities. All I'm asking is that you think about it."

"I will, and Joe, I don't think I ever told you how rotten I felt that your former partner was killed by my uncle. I hope he rots in prison. For what it's worth, I don't think my mother will ever get over the tragedy. You were like another son to her when we were growing up."

"It's been almost three years, and it still hurts, but I know you cared. We aren't responsible for our relatives, but we both come from good and bad. Our mothers are saints, right? Some of the others, however—not so good. All the more reason we need to keep the young ones on the straight-and-narrow. I'll get back to you with a reunion date. Say hi to Erin for me. Maybe we could get together for dinner before then. Elena would like that... and so would I."

Mike sat at his desk for quite a while after he hung up with Joe. How could one call mess up his carefully planned day so thoroughly? His office door was still closed. There were several client files in front of him and he had a luncheon appointment for one-thirty, but he found, for the time being at least, he couldn't concentrate on any of that.

He had always been proud of his ability to compartmentalize his life—not to let the personal intrude on the professional. But playing it safe so as not to get hurt didn't seem so attractive now. The truth was that he loved Erin very much, missed her a lot, and Joe's call had only intensified that fact. He picked up his phone and dialed a cell number he knew by heart. As it rang he practiced saying, "Erin, it's me. I've been a fool. I'm sorry. Can we try again?"

# 24

After she has finished eating, visited the trash bin, and used the public restroom, Serena wanders back up to a grassy knoll on the Marina Green where a few artisans have laid out their wares on small blankets or rugs.

She goes a little closer and watches as a pleasant-faced, short-haired blond woman is stringing colored beads and costume gem stones. Her slender fingers move quickly, yet there is nothing hurried about her actions. Serena thinks she is beautiful in her full-length, rainbow-hued skirt and cream-colored peasant blouse. A man lies dozing in the sun close by.

Serena is drawn to her, wants to sit by her side and watch her work, and wants to own one of her creations. The woman looks up and catches Serena's eye—seems to read her mind. She knows about me, Serena thinks, in a panic, and almost blindly, runs back down the hill.

She is confused. Ultimately she must trust some adult if she is ever to get back into a normal life. What if that woman was the one?

Still shaken, she decides to watch some rollerbladers doing tricks while she ponders her dilemma. Before long a yellow Lab, tail wagging, takes a shine to her, its owner follows and she and Serena chat briefly about the dog. By the time they leave and Serena climbs again to the grassy knoll where she had seen the jewelry maker, the woman and the man who had been lying close by are nowhere to be found.

Serena can't help feeling a sense of loss, but she concentrates on gazing at the Golden Gate Bridge, so often pictured as rising *out of the fog, but on this sunny afternoon, magnificent in the sun-light.*

*Perhaps tomorrow she will join the throngs of locals and tour-ists who make the roundtrip across the bridge by foot every day, but now it is getting late. Having seen nothing better she decides to spend at least one more night on a boat like the one that had previously sheltered her. But that is not to be.*

*As she rounds a corner heading back to Pier 39 she hears the sound of a steel band. A small crowd has gathered around five men in dreadlocks playing reggae music. As a result the sidewalk is partially blocked.*

*That type of music, reminds her of the time in San Diego, when she was kept in the factory basement with Alicia and the others. She starts to give the musicians a wide berth. Suddenly, one of them looks directly at her, and says in a lilting Jamaican voice, "Why don't you come closer little girl. We won't bite."*

*He looks and sounds just like Dion, the pimp who beat her so badly back in San Diego! It couldn't be him. Or could it? All reason is gone. She turns and runs back the way she came until she thinks her chest will burst, oblivious to the startled pedestrians who step hastily out of her way.*

*"Whoa, what's the hurry?"*

*Serena looks up at a tall man, with sandy-colored hair and small beard, who looks to be in his late twenties. He is wearing khaki shorts with lots of pockets and a T-shirt that says Property of the Army. A medium-sized short-haired dog lies nearby, guard-ing a large duffle bag and a walking stick.*

*"You almost plowed me down, kid," the man says, in a tone more amused than upset. She tries not to stare but she can't help noticing that one of his legs is much thinner than the other, and that fading, but still obvious, scars cover much of its surface.*

*She still hasn't said anything. "Are you trying to catch up with* your folks," he begins, "or running away from a ghost?"

How does he know? Serena wonders. Maybe the street musi-cian she thought was Dion was a ghost. Her Mexican grandmother believed in them. Perhaps she had been right?

"Cat got your tongue?" No response. "Guess you never heard that expression. My grandmother back in Oklahoma used to say that all the time. I was kind of shy like you, see—didn't talk much. My name is Peter, by the way, but my friends just call me Pete," he says, offering his hand. "In any case, I think I better find a police-man. Someone must be very worried to have lost such a small girl like you."

The word policeman has its usual bad effect on Serena. She is suddenly bone-tired and unable to think straight, the lovely day gone forever.

"Did you run away from someone?" He lights up a skinny ciga-rette as he talks. Serena recognizes the smell and it brings back bad memories of pimps and johns but Pete has kind eyes and a warm smile. She is tempted to tell him everything.

"Are those tears? Please don't cry. I'm not good at handling ladies tears." Pete is bending down to her level now.  He hands her a clean-looking handkerchief. "You can talk, can't you?"

She nods, gulps, and blows her nose.

"How about we go to the Jack in the Box for something to eat? Then maybe you can tell me what's going on with you, and I'll an-swer any questions you may have about me. Fair enough?"

A few minutes later the two of them are seated in a booth at the brightly-lit, fast-food restaurant. The dog, Rocco, is tied out-side.

"How are those tacos?" Pete asks, offering her some of the fries that came with his chicken sandwich.

Her mouth is almost full, but she manages a "Great!" along with a smile. "But you didn't tell me how much I owe you. I have over forty dollars with me."

"Keep your money, kid. This is my treat. Now, how about fill-

*ing me in a little here. Hopefully, I'll be able to help, but I've got to know more than I do now."*

And so it happens that Serena comes to trust the first adult stranger in her life since being snatched by Nestor from her home in Campo.

The words come in fits and starts—the story is appalling. Pete is a good listener. Finally, she comes to the end. "You do believe me, don't you?" she pleads.

"Every word," he responds. "Even that you are eleven instead of the eight I had you pegged for, and why you don't want to involve the police. I could tell you how terribly sorry I am that you had to go through all that, which is true, but more importantly, what can I do to help with your future? You can't just go on living alone on the streets. Unfortunately, there are some pretty bad dudes out there—and not just gang members."

She nods in agreement. "Then can I come along with you and Rocco—at least for now?" she asks.

"Speaking of my dog, we'd better take him his supper," Pete says, ignoring her request, and wrapping the leftover chicken in a napkin. Once outside, he looks for a more private location, and settles for a curb edging a small grassy area.

The dog eagerly wolfs down his food and then lies quietly nearby. Pete addresses Serena's question by first filling her in on the events that led up to his current living situation. He tells her that his withered leg is the result of a childhood accident when he was hit by a car which shattered his leg and broke his pelvis. Unfortunately, the bones weren't set right, and he was left with a permanent limp.

The resulting physical problems limited him as to job prospects, and meant that he had no chance to enlist in any branch of the service.

"Does it hurt anymore?" Serena asks at this point in his narrative.

"My leg? Not usually, though if it rains a lot or I sleep funny, it *does bother me. Which now brings you almost up to date with my rather sorry life. I worked odd jobs in Oklahoma for years, and after my dad passed away, came to California and did the same here. But these jobs are always temporary. No regular paycheck, so no way to save." He shrugs.*

*"And then?" Serena looks at him expectantly.*

*"And then, one day two weeks ago I was walking near Golden Gate Park feeling sorry for myself. I turned a corner and in front of me was an old, down-and-out-looking guy in a tattered army shirt. He stopped me as I walked by and asked if I had any spare change. He had a dog beside him and a cardboard sign that read 'Please Help a Homeless Vietnam Vet—God Bless.'*

*"Usually I would have ignored him, but for some reason I gave him a couple of bucks and we got to talking. To make a long story short, he said he made surprisingly good money begging, but he had to go into a nursing home, and so he needed someone to keep his dog."*

*"So you agreed to take Rocco and get into begging?" Serena asks, wide-eyed.*

*"You got it, so, if you want to go with me, it means sleeping in my little tent and hanging out while I try and make a few bucks—at least until we can figure out what to do with you."*

*Serena seems to be mulling this over. "Do you have a cell phone?" she asks.*

*"I do. Why, you got someone you could call? Someone you could stay with?"*

*My abuela may still be in the hospital, but Carla may be back in Campo now, she thinks. She'll know how I can get back. "I hope so," she answers. "I can dial in the number myself." Pete holds out his cell phone.*

*She realizes she is holding her breath. How long should she let it ring, and should she leave a message if no one answers? Her questions are soon answered when she hears a hated voice. It's Uncle Mateo! She freezes, but she can't hang up.*

*There is a pause, and then a stream of swear words. "Nestor, are you playing games? You know I just got out of another drug program, but I'm still on parole. Tell me where we can meet so I can pick up some stuff. You can't come here. They could be watching the house."*

*Her worst fear has come true. Not only is her uncle back in the family home, but he still does business with the pimp that stole her and Carla!*

*She hands the phone back as if it here a snake. Now she has no choice but to follow Pete, despite his questionable lifestyle.*

*Her bed this night is similar to the one on the boat, except it is under an old tarp in a remote corner of Golden Gate Park. She shares this with her new friend. The dog remains outside, guarding them both.*

Serena lies awake, shivering in the damp, morning air. She's anxious to stretch her legs, but she's afraid that if she ventures outside Rocco might bark. Pete is still asleep. He had gone out somewhere after he got her settled and hadn't returned for several hours.

Finally, he groans and rolls over. "You still here?" he kids.

"You snore." she counters.

"I had kind of a rough night," he says, by way of explanation. "Let's get something to eat, and then we'll get to work. Bring all your stuff with you," he says, indicating her backpack. "You can't really trust anyone around here."

Serena follows dutifully behind as they make their way to Martin Luther King Jr. Drive and out to the more bustling panhandle area of the park.

"There are some really neat things to see and do in the park, kid, but today we're here to build up the old bank-roll. I promise you I'll take a few hours off in a day or two and show you the sights—the aquarium, the planetarium, the zoo, maybe even have some refreshments in the old Japanese Tea Garden. I think you would like that.

"This is the corner where I met the Vietnam vet," Pete continues, unloading a few things from his duffle bag. "And it's been a good place for me, too. Now, why don't you and Rocco settle down around the corner? I have some comics you can read." And with that Pete, carrying his 'Homeless Disabled Afghanistan Veteran' cardboard sign, begins a slow hobble up the sidewalk.

The hours pass slowly for Serena, but Pete does check in every so often, and brings a soda and sandwich for her, water and, from somewhere, a bone for the dog.


At some time she must have dozed off, because she hears Pete's voice as if in a dream.

"Let's go. I've got a game lined up."

"What kind of a game? Can I watch?"

"Nah, it's not that kind of a game, but as I said, I'll take you some places soon. Be patient."

They are reversing their morning walk, full of twists and turns. This is such a confusing place, Serena thinks, though she is enjoying just stretching her legs in the fresh air, pretending she is a tourist.

Pete seems preoccupied and in a hurry so it's hard for her to keep up. Suddenly, he turns and says, "I have a favor to ask. I need to borrow some of your money. I'll give it right back after the crap game."

Serena is taken aback. She hates to part with any of her precious savings, but that's being selfish, she reasons, after all he has done for her. They are now standing, half hidden, in a small grove of Monterey pines. She takes her small purse out of her backpack and hands him all but a few singles and the loose change.

"Thanks, kid," he mumbles, avoiding any eye-contact. They continue walking. "What is a crap game?" she asks.

*"It's the same as shooting dice," is his non-answer. Then: "You really don't know anything about it, do you?"*

*Serena sighs. Adults can be so strange, sometimes. "No," she admits, "are you going to explain it to me?"*

*So he does—shows her his lucky red dice, tosses them against the base of a fountain, and calls out a number before they stop rolling. A different number turns up.*

*It sounds like a dumb game to her. "You're saying that the players bet on which numbers come up, right? That's gambling. Do you win much?"*

*"I do alright," he answers, and then adds, "Why, you worried about your money?" He sounds defensive.*

*She shakes her head, but she is worried. Uncle Mateo was always gambling on something, and he never seemed to have any money. Pete abruptly starts walking again and stops only when they get to a hill which looks down on a small, out-of-the-way, paved area, containing what seems to be an abandoned utility shed of some kind. Several other men are already there, including one wearing a business suit, and several others, shabbily dressed for the most part.*

*Pete hesitates, and then starts to lead her back the way they've come. "We passed a playground just a short distance from here.  Why don't you go hang out there for a little while and then, later on, I'll come back for you," he suggests. "I'll take Rocco with me. They don't like dogs around little kids or in those family parks."*

*"Good luck," she calls out, sensing his impatience, before turning away.*

*"Take care, Serena," he says in return.*


*The storm comes on quickly. There are a few flashes of lightning, then rolls of thunder, getting louder and closer together. A few of the younger children start to cry as parents and other caregivers* swoop in to hurry their charges off the playground equipment, everyone scurrying for shelter from the elements.

When the rain is over, only a few muddy puddles, some trash bin overflow, and a handful of overlooked clothing is left.

Serena, who had taken partial shelter under a tree, is soaked to her skin. She looks frantically around for her backpack, but it's nowhere to be found. Someone probably picked it up with their own belongings by mistake. Everything precious she had is gone, including her beloved yellow bunny!

She waits a bit more for Pete and makes another search for her belongings. She reasons that he and the other players probably got caught by the storm, which naturally interrupted their playing. Now they are probably trying to get in some more games before it gets dark.

She is uncomfortable being the only one in the deserted playground, so decides to go back to the hillside overlook and wait until Pete is ready to call it a night. As she walks, she begins to feel a little better. When Pete gives her back her money she'll ask him to take her to the Salvation Army store for clothes. She can easily get more brochures almost anywhere to replace the ones she lost. She even dares to imagine that some little child from the poor family who now has her possessions will come to love her bunny the way she did.

But all such hopes are dashed when she gets to her destination. It is deserted. And she is faced with the harsh realization that Pete is probably not coming back for her. Perhaps he never intended to, or he meant to, but lost all her money and more, and is now too embarrassed to face her. The truth, in any case, is that he and his dog will go back to their life without her. She has now become an unnecessary and unwanted burden.

Dusk has now turned into inky black with only a sliver of moon for light. The trees, bushes, and flowerbeds, which only a *few hours ago made this park a thing of beauty, now cast ominous shadows from which comes the chilling sound of a screech owl and the scurrying of its potential prey.*

*Serena has hit bottom. Any hopes she has for finding her family no longer exist. She seriously considers finding her way back to Angel in the Mission district. Can regular meals, a roof over for her head, and the company of other young girls, make up for the beating she has coming, and the degradation she must endure from the johns? If not, what else is there?*

# 25

So far, the day was going well, and the news at the doctor's office was encouraging. Now, Carla and I were looking forward to working a shift at my favorite bookstore.

"Before we go in, give me a minute while I check my cell for messages," I said, as we drove into the parking lot.

Carla leafed through a copy of *Elle* while she waited. I smiled, as I put the phone back in my purse. It was very good news.

"There was one from Mike," I explained. "You and I may have to change our plans for tonight."

"Did he beg you to come home?" the teenager asked, excitedly. "I bet he'll fill the house with flowers and ..."

"Carla, this is not one of your Mexican telenovelas. When we talked at the restaurant I told you that the reason I was staying at the motel for a few days was that Mike and I needed some time apart to work out a few differences between us. I had only just checked in when you called me to get you at the Carlsbad Outlet."

"Have you told him I'm with you?"

"No," I admitted, "but ..."

Carla broke in. "*I'm* the reason you had the argument, right? I'm such a dummy! You got hurt because of me, and now I've come between you and Mike," she said, despair in her voice.

"Please don't look so sad, honey, you mustn't blame yourself. Our disagreement was *not* because of you. Mike did think that my involvement with the human trafficking movement, in general, was getting too intense, and that maybe I was somewhat neglecting our life as a couple. But there were other issues and differences that we needed to address. That's why we spent some time apart.

"And it worked. We missed each other a lot, and now we just need to clarify a few things, which we plan to do tonight. That's what Mike's cell message was about, so please, let me see a smile, and let's go in and get to work."

Carla opened her passenger door, but paused to say, "But Erin, from what you've said, you and Mike *could* be in a novella—you know, boy gets girl, boy loses girl, boy gets girl back."

"Okay, Miss Smarty, you win," I conceded. Both of us were smiling as we entered the Reader's Roost.

As usual, I couldn't get enough of the sights, sounds, and smells of the bookstore, but I was concerned that yet another new situation with different people involved might prove a little formidable for Carla.

I needn't have worried. The book store owners, Judy and Dave, were there, and went out of their way to make my young friend feel welcome.

Carla was a quick study, and eager to please. "I can see why you love it here," she told me, as we unloaded stock, refilled shelves, and set up exhibits. On a break, the teenager was encouraged to pick out a few books from a markdown bin. I was pleased to see how almost reverently she handled her choices.

I did wonder though, just how far behind in grade Carla was academically, but from what I observed in our time together it wouldn't be hard for her to catch up—to even excel. If she gets to lead a normal life, that is. But then, she also needs to give a statement to help the police and district attorney prosecute the gang members—and thus hopefully to locate Serena. Certainly, a normal life for Carla will thus have to be deferred.

On the other hand, at this point, there didn't seem much left of her old life. I owed her a call to Campo to find out more about that, but for now, I needed to answer Mike's message.

When my coworker, Pam, took Carla off to check out some new young adult fiction, I called up Mike's work number.

As the receptionist put me through I rehearsed my words, but I needn't have. When he picked up I blurted out, "I'm sorry," a half beat before he did.

And then we both said "I love you," at the same time. I told him that Carla was with me, unsure what his reaction would be, but he countered that he was glad, and that he should have been with me in Oceanside when I first tried to rescue her from the pimp. Of course, there was much more to be said, but that could only be done face to face, so we agreed to meet later at an Ocean Beach Denny's.


I stopped at a deli on the way back to the motel so that Carla could order a favorite wrap and a salad for her supper. Once she was settled in, I said, "I won't be long and, just think, you can watch one of those Spanish soap operas, if you like."

"I just might. You and Mike should watch them together to get some pointers. Put more passion in your lives—we Hispanics are passionate people!"

I pretended to be shocked, but I couldn't help but grin. Seeing her happy, even if it might be only temporary, was worth a lot.

Carla continued on a serious note, "And don't worry about me. Take your time. I won't open the door for  anyone. I'll be fine. Honest."

A few minutes later, I arrived at the restaurant and saw Michael waiting in his car. He stepped out to greet me as soon as I parked. We kissed only briefly, in deference to our surroundings, but the longing for more was evident to both of us. It was very hard to pull away.

"I missed you so much," Mike murmured against my throat. "I was such a ..."

"No need to apologize," I said, touching his lips with my fingertips. "If I hadn't . . . but let's go in. I want to get a booth. There *are* a few things we need to discuss right away."

Now that he was near it would be so easy to let our natural chemistry and the unspoken promise of our upcoming lovemaking take over and, yet again, push all issues aside.

I had been encouraged by his phone message, but I still feared that the main stumbling block to any permanent reconciliation might remain. Now that Carla was with me I knew more than ever that I couldn't give up my involvement with the human trafficking movement, no matter the personal cost. Would he still ask that of me?

But my fears were allayed when Mike spoke of his conversation with Deputy Cruz. That conversation, and our separation, seemed to have made a profound change in his outlook.

"So you do understand," I said. "You're even okay with Carla staying with us a bit until I can make a better arrangement?"

Mike reached out and covered my hands with his. "I'm fine, really. In fact, as I said, after talking with Joe Cruz, I think I can even be of some help with the effort to stop trafficking, especially the gang part of it. As to our personal plans—the wedding— I'll leave all that to you. Just wake me up when it's time for the ceremony, or we can elope, or . . ."

"Just so we're together—deal?" I finished for him, feeling a profound sense of relief.

"Deal!" Mike answered, with conviction. "Just come on back to *our* home."

Mike returned to work and I headed for the motel. What a whirlwind these past few days had been! And there were probably many more to come, but soon I would be going home, to *our* home, to the man I loved, and now, hopefully, a true partner.

I put the car in my safe spot and approached the unit as unobtrusively as possible. I gave our special knock and saw the curtain move an inch before Carla let me in, then locked the door and slipped on the chain-guard immediately. I can't wait for this secretiveness to be over, for all our sakes, I thought.

Carla turned off the TV. "Tell me all," she said, sitting cross-legged on her bed. "How did it go?"

I eased off my shoes and perched on my bed. "It went very well, in fact, how would you like to pack up and move in with Mike and me for a while?"

Carla's reaction was one of pure joy—all youthful exuberance. I only wished that I could be as unencumbered by practical considerations such as her long-term future and the whereabouts of Serena. But for now, I put them aside, and joined hands with her as she whirled around the room.

"We could go tonight, but Mike has a work-related seminar which will last until very late. Also, I need to go into the office tomorrow, so we decided to put off my returning until later when we're both free. I hope you're not too disappointed."

She sighed dramatically and said, "I'll live! We could stay up all night telling ghost stories or something like that."

"Or something like that," I echoed.

We both slept late next morning, then finished packing and, before stopping at the newspaper, went out for breakfast. Carla's spirits were so high that I hated to bring her down, but I knew that the uncertainty of the Campo situation remained.

When I was alone with her at work, I brought up the subject. Carla was anxious for us to make the call. Before handing the phone over, I had learned from the dispatcher that the grandmother, though conscious, wasn't doing well, and that Mateo has been released from drug rehab. He remained on parole, but was living back in the family home.

Lorena told Carla the same thing, but added that her grandmother had expressed great joy when told that her granddaughter had been found, and was safe.

I had left my cubicle to give Carla privacy. When I returned I found her wiping her eyes. "I want to see my abuela so much," she said softly, "but Lorena told me that the doctors are working to build up her strength so that soon she will be able to have visitors. And did you know that my uncle Mateo is home and that Nestor is back in the area?"

"She told me."

"Then I may never be able to go back!" Carla agonized, shaking her head in despair at that possibility.

"Not for now, but the situation may change, as I mentioned before there are many people, including the police, who want to put these criminals out of business.

"Now let's get out of here. We need to pick up some groceries on the way home. Do you have any suggestions for dinner?"

Carla brightened at the mention of home. "Can we have tacos? I make really good ones. Do you know where there's a Mexican grocery store?"

I shook my head. "Would a Ralph's market work? I know of one nearby."

An hour later, loaded down with grocery bags, we pulled up to the condo and into the garage, Carla wide-eyed from the time we turned off I-5 onto La Jolla Village Drive.

"We'll put some of the perishables away, and then get you settled in the guest room," I said.

The coffee maker looked as if it had been used and there was a mug and a dish in the sink, but otherwise no sign that Mike had eaten until I opened the under-counter trash compactor to discover several empty boxes of ready-to-eat meals. The thought of him eating alone in our dream home was touching, no matter which one of us was more at fault for our rift.

Once the groceries were stowed, I gave Carla a brief tour of the house, seeing it once again through someone else's eyes. It *was* stunning, but might it appear too pretentious to someone like Carla with her background? She was taking everything in, but hadn't said a word until she saw the oversized aquarium.

"Erin, I didn't know you could have something so magical in

your own home! I want something just like it one day."

"I hope that comes true. It *is* beautiful and peaceful. I even talk to the fish sometimes. They're great listeners."

The study, with all the books and Michael's massive desk, impressed her as well. "Erin, this whole place is right out of a magazine," she commented, as we climbed the spiral staircase to the upper floor. "You guys must be very rich."

As had been the case with Amy, there was no hint of envy in her voice. She continued, adding shyly, "I guess I thought rich people were kind of stuck-up but you're so nice."

"We can all learn not to be too quick to judge others," I told her, hoping that didn't sound too preachy. Actually, I was thinking of myself, how I had misjudged several policemen, for example, or worse yet, perhaps even Mike. Before I packed up and left had I really given him a chance to come around to my way of thinking?

We took our time looking around upstairs and putting Carla's few belongings away in the one extra room we had furnished. She seemed most taken by the shared bathroom, which included two sinks and a walk-in shower, as well as a bathtub with jets. I filled one of my spare cosmetic cases with some toiletries and insisted she pick out a few items of clothing from my walk-in closet. It was easy to lose track of time.

"When do you expect Mike to get home, and do I look alright?" she asked suddenly, after she had changed her outfit for the third time.

"Where did the time go? He'll be here any minute. And you look just fine," I answered, in approval of her current choice of capris and coral crop-top. "Now, let's go downstairs and get out the fixings for those tacos."

Carla had been chattering away until we heard Mike's car approaching. Then she grew silent and slumped against the center island. Her need for his approval was palpable. He knew about the real her—the soiled her. The pimps had done their job well.

Mike walked in a few minutes later, carrying two bouquets of mixed flowers. Carla looked up hesitantly. He walked directly over to her. "You choose," he said. "Next time I'll know your favorites."

She beamed as she reached for the bouquet containing mainly blooms in pinks and purples. I could have kissed him. Well, actually, I did.

Carla's suggestion for dinner was a big hit. We sat around the counter eating our do-it-yourself tacos. I noticed, while eating, that the physical resemblance between Mike and Carla was striking as they sat side by side, passing hot sauce back and forth.

I offered to clean up while the two of them checked out a pay-per-view movie. I also made up a big bowl of popcorn and carried it into our living room.

When she saw me, Carla said to Mike in a challenging tone, "Erin boasted that you were really good at tossing these up in the air and catching them in your mouth."

Mike raised his eyebrows, but then my usually serious, somewhat neatnik, fiancé put on a skillful demonstration of this talent. Before long he was coaching Carla who proved to be an apt pupil.

"I'll be your manager," I said, shaking my head in mock consternation. "I see big money to be made. Now what did you choose for tonight's viewing?"

The third installment of a blockbuster adventure series proved to be just the mindless escapism we all needed, and capped a memorable day—one of many to come, I fervently hoped.


It was very nice, once again, to fall asleep at night with Mike holding me close. I even welcomed our typical weekday morning ritual which had me responding groggily to his declaration of love as, at five-thirty, he headed to his office and the upcoming New York stock exchange openings.

I decided to spend some time each day helping Carla explore our immediate neighborhood as well as the many other wonders that La Jolla had to offer. I found her curiosity to be boundless and her stamina to be awe inspiring. I could see myself getting in the best shape of my life as we walked, hiked, and rode bicycles everywhere.

I had taken some time off from work for a few days so that we could visit the famous local beaches in leisurely fashion. We stood well back on the jutting rocks watching talented surfers brave the fierce waves at Windansea, joined the tourists at La Jolla's Children's Pool where the harbor seals had long dominated the scene, and had become a major, if somewhat controversial, attraction. The seals tended to be smelly and noisy, but their antics, as they lolled about or fought for prime sunning spots, held Carla's attention for quite some time.

But whether at those two ocean spots or at the La Jolla cove—calm surf good for swimming, snorkeling and diving—or the long, wide, sandy beach stretch known as the Shores, or at any of the myriad other spots which offered an ocean view, Carla could not get enough of looking out to sea to try to catch a glimpse of dolphins.   When we spoke at the motel Carla had said that one of her fondest memories, one she returned to over and over when things were the hardest for her to bear, was when her grandmother took her and Serena to the San Diego waterfront to watch the whale migrations and to enjoy the antics of the dolphins. Now, she was living in a place where such sightings were routine and she couldn't believe her good fortune in being able to live nearby.

On Mike's poker night, I rented a PBS educational special on dolphins, showcasing those magnificent mammals in the wild all over the world. And also, for the pure tug-at-your-heartstrings effect, we also rented *Whale Rider,* that amazing Maori film. It was a good thing that Mike wasn't there. It was easily a four-tissue viewing!

To keep our strength up during these outings, of course, we needed to eat. But while La Jolla has more than its share of famous, trendy, eclectic and gourmet-type places to eat—and we did try a few—Carla seemed most pleased to discover a Subway and a 7-11, the latter open around-the-clock and no more than a long walk or an easy bike ride away from our condo.

"I think I could have a Slurpee every day," she said on one occasion, while downing a version called Blue Shock. "I'd be a cheap date."

The time passed quickly, too quickly. But despite the ease with which Carla fit in, and the pleasure we derived from her company, Mike and I knew that, in general, we were just postponing her long-term future, but more immediately, her working with the police to pursue prosecution of the gangs.

"Have you spoken to her yet?" Michael asked, as we did some bedtime reading a few nights after her arrival. "You know Joe Cruz is anxious to meet her."

"I will tomorrow. I admit I've been avoiding the subject after her initial negative reaction when I mentioned the police. But speaking of Joe, aren't we supposed to go to dinner with him and his wife next Tuesday or Wednesday?"

I was looking forward to meeting the couple on a social basis. In a way it would be the first time that Mike had ever let me see into his past, but at the same time I knew that somehow Carla's situation might come up, and, in all honesty, I wasn't ready to deal with what that might mean.

Meanwhile, I was determined to build fond memories for Carla as long as she was with us. The La Jolla chamber of commerce had published a very full calendar of area events for June. One I especially was looking forward to is called bouTEAque-A, a shopping-for-self-confidence event.

The flyer billed it as an English tea, complete with mini-sandwiches, crumpets, and cookies, for mothers and daughters, with a local designer's fashion show to follow. There would be prizes and raffles and all proceeds would go to benefit Children's Smiles—a non-profit agency which offered programs to build confidence in girls who had been victimized by trauma or abuse.

I got myself assigned to cover it for the newspaper and, true to his word, Malcolm gave Carla an intern's press pass, and she would accompany me as my photographer.

It was a truly memorable afternoon and, since Carla herself had suffered both trauma and abuse, opened the door for her to share some more of her own stories with me during our time together in the car. Once again, I tried not to think of what she had endured.

The event also served as an example of the good that can occur when the more fortunate work to improve the lives of those not as blessed.  The several thousands of dollars raised would go a long way to help the cause. There were many ways to make a difference, and I would do well to remember that, lest I continue to make the mistake of pre-judging Mike's clients and coworkers as dilettantes.

On Saturday Mike even gave up his golf game so that the three of us could attend the San Diego County Fair held in nearby Del Mar. We toured the Future Farmers of America and garden club exhibits, petted the 4-H animals, watched tractor pulls and equine exhibitions, and ate giant portions of fried dough sprinkled with cinnamon sugar. We each accompanied Carla on a carnival ride, then watched and waved while she went alone on a particularly stomach-churning ride. At night, we listened to Darius Rucker, reunited for a summer tour with his old band, Hootie & the Blowfish, and then to a tribute band playing rock and roll favorites.

"That was my best day ever. Thank you both so much," Carla

said later, as she headed up to her bedroom.

That evening, as Mike and I climbed into our own bed, he said, "I'm exhausted, but that *was* fun," and then, "Honey, are you crying?"

"Oh, Mike, I wish she really were my sister. I can't bear to think of her not being a part of our lives."

"I don't know what to say. I was afraid this would happen. I understand. I really do, but we have to be realistic. At this point who knows how things will turn out? I just hate to see you get hurt. Now scoot over."

I don't know how long he held me. I just know that at some point we both fell asleep.

"Now stay out as long as you want. I'll be fine," Carla said Tuesday, as she saw us to the door of the garage. "I don't want you to change your social life because of me."

We were on our way to dinner in Oceanside, but we hadn't told her that our dining partners were to be Joe and Elena Cruz. As soon as we arrived, Joe made the introductions all around. "Hope this place is alright with you," he said, as he led us into The Flying Bridge Casa De Villa. "Their menu is quite varied." Then to Mike: "I was tempted to go to one of the taco shacks, for old time's sake, but my wife talked me out of it." Elena shook her head as if to say, "*Men!*"

Our booth was ready. A waitress came by immediately with a wine and liquor list. "They make delicious margaritas," Elena suggested.

"Perfect," I agreed, and we ordered two on the rocks, with the men going for Dos Equis beer. The food was good and the conversation flowed easily.

The upcoming high school reunion was mentioned and I found that I was looking forward to attending. It turned out that Elena had graduated from the same high school, but several years later.

"Then she went to the Northridge campus and majored in business, but she couldn't stay away from her old neighborhood. Now she's head of the Solutions for Change HR department in Vista," Joe said, proudly.

Attractive, intelligent, and gracious, I thought. I could envision Carla becoming like her one day.

Shop talk was avoided by a mutually unspoken agreement. Mike did tell me on our way home that, while Elena and I were in the restroom, Joe *had* mentioned Carla. Joe remained convinced that statements from her, as a former victim of gang sexploitation, could help his office procure an indictment and lead to an eventual prosecution. The county grand jury, after reviewing Carla's statement, would then make the final decision. Then, in conjunction with the district attorney's office, a decision would be made as to handing down an indictment against the traffickers.

So, at least temporarily, we had to decide Carla's future ourselves. In the fall there would be schooling to consider, and perhaps even legal custody matters, and the continuing question of Serena's whereabouts. We had taken Carla into our lives and, for now, accepted all that entailed. Her future rested with us— awesome responsibility, but nothing we wouldn't be able to handle.

Now, if I could only stop being suspicious of men who looked at Carla in a certain way, or of large, black, American-made cars which seemed to appear unexpectedly. Nothing concrete, paranoia on my part, no doubt, but just the same, disturbing.

# 26

They ran hand in hand—she toting a mammoth canvas beach-bag—he with two small rugs tucked under one muscular arm—down the grassy slope, across the paved walkway, and into an older white Volkswagen Vanagon camper just as the first fat drops of rain began to hit the pavement. Lightning lit up the sky, followed closely by a sharp crack of thunder that sounded ominously close.

"Where did *that* come from?" Melody winced, as she flopped down on the back seat of the camper, Jimmy following.

"I think the weather channel nowadays calls these rain bands," he answered, putting his arm around her and pulling her close as there was another lightning and thunder combination while the wind-driven deluge rattled their vehicle. "They don't last long but doesn't this make you wish you were back inside a real house?"

"This *is* our house—our home, and some days I still have to pinch myself to believe it. Look around, we have everything we need—propane two-burner stove and small refrigerator, tiny sink, sleeping for four, a closet, storage area and a pop-up top," she said, enthusiastically as she pointed toward each.

"You forgot the auxiliary battery and the port-a-potty, but that *was* impressive! You could always get a job selling used cars if we're hurting for cash. But seriously, honey, I'm glad it's working out for you. And we've spruced it up with new carpet and those rainbow-colored curtains my sis donated."

She nodded. There was another flash and rumble. "I could do without that," she said, with a shiver, "but actually I have always liked the sound of rain on a rooftop, and we're snug as can be in here. However, I can't help feeling especially sorry for anyone who doesn't have a safe, warm place to be at times like these. Speaking of the homeless, or those that appear to be, did you happen to notice a small, disheveled girl who came by to look at my jewelry the other afternoon?"

"A lot of people come by to admire your jewelry. Some actually turn out to be customers. Anyhow, I was probably dozing off. Why, was there something special about her? You have that wistful look."

"It's hard to explain, but it was late afternoon and sunny. I may have been dozing off too, or at least day dreaming, when I looked up and there she was staring at the jewelry. Suddenly she raised her head, and I got the strangest feeling that she wanted to speak to me—to ask me something or tell me something important, or . . ."

"Or steal something . . . sorry," he added, when he saw her disapproving look. "But that has occurred in the past. So what happened then?"

"Then, she just ran away before I could say anything."

"Probably ran back to her family. Maybe she even has a pink bedroom of her own, while you make do with a backseat that converts into a bed!"

"You're probably right," Melody responded. "Most all kids look scruffy after playing outside for a while. Guess we'll never know, in any case.

"It's still raining a little, but I think the storm has moved on. It's safe to remove your arm if you can. It's probably gone to sleep by now."

Jimmy was aware that holding his wife close during thunder storms was as much for his benefit as for hers. After twenty-two years in the Marine Corps—which included many tours of duty in war zones, the last in Iraq and Afghanistan—loud noises still had the power to set his heart racing.

Melody knew of his occasional nightmares, but he hadn't shared much about them or any other stress-related symptoms with her yet, despite the fact that she felt she was an excellent listener and the shrink at the VA had urged him to be more forthcoming.

He would in time, but for now he just wanted to protect their love and their new life together. Almost a year ago, when he had asked her to marry him, he had been so sure that she would say no that he had prepared an I-understand-why-not speech.

He was only forty-one, but the saying was that being on active duty for a long stretch causes one to age in dog years. What did Melody see when she looked into his face with its strong nose and jaw, the hazel eyes that contrasted with skin dark and leathery from years spent in desert climates? Handsome, he was not. Grizzled was perhaps a more apt description.

She, on the other hand, at thirty, with cornflower-blue eyes, peaches-and-cream complexion and flaxen-colored hair, was an old-fashioned beauty. Even though she had recently put on a few pounds and cut her hair, in his eyes she remained his fairy tale princess.

Melody's voice broke through his reverie. "I don't think there's any sense in setting up again today. Besides, didn't you promise Jerry at the deli that you would help him rearrange the back storage room?"

"I did. It shouldn't take long. Maybe you could check on your consignment pieces and then we can meet at Club Rouge for happy hour?"

"Excellent plan," she agreed, reaching across to give him a kiss before they buckled themselves into their front swivel seats.

The drive from Marina Green to the iconic Haight Ashbury section of San Francisco took only minutes. The Millers were, at least temporarily, part of the neighborhood's vibrant, eclectic culture. As such, they had a parking arrangement with one of the clothing boutiques where they could leave their camper overnight behind the store. Melody's lovely, unique costume jewelry was prized at several of the vintage shops, while Jimmy's physical strength and ability to fix almost anything kept him in great demand. They had bartered for nearly everything, including their overnight parking place and most of their food. It worked well.

After parking, they went their separate ways. Melody got good news at Piedmont Boutique and Ambiance's—both specialty stores had consignment money for her, and the former asked if she would make an original bracelet and earring-set for a customer. It was very rewarding to have a former hobby of hers recognized in such a positive way. It had worked out perfectly with the semi-gypsy life she and Jimmy had adopted shortly after their marriage.

Melody and Jimmy's youngest sister Lynn had been friends since their days at Davenport high school in eastern Washington, so Melody readily accepted when Lynn invited her to be part of a Thanksgiving celebration. Melody's mother had died a few months earlier after suffering through a long illness, and friends and neighbors were still showing her, as the caregiver daughter, typical small-town help and compassion.

She also knew a number of other family members and guests, and fit right in, though she became increasingly uncomfortable when several commented favorably on her work with special-needs children. What would they think if they knew that she was facing burnout, and had considered leaving her position, though she still cared deeply for her difficult charges? She had celebrated each small gain, and empathized with the often frustrated parents, but in the past year she had been bitten and spit at, and devastated when a former pupil committed suicide. It was high time to consider other options.

She had tried to put that out of her mind and just enjoy the friendly, festive atmosphere. Lynn's mother had taken her under her wing and introduced a new son-in-law and the latest grandchild. And you remember Jimmy, she had said. Melody had heard that Lynn's oldest brother had retired from active duty, was receiving a pension from the government, and was now working in the family construction and industrial equipment business. However, she hadn't seen Jimmy in years.

Other than that brief introduction and being seated at the same table for the meal itself, she had barely seen him again that day, absorbed as he and most of the other males were with football, so she was totally surprised when he called the next day to ask her out to dinner.

Half intrigued, because it was the most hesitant request for a date that she had ever heard, she accepted. "I couldn't stand the thought of eating any more turkey just yet," he had explained. And that was the inauspicious beginning of a friendship that grew rather quickly, and, to their mutual surprise, into something much more.

They realized that they were both at a crossroads in their lives; he, having trouble returning to his hometown and going to work in the family business, she, no longer a caregiver, but now also suffering deep dissatisfaction with the teaching career she had worked so hard to attain. The only solid thing they had going forward seemed to be their increasing love for one another.

They became engaged, and she finished out the final year in her teaching position, while he spent most of his free time working on an old VW camper he had bought from a friend, with the idea of doing some traveling in the future.

On the fourth of July they hosted a wedding ceremony and reception amidst the lush, backyard plantings of the old Victorian that had been her family home for generations. A retired judge presided, the weather cooperated, and all the well-wishers who attended seemed to enjoy themselves immensely. Melody remembered it as a perfect day.

The couple spent overnights and weekends in the camper at first—working out the kinks and getting used to married life in small quarters. And then, one day, Jimmy had suggested a no-timetable, fancy-free trip down the Pacific Coast Highway to Baja California. In short order, they put Melody's family home on the market, packed up her jewelry-making supplies, and headed toward the coast.

Melody never tired of reflecting back over the past several months and she was still smiling as she neared the Club Deluxe. The cool sound of a jazz CD, and the familiar murmur of tourists and locals alike easing into happy hour, made her feel at home. The place would most likely be jammed and very noisy by nine-thirty when live musicians took over the small stage, but for now it had the small, intimate feel that made it one of her very favorite places in which to relax and socialize. She walked over to Jimmy, who stood at the bar nursing a draft beer.

The bartender spoke up immediately. "Hi, Melody, the usual?"

"With vodka, please," she answered, as he quickly blended the club's signature Spa Collins—a refreshing drink which included cucumber, lemon, fresh ginger and club soda.

She and Jimmy took their drinks to a booth in the back of the room. Melody decided to sit close beside her husband instead of across from him. She gave him a hug as she slid in.

"You two celebrating something?" a waitress asked, as she paused by their table on her way to put in an order.

"Just our being together, I guess," Melody answered, as she covered Jimmy's hand with hers. And how unlikely that would have been less than two years ago, she thought.

Jimmy looked a little uncomfortable at this public display of affection but he didn't pull his hand away.

"I'm sorry if I embarrassed you," Melody said softly, when they were alone again. "But what I told her was true."

"Don't be sorry. Remember, you are my lifeline. Besides, I'm working on my inner romantic, but really, you know that our being together is the best thing that ever happened to me."

Melody began to choke up at those tender words, coming from her usually unsentimental husband—the   retired marine master sergeant, with the brush cut he refused to let grow out.

"Ah hell, Melody, don't go getting all teary on me," Jimmy said, apprehensively.

"Don't tell me one of your sisters never explained to you that a woman's tears depend on a number of circumstances, happiness being a major one. And *you* make me *very* happy."

"Okay, if you say so, but speaking of togetherness, our anniversary is coming up. Have you decided where we should go to celebrate?"

'Well, our stay here has been wonderful, but since our plan was to eventually go all the way to Baja California, I was thinking that a great anniversary would be going down to Big Sur country and spend some time there. Everyone raves about the area."

"Sold," he said. "I just need to fulfill a few commitments and you have a handful of outstanding orders left to do, right?"

"Yes, but I can easily see us coming back here at some point, can't you? We seem to fit in well."

"I think that the camper paved the way for us to be readily accepted here, even though a few old-timers considered us to be just wannabes since we hadn't been around for their hippy glory days."

"Well, of course not, but we do like a lot of the music from that era—even own an anniversary DVD from Woodstock, and I think my dad took part in a few sit-ins when he was at UC Berkley. Everything seems to be retro nowadays anyhow."

"Actually, you won them over with your long skirts and fringed shawls, and when we first got here your hair was down to your . . ."

She finished his sentence. "My hair *was* very long. But it was usually clean, as were my feet. And I'm too much of a feminist to be the subject of a Bob Dylan song. In addition I have never inhaled—even incense makes me sneeze—and I still want to wash and cut the hair of anyone I see with dreadlocks.

"As for you, you actually enlisted, and then made a career of the military! We're not exactly typical Haight Ashbury inhabitants. But the fact is, we're in a vibrant, diverse community—interesting to visit as a tourist, but even more special once you become a resident."

"Well said," he nodded, and leaned back in the booth contentedly.

"Had enough?" Jimmy asked, a few hours later as the noise level continued to rise, and a not-very-funny comedian added yet more bodily-function jokes in a mistaken attempt to win over the tough audience.

"I almost felt sorry for the guy," Melody said, as she and her husband walked hand-in-hand back to their camper. "I heard someone say he was related to one of the bartenders."

"They needed one of those hooks from the old gong shows," Jimmy commented, as he unlocked the side door and slid it back.

They had made up their bed earlier and pulled the curtains closed all around. It was cramped—especially with the top down—but they were used to it, and prepared to settle down for the night, quickly and efficiently. As a concession to the rather public nature of their parking spot she wore a Haines, amber-colored, sleep-set, and he, plaid boxers, but that hadn't proved to be much of a hindrance to their lovemaking.

While on leave, and still in his teens, he and a former classmate had eloped—only to regret their impulsiveness and get an annulment shortly afterward. Since then, while hardly what would be called promiscuous, he had been intimate with a number of women in several countries, but he hadn't been in a serious relationship until he had started dating Melody. And, unrealistic as it might seem, his love for her was such that he regretted all his encounters.

He knew she would laugh if he told her such things. "I'm not going to break," she would say, as she led him in ways that guaranteed she would be as satisfied as he would be. He loved caressing every inch of her and then lying entwined when they were spent. Tonight was no exception.

"I had a lovely day," she said, sleepily. "And I can't wait for our anniversary trip."

Together and fancy-free, he thought, just before he fell asleep—his features softening in contentment.

Next morning Melody laid a rug down on her favorite spot on the Marina Green and set out a varied assortment of her jewelry—preparing to work on one of the custom orders she needed to complete and, hopefully, also selling items to passersby.

Jimmy helped her set up. "I'll be back in a while," he said. "I'm going to go watch the remote control airplane exhibition they have set up over the hill, near the basin."

The fog was burning off early and a number of tourists and early walkers had already appeared. Melody was very fond of this place and was glad to know that they would probably be returning one day, but since they had started out they had been to many other lovely and interesting spots, especially driving south along the Coast Highway.

The scenery had been spectacular and they had taken the time to do a lot of off-road exploring—much of it physically challenging. Melody was glad that she had been working out regularly at a gym so she was able to keep up with her ex-Marine husband.

But so far, if she were to choose another area to settle in for a while, charming Old Town Florence in Oregon would win hands down. There, she had been able to sell some of her jewelry, and she and Jimmy got to be tourists; staying for two nights in a bed and breakfast, eating most meals in different places, exploring the unique shops, and, in general, just enjoying the laid back, friendly atmosphere.

What a country! What a life she thought, as she assumed a yoga balance pose by her rug. And then, out of the corner of an eye, she saw the girl again—the pose and the proper breathing quickly abandoned as she eased slowly back to a seated position.

The child looked worse than ever. Haunted eyes stared out from a dirty face almost covered by matted hair.  She's starving, Melody thought, and turning into a feral animal. But you've dealt with frightened children before, she reminded herself. You *can't* let her get away again.

Carefully, she took some peanut butter cracker-packs out of her bag, added some grapes and placed them on a napkin at the edge of the rug near a pile of brightly colored bracelets. Then, holding her breath, she motioned for her visitor to come and help herself.

Slowly the child crept forward, snatched the food and began to gobble it down.

"My name is Melody,' she said, very softly. "Can you tell me yours?"

Slight hesitation, then—eyes filling with tears but chin held high—"Serena."

# 27

It was surprising how quickly Mike and I had adjusted to having a third person in our house. Arriving home after our evening with Joe and Elena Cruz, we whispered as we entered the hallway from the garage, in case Carla had fallen asleep. Sure enough, she was lying down on one of the couches in the den, breathing evenly, the television playing to its absent audience.

"I'll just cover her," I said, softly to Mike, then "You coming up?"

"As soon as I have a little juice, you want anything?"

I shook my head and went upstairs to get ready for bed.

When Mike joined me he was laughing. "She's been at it again. Wait until you see how she's organized the refrigerator. No more searching for the dill pickles or wondering what leftover is in that little opaque plastic container."

"I thought you *liked* my little mystery containers," I said, pretending to have had my feelings hurt.

"Erin, I hope you're not taking this as a criticism of your housekeeping skills?"

"Heck, no, I'm glad for all the help. I just wish she didn't feel almost driven to pull her own weight so we won't turn her out." We exchanged kisses and murmurs of love then turned out the light—I quickly fell into a deep sleep.

It was still dark when I woke with a start, not sure if the sound I heard was part of a dream or not. Mike was sleeping soundly beside me. There it was again and I remembered that Carla was downstairs. I crept down the stairs quietly, and as I approached, I heard her mumbling unintelligibly except for when she clearly cried out, "Serena!" She had thrown the afghan off and one foot dangled over the side of her makeshift bed.

I hated to leave her alone, so I arranged some large throw pillows on the floor and lay down nearby. Mike found us both asleep, a few hours later, when he tiptoed through the room on his way to work.

"Darn! I wanted to be awake when you came in last night," Carla exclaimed, as she stretched herself awake and saw me just getting to my feet. "What were you doing down there? You must have been uncomfortable. Was I calling out in my sleep again? I am *such* a bother," she finished, dramatically.

"It was *not* a bother," I assured her. "It did sound as if you were having a nightmare, so I plopped down nearby in case you could use some TLC."

We were both standing now. "Oh, and Mike noticed what you did in the fridge. Thanks. Now let's have breakfast. How about scrambled eggs?" We headed for the kitchen.

"And the eggs are?" I asked her, as I peered at the rear-ranged interior.

"In that big bowl," she answered, pointing them out. "I need-ed the carton for a project. I hope you don't mind. It's supposed to be a surprise for you, but I didn't get it finished yet."

Another Martha Stewart marvel, perhaps? Someone had given me a subscription to her magazine—as a joke, no doubt—but Carla had become totally smitten with Martha and was read-ing the back issues cover-to-cover. There was no doubt in my mind that one day she could have a charming home of her own, furnished on a shoestring. *Could* have—but *would* have? I was less sure about the latter.

Later, I caught up on some e-mails, while Carla read from Austen's *Pride and Prejudice*. I was no psychologist but I recog-nized that Carla's bad dreams, as she called them, stemmed largely from the very real bad dream she had been living.

She had revealed a little about her former life when we were together at the motel, but had pretty much clammed up since—as if she was reluctant to diminish our opinion of her in any way. Or perhaps so as not to interject anything negative in what she saw as our perfect life together.

Not realistic or healthy for her in any case, but now there was an even more pressing reason for her to face the past—the chance to help put some local gangs out of business by meeting with the police and ultimately testifying before a grand jury.

I still needed to address this issue, but perhaps easing into it would be better. "Carla, I would like your help with my current newspaper assignment," I said.

She set her book aside immediately. "Super. When do we start?"

"Most any time, but don't you even want to know what it's about?"

"Well, sure. I guess." But it was obvious that she trusted my judgment implicitly. Would her trust turn out to be misplaced?

I showed her the article I had written about her and Serena, and told her truthfully that it had been a huge success as a wake-up call for a great many readers. Now, Malcolm, my editor, was urging me to do a follow-up.

"So that he can sell more newspapers?" she asked, with maybe a touch of bitterness creeping into her voice.

Ouch! I thought of my earlier talk with Malcolm about the bottom line. "I won't lie to you, Carla. That too, but mainly this is because we hope that by inspiring more people to get involved we can help keep the pressure on the gangs so eventually they will be forced out of the pimping business. You said one day you wanted to work with other young victims. In a way this could be your chance to get an early start."

Her silence was making me uncomfortable. "Of course, I will totally understand if you turn this down," I added.

"What do you want to know?" she asked, and I was relieved to see a defiant look. "After all, as you pointed out from the beginning, it wasn't me who did anything wrong."

To make it easier I suggested that she jot down some of her own thoughts. Then we could talk them over and edit and personalize the highlights, hopefully resulting in an informative, provocative article.

For the next two hours or so Carla wrote and scratched out and wrote some more. I kept a glass of   fruit juice filled within easy reach.

She spoke aloud as she wrote of the pimps and the johns. Of dressing provocatively to attract the men she and the other girls despised. Their forced occupation often putting them in danger—working at night, standing idly on street corners, getting into the cars of strangers, walking through dark alleys—only to give the money they earned to the pimps who, at best, treated them as prisoners within a harem. But more often as an expendable commodity, kept in line through beatings and coercion, and threatened by their captors of violence against members of their families, as well.

Friendship among the girls was discouraged, rivalries encouraged. And it was constantly emphasized that they were damaged goods—sinners, even—looked down on by good, decent, people everywhere.

We read her words together when she was finished, she, sometimes speaking so softly I could hardly hear her—then abruptly exclaiming in anger and frustration. And there were tears shed from both of us. I was unable to be a dispassionate professional!

Trite or not, the phrase 'emotionally drained' seemed to most appropriately describe our condition when Carla finally ran out of words. Above all else, I hoped it had been cathartic for her. I couldn't help it. Prosecuting the gangs was terribly important. Enlightening a complacent public was certainly worthwhile, but potentially at the cost of a girl's fragile psyche. Was the latter also worthwhile? I was not nearly as sure. That ancient dilemma "Does the end justify the means?" remained unanswered.

# 28

Stay calm and try to move slowly, Melody reminded herself. "Serena, I would like it very much if you would sit down on the blanket with me for a few minutes. It's hard to talk with you over there and me over here."

The child seemed to be weighing her options carefully. Perhaps it was simply that exhaustion finally won out over the obvious fear and mistrust that could be seen in her eyes, but in any case, while Melody held her breath, Serena came and sat on the part of the rug that had been cleared for her.

"Serena, that's a pretty name. Do you have a last name?"

No answer. "Just asking, because mine is Miller, now that I'm married, and I'm thirty-years-old, and I used to be a teacher, and now I live in a camper, and I make jewelry, and sell it in many places like this."

Serena appeared to be listening intently—head cocked, lips pursed. At the mention of the jewelry, she seemed to relax a bit, so Melody tried again to find out more about her waif-like visitor.

"I was just wondering where you slept last night and if there is someone who might be worrying about you right now." No response. "Or perhaps you are running away from someone you are afraid of?" she gently asked.

No answer again, but Melody knew she was on the right track when the child shuddered and looked around as if to check that no such person was in sight.

Don't overdo the questions too soon, Melody admonished herself. "Tell you what. I was just going to walk to my favorite restaurant for a big breakfast. I'd be pleased if you could join me. Maybe later you could tell me a little about yourself." Melody stayed perfectly still, though she wanted in the worst way to reach out to the child. Instead, she just opened a hand in the child's direction.

Then, a small, grubby hand reached towards hers, and a slight nod of the head signaled Serena's acceptance.

"What will Jimmy say?" thought Melody, though it was obvious there would be no worried family member appearing suddenly to claim the child. Something was very wrong with Serena's situation, but what? In any case, Melody felt she couldn't just abandon the girl. She was at least temporarily involved, and had a responsibility to find out more, like it or not.

Melody gave it one last effort, "Serena, is there someone I should call so they will know you are going with me?"

The wariness in the child's eyes returned. She looked ready to bolt.

"It's okay. I won't call anyone now. I promise." Melody said hastily, and began to pack up her jewelry. She noticed that Jimmy was coming down the hill toward them. She took a deep breath and said matter-of-factly, "My husband will be hungry, too, and here he comes now."

"Jimmy, meet my new friend, Serena. I've asked her to join us for breakfast at the Buena Vista."

"Nice to meet you," Jimmy said, keeping his questions to himself and wisely choosing not to offer Serena his hand, or touch her in any way. She had visibly flinched and recoiled when he came forward and joined the two of them.

Melody led the way to the parked camper to stow the rugs and her inventory—chattering all the time about the great meal they were about to have. "I told Serena we would walk up to the restaurant and then afterward, perhaps, get some chocolate in

Ghirardelli Square," she explained, deliberately walking in the middle of the three of them as they headed toward Hyde Street—Serena's hand holding surprisingly tightly to hers.

As a famous landmark, the old Buena Vista was one of San Francisco's top tourist attractions with its swinging entry door, plank floors, mahogany bar and heavy use of brass throughout. It was often packed with people who had hopped off the cable cars at the turnabout across the street.

Today was no exception, but the Millers weren't tourists, and soon, one of the older waitresses made room for the three-some in a back corner. Melody was glad that they were in a relatively private area. Serena huddled against her. The noise and the rather hectic atmosphere could be daunting to a child. Also, Melody thought, their out-of-the-way location should cut down on any negative assessments of Serena's condition. With her rumpled clothes and dirty, tangled hair she was so disheveled she could pass for one of the orphans in a production of *Annie!*

But there was probably little cause for concern because, as usual—at least for the first-time diners—most eyes would be on the white-coated bartenders. In addition to serving a variety of other drinks, they ritualistically turned out as many as thirty of their famous, authentic Irish coffees in as many seconds— elegant little glasses set in a row with two sugar cubes in each, coffee added from endless pots, then some Jameson whiskey, and finally a layer of aged-cream poured on just the top of the coffee (and never stirred) from silver shakers. It was quite a show, and the drinks were delicious, if pricey. Few customers left without having at least one.

"Anything special you want, honey?" Melody asked, shortly after they were seated, but Serena just shook her head.

"Then why don't we let Jimmy choose. Lots of everything including a fruit cup for our young friend and the usual, plus

Irish coffee for me" she suggested to her husband. "Serena and I are going to the ladies room."

Down the stairs, through a long corridor and into the bathroom they went. "I'll let you wash your own hands but would it be alright if I helped with your face and hair? I know you're hiding in there somewhere." At Melody's words, Serena managed a shy grin.

After a few minutes of gentle washing, Melody remarked playfully, "Ah, there really was a little girl under there. Does she have a last name and a birthdate, by any chance?"

Once more, Serena seemed to be weighing her options—sizing up Melody.

Then she answered quietly, "Flores, and I'm not a little girl. I'm eleven!"

A few minutes later they emerged and rejoined Jimmy at the table. Melody had been able to do little with Serena's hair, but her face shone, and her hands and nails were clean.

The coffees, and most of the food had arrived, and Serena didn't need much encouragement to dive in. She ate fast and indiscriminately, as if she hadn't eaten well in quite some time, and had no idea when she would get to do so again.

Melody and Jimmy ate their breakfast combinations and sipped their Irish coffees in a leisurely fashion, making small talk and trying not to stare at their young guest as she literally shoveled food into her mouth. Halfway through her second plate, Serena began to nod off. Jimmy moved the dishes aside and she was asleep—head on the table.

"Poor child," he said softly, "let's carry her back to the camper and see if she will take a nap. We can talk about our options while she's sleeping."

# 29

Carla went up to her room to take a nap after our grueling, emotional session. I settled down at my PC to work up a feature article, based on her experiences in the 'life,' as the girls call it: out on the streets, working for the pimps, an innocent victim of sexual exploitation, wrenched out of her home and away from her younger sister and grandmother. I hoped to be able to bring the reader into her world, as it had been since that initial kidnapping, in a way that would make them angry and uncomfortable.

Some two hours later I was satisfied that I had accomplished my objectives and faxed the article to my boss. It might be awhile before I heard back from him, and Michael wasn't due home for a few hours, so to fill in the time, I checked the refrigerator and freezer to be sure we had the basics for our dinner.

Bless Carla, I thought. She had volunteered to be in charge of most of the dinners we ate at home. All, so far, had been delicious, and many were cooked ahead, needing only to be reheated. Tonight, we had a choice between green chilies and beef enchiladas, or pollo en salsa. Side dishes of rice and a salad—probably her favorite, a simple avocado and tomato—would complete an outstanding meal.

I was restless while I waited for my editor's reply so I began to read a mystery I had earlier put aside. A few minutes later, my cell rang.

Malcolm was on the line. "I'm impressed," he said, then paused. "That was powerfully written. You should be proud, but..."

"But—the dreaded but," I said, confused and somewhat dismayed, as to his reaction.

He continued. "I meant what I said, but I *am* concerned that it might be a little raw—too unsettling for some of our readers. What if you toned it down a little? Sanitized it a bit?"

He had missed the point. Or was this mostly about the finicky advertisers again? "Yes, it *is* raw," I responded, "but that is how those poor girls live! I *want* the readers to be uncomfortable—to get angry. I want them to feel that doing nothing is not an option. Please, Malcolm. Back me on this. You said it was good. Why not run with it?"

I thought I heard a sigh. "You make a good argument, but it's not that simple for me," he said.

Here we go again, I thought. "You said that the first feature was a big hit with readers and the bill-payers alike," I reminded him. "Now, we owe them the follow-up. Come on, Malcolm!"

"We owe it to them, huh?" Malcolm gave another sigh, followed by a long pause, while I impatiently waited for an answer at my end of the phone.

"Okay," he finally said, "I'm not really sure the publisher will be happy about this but you sure can be very convincing at times."

I smiled to myself, as I imagined the gesture of surrender that went with those words.

He continued. "I'll proof it and fax it back for your approval. When we're both satisfied, next week it will probably be my lead, with your byline. Congratulations."

"Yes!" I exclaimed aloud. We both laughed and clicked off.


I was elated, but that feeling was dashed as soon as I answered another call. "Erin, Joe Cruz here. I hate to pressure you, but the DA is after me to speak with Carla immediately so I can judge how credible she might be as a witness. As I mentioned before, we've learned that not only are some of the girls Carla knew, about to be moved, but there is some shake-up going on within the gangs themselves. We might lose jurisdiction over Emilio and some of the other local sex-trafficking offenders if we don't act now. As you may know, a federal statute with stiffer penalties for human trafficking was passed recently, but we still have to win a guilty verdict."

"I understand," I told him, recounting the agonizing session Carla and I had just been through, but confessed that I still had not urged her to take the next step, to arrange a meeting with him. "What if she flat out refuses?" I asked.

'Tell her that if she agrees to talk with me and then the DA, we will most likely have enough evidence to convince the grand jury to indict and ultimately prosecute the gang members she identifies. If it gets to that stage we may well be able to offer them some deal if they tell us where her sister, Serena, is being kept."

He let that last statement hang. I tried to keep my voice steady. "Is that true?"

"No guarantees, Erin, but it's certainly a possibility. None of them would welcome a prison stint just now—it puts a crimp in their lifestyle. What's one more girl to them? They have a grapevine. Someone must know where Serena is."

The deputy had been speaking in a conversational manner, but now his voice took on a brusque tone. "Oh, and Erin, it's important that Carla note as many specific times, places, and names as possible that relate to her experiences. Without those facts her statement will be meaningless."

I assured him that, while we had not included the latter information in the article, we had already compiled quite a list, and that she continued to add to it as memories came flooding back.

"Good. Well, that's about it, Erin, but it's urgent that we act. Think about what is at stake and get back to me."

*    *    *

The long nap had been just what Carla needed. She awoke re-freshed and famished—showing the resiliency of a typical teen. Oh, if only she could be! I dreaded the talk we must have before the day was over.

Mike came home shortly and the three of us settled into one of our routine pre-dinner rituals—interactive TV news watch-ing. Carla had been so out of it, as she categorized the past months, that she had accumulated a monumental thirst for world and local events—and opinions to match. Her latest ambi-tion was to become an investigative journalist exposing crimes against humanity. I had no doubt that she could become what-ever she desired.

Later, with Carla putting the finishing touches on dinner, I managed to get Mike alone. "Joe Cruz called," was all I needed to say. Carla must be confronted as to the role she might play in prosecuting the local gangs for human trafficking. "I'll bring it up," Mike promised.

"Those enchiladas were delicious, Carla," Mike remarked later, adding, "I am *so* spoiled," as I brought him an after-dinner coffee into the living room and Carla consulted him as to a DVD we might all agree to watch. He cleared his throat. "And I really hate to spoil everyone's good mood, but Erin and I need to talk to you about something important. I'll let her fill you in." He gave me an encouraging look.

Carla, who had been sitting on a couch with her feet tucked comfortably under her, began to nervously twirl a lock of her hair.

When I had finished discussing the conversation I had with Deputy Cruz, Carla looked sad, but resolute. "I would like to see them all rot in prison," she said, "but if the only way they will lead us to Serena is to have them tell us where she is so they can bargain for lesser sentences, I'll be sorry, but I'll live with it. You know that I want to find my sister above all else!  Is that wrong?"

Mike and I both reassured her that her feelings were totally understandable "I think it's safe to say that we hope and believe that your testimony may help rescue many other girls," said Mike, "but the bottom line is that this may well be the only realistic way to find Serena."

"Then set up the meeting," she instructed, "but I have a few conditions of my own."

There was a new strength in her voice and she sat up straighter.  "First, I insist that you are in the room with me through everything, Erin.  And the police have to put in writing that they won't turn me in to child and protective services. They might want to send me to a group home or some type of victim's rehab place while I am testifying, or afterward. I refuse to go," she said. "You wouldn't let that happen anyway, would you?"

Could an officer of the law make such promises? We hadn't really discussed Carla's legal status with Joe Cruz. Her grandmother was her next of kin and guardian, but she was very ill, and her future ability to care for either, or both, of her granddaughters was very much in doubt.

Mike and I had some serious issues to face. We had gotten too close to Carla to let her become a ward of the court—no matter how well meaning the agencies were. Perhaps a trip soon to Campo to visit Mrs. Flores was in order. Carla had chosen us, and we had gone into this temporary custodial arrangement with open eyes. Now we needed some legal advice.

But all that would take time. Joe knew we had Carla. Would he continue to look the other way until we could work something out?

"No, we would never let that happen, honey," I said—hoping that Mike would back me up on my risky promise. "Not a chance!"

# 30

"How long do you think she'll sleep?" Jimmy asked, in a low voice as he and Melody stood outside the camper. Serena had barely stirred when he had placed her gently on the backseat after carrying her from the restaurant.

"Who knows?" Melody shrugged, answering in a whisper. "But it may be quite a while. Poor little tyke is obviously exhausted. Why don't you go and help finish building the new display cases. I'll stay here, and when she wakes, take her to pick out some new clean clothes. Afterwards, she can help me sell some jewelry on the Green."

"Sounds good, but before I go, are you sure we're doing the right thing by not taking her to some authority?" They had been avoiding the issue of Serena's near future, but the agonized look Melody gave him was argument enough against making a hasty decision.

He tried another tack. "Okay, look, before we decide anything, why don't you see what more you can find out from her."

"I need to take it slow, but I'm fairly confident she *will* open up for me," Melody agreed. "But I've been giving it a lot of thought. I'm probably crazy, but I remember several cases in years past where some crazy person abducted young people and kept them prisoners on his property and even got one pregnant and . . . anyway, maybe Serena was part of something like that and she somehow escaped, or maybe just some sick family member has raised her like an animal in captivity, or . . ."

"Or . . . what about the gangs?"

"The gangs? What would they have to do with it? Don't gang

members usually have turf wars over illegal drugs? Lots of guns involved—drive-by shootings? Why would you mention gangs?"

"The gangs who run prostitutes," Jimmy explained.

"You don't mean—but Serena's practically a baby, she couldn't . . . they wouldn't . . ." her voice trailed off.

"I told you a little about the child exploitation that I saw when I was doing duty on a couple of my deployments. Unfortunately, sexual exploitation of minors and other forms of human trafficking, occur all too often in this country as well. And this *is* San Francisco—international ports, service men, foreign visitors, all   looking for a good time. Some of those perverts who seek girls prefer them to be very young."

"Jimmy, please stop! I couldn't bear it if that were her story." Melody was on the verge of tears.

Jimmy held her close. "I'm not saying it is, but we agree that something very ugly might have happened to her. It's only natural that you want to protect her against any more hurt, but we may be in over our heads. She may well need professional help. And then, what about the people who did this to her? They need to be punished. Right?"

"Of course you're right and I know you just don't want me to get hurt. But for now we don't have enough to go on. For the time being we have to be her buffer. Please, Jimmy, even if it makes the most sense, promise me you won't turn her in to anyone just yet."

"I would never do that unless we make that decision together. We're in everything together. Now, I better get going." He tilted her chin up gently. "Are you going to be alright?"

Melody nodded. "I'm going to concentrate only on the positive for now. My little friend and I are going shopping, and then we'll wipe out the biggest sundaes they can make at Ghirardelli Square. No matter what happens down the road I'm going to see that she has a day to remember!"

Jimmy grinned and pressed some cash into Melody's hand.

"Buy her something for me," he said, before heading off toward Haight Street.


Melody stayed outside reading a magazine for a few more minutes, then quietly slid the side door of the camper open and slipped inside. Serena still slept, but she had begun to stir, making little mewling sounds as her eyes fluttered open. She was bound to be disoriented, probably even frightened, by her unfamiliar surroundings, and Melody hoped that by staying nearby she could provide some reassurance.

"Hi, sleepy head! Hope your rest was a good one, because I have some plans for us, if you're up for them," she said encouragingly, when the child appeared to be fully awake.

Serena sat up and looked around the interior of the camper, then back to Melody. "This is like a little, cozy house—and you are the lady who makes the beautiful jewelry. And the one who saved me and bought me lots of food." She patted the seat beside her and looked intently into Melody's eyes. "Did I thank you properly? My grandmother would want to be sure I minded my manners."

Amazing that the child, who was almost mute a few hours ago, was now concerned with manners! "You certainly showed us your appreciation," Melody replied. "But you mentioned your grandmother. Won't she be worried about you?"

Serena looked concerned and fearful at the same time. "I tried to call, but *he* answered." Then, as if she'd already said too much to a stranger, she stated firmly, "I don't want to talk about it!" and pulled slightly away from Melody. The guarded look on her face returned.

"I'm sorry I upset you, honey. We'll only talk about what you want to, but I did have some fun plans for this afternoon if you'd care to hear them."

Curiosity won out and when Serena heard that the plans included a clothes shopping spree and ice cream, she brightened up. "But I must look awful," she remarked, looking down at her raggedy clothes.

"I have an idea," Melody said, reaching into the back of the camper's small built-in closet and coming out with   a pale yellow oversized T-shirt. "I'll go outside while you get out of your clothes and try this on. Oh, and you probably need to use the port-a-potty by now," she added, pointing to the latter.

On Serena, with the addition of one of Melody's handmade woven tie-belts, the Tee became a creditable and comfortable dress. She was smiling again. "Yellow is my favorite color," she remarked, looking at herself in the mirror on the back of the closet door.

"Mine, too," Melody echoed.

"No way! Why?"

"Why is yellow my favorite?" Melody mused, as she brushed Serena's hair and gathered it into a ponytail. "Well, for one thing it's a sunny color. Did you ever get happy-face stickers on your school papers?"

"In the second and third grade I got a lot of them," but then her voice trailed off. The veil had dropped down over her eyes again.

Better to get back on safe ground, Melody decided, but Serena's words had revealed that at least some things in her life had, in the past, been normal. "Actually for me I think the main reason I love yellow is because that's the color of baby chicks. One Easter when I was a little girl my dad bought me six of them. They were my pets. Later, when they grew into hens, we added a rooster and soon we had enough eggs to sell to a few neighbors, and I got to keep the money."

"I had a yellow pet, once," Serena said, sadness in her voice—"an Easter Bunny. Well, it wasn't alive, but sometimes I pretended it was. It was in my backpack when it got stolen," she explained, and then she began to cry.

As Melody took her in her arms she vowed, you may break my heart one day, little girl, but meanwhile I'll do everything in my power to protect yours.

Fortunately Serena's sadness was significantly assuaged, for the moment at least, by the shopping expedition. Melody knew the area well so it didn't take long for them to find appropriate girl's clothing and shoes for her that pleased them both.

Melody had suggested that perhaps Jimmy could join them to help with the selections but, somewhat to Melody's surprise, Serena had been totally against that and she further made it plain that her negativism was entirely due to his gender. She had also stated firmly that she was glad that she was finally able to pick out clothes that reflected her own taste and suited her age.

Who had been choosing the clothes she wore in the preceding months, Melody wondered. The more she thought about it, the more she came to believe that Jimmy's theory about a gang abduction and sexploitation might be on target. There were still many unanswered questions, but she felt she was getting closer to finding out how the child got into these circumstances.

There were two more items on their list. The backpack was easily come by. It came down to a flower splashed print, or a royal-blue number with leather trim. Serena chose the floral one, in good part, because it had the most zippered compartments.

The stuffed animal proved to be more of a challenge. There were bunnies, but no yellow ones. The twenty-something clerk asked Serena if she was buying for a young sibling. When she answered, in an embarrassed way, that she was shopping for herself, she was assured that this was entirely normal. "I took three of my animals to college with me," the clerk said. "Still have them. Someday, I may pass them on to my daughter."

Serena beamed. Melody suggested that she choose another kind of animal. "Remember, this morning when you told me about the children you saw at the playground, before the thunderstorm hit, and your backpack with the bunny in it was probably picked up by some family by mistake?" Serena nodded. "Well, I bet some other little girl is taking care of your bunny now. Why don't *you* start over with something different?"

"Okay, but it's got to be soft and small enough to fit in my backpack," Serena said firmly.

There were many animals that fit those requirements, but she finally chose an incredibly lifelike, dark brown puppy, which after she considered other possibilities, named Brownie. "Easy for everyone to remember," she reasoned.

"Are you ready for some ice cream?" Melody asked, as they exited the toy store. Serena returned an enthusiastic nod and continued to thank her for the gifts. Serena's grandmother would be proud, thought Melody.

Jimmy met them in Ghirardelli Square. They ordered three sundaes—two with hot fudge syrup, one with butterscotch, and all with whipped cream—then took them outside to sit on a nearby bench. Serena seemed to grow more comfortable with Jimmy as they ate, though she glanced back and forth from him to Melody several times.

"I give up!" Melody said, as she laid down her spoon. "Where are you putting all that?" she asked, looking at the child's slight frame. Serena just smiled to herself and kept on eating.

"Can I have the rest of yours?" Jimmy asked Melody innocently. He knew she was always trying to lose a little weight. The ice cream binge was strictly for the child.

"Sure, but don't blame me if you have to roll down to the VW," Melody said, sighing dramatically. Serena smiled once again and cast Jimmy a conspiratorial look.

"Thank you, kind lady, "Jimmy said, leaning over to give Melody a gentle kiss as he added her melting ice cream to his own.

The trio headed back to their home-on-wheels, containers licked clean and tossed into a nearby trash receptacle.

Later, as promised, Serena helped Melody set up her unique jewelry on the Marina Green. Jimmy had headed back to continue helping with the display cases.

Serena had brought her stuffed animal along. "Would you be able to make her a collar?" she asked Melody.

"Well I could, but what if I show you how, and then you could make one yourself?" Melody suggested.

Serena was thrilled, and before long the puppy's neck was circled by various colored beads strung on leather. The dog collar was quite a hit. Some of the customers even asked if they could buy something like that for their own stuffed animals. Melody could see Serena having a little business of her own someday.

When they were alone, Melody said, "Be sure you show Jimmy your handiwork when he comes back for us. You did a super job."

"You're a good teacher," Serena countered. "Did you ever teach Jimmy to help you make things to sell?"

"Jimmy is not at all interested in trying to make what I can. He says his hands are too big. But those hands are also very strong and he can do a lot of other things I can't, so it works out well."

Serena gave that some thought and then said, "He seems like a nice man and he *must* be strong. He carried me when I fell asleep, didn't he?"

"All the way," Melody answered. "He was glad to—you were *so* tired."

Her next question stunned Melody. "He would never hurt you, would he?" Serena asked.

Or me, seemed to be implied, Melody thought. "No, Serena. There are men out in the world that would, but most men are good and loving. Have you met some of the bad men who hurt instead of love?"

Serena once more got that wounded, far-away look in her eyes. "They said they loved me, but then they hurt me, and made me do bad things. I didn't want to be with them, Melody. I just wanted to be back with Carla and my grandmother."

Hanging in the air was, 'you believe me, don't you'? And how about Jimmy—men were not to be trusted.

Melody took a deep breath. "Serena, my guess is that many men, and maybe even some women, have lied to you and hurt you a lot. I wouldn't blame you if you didn't even dare trust me, but I hope you can. If you tell me more about the grandmother you mentioned and now someone named Carla, I think Jimmy and I might try to help you find them. Will you tell us more?"

"I want to, but how do I know you won't turn me in to the police, or a priest, or somebody else like that?"

"Oh, honey, I would never in a million years do that to you. I know people have pretended to be your friends, but weren't, so I don't blame you for worrying." Unsaid, but in the back of Melody's mind was the nagging thought that she and Jimmy could be the ones in trouble if, for any reason, they were questioned about their situation by having Serena with them.

It was becoming apparent to Melody that Serena was an eleven-year-old, possibly street-smart kid—not the helpless waif of about eight that she had appeared to be at first. But she was still a child in desperate need of an adult intervention.

Serena seemed to be mulling Melody's comments over in her mind, but the arrival of several customers postponed any further conversation.

* * *

It had been a very long day for their young visitor. Jimmy picked them up in the camper and now they were parked for the night in their complimentary spot behind the Ambiance dress shop. He had brought back deli sandwiches from his carpentry job, so no cooking was required. They had raised the top of the camper and made up the upper bunk for Serena. She had chosen that arrangement—said it reminded her of a similar place she had once considered a haven.

"Some of the guys are going to the Club Deluxe for a couple of beers," Jimmy said, after supper. "Why don't you and Serena watch a movie? I won't be late." He gave Melody a hug and looked to the child, who stood close by observing everything with her dark, needy eyes. He wanted to hug her too, but knew it might not be received the way it was meant, so instead said, "Pick a good one. You can tell me all about it in the morning."

Halfway through the DVD they had been watching on Melody's computer, Serena fell asleep. Melody gazed fondly at the sleeping child for several minutes. For now she would let her sleep where she was. Jimmy could help move her when he returned.

# 31

Carla's appointment with Joe Cruz was not until ten in the morning. I wished it were earlier. There was too much time for her to get nervous—maybe even change her mind. I hadn't slept well. I could just imagine how the night had gone for her. She was about to relate all the sordid details of her life as a human trafficking victim to yet another stranger—for the most part in the hope that her sister could be located.

I was sitting at the kitchen island counter nursing a cup of coffee, trying to concentrate on the contents of an article in the Wall Street Journal that Mike had left for me to read, when Carla walked in. I noticed dark circles under her eyes. She wore her shorty blue bathrobe, and her hair was still wet from showering. I poured her some orange juice. "Can I make you a fried egg sandwich?" I asked. "We still have some of that Canadian bacon left."

"If you want to," she answered, with little enthusiasm, and began to drink her juice.

While I made our breakfasts I tried to make conversation—bringing up incidents from the bookstore and *The County Voice*, hoping to engage her in a mundane conversation, but she was having none of it.

"Erin, I know you're just trying to get me to think of something besides the meeting, but that's *all* I can think about!"

"You're right," I said. "I'm sorry. I seem to be saying that a lot to you lately. Sorry to cause you pain when what I'd really like to do is see that you never feel pain again! But I also know that ev-

er since you and Serena were brutally separated your main focus has been on getting her back. We agreed that this is your
best chance."

I had to believe that Joe Cruz and the justice system would
make every effort to see that happen. Nothing that Mike and I
hoped to eventually be able to do for her could make up for the
loss of her sister.

"It's not your fault, Erin. It's just . . . the breakfast sandwich
was yummy. Thank you. I'll go up and get ready now."

Later Carla came back downstairs, hair in a low ponytail,
wearing a teal-colored pant suit. She looked like a composed
young professional—any nervousness, for the moment, well
hidden. But I knew the vulnerable young teen underneath, what
it was costing her to go through with this, all in keeping up the
hope of a reunion with her sister and grandmother.

We were ushered into the Deputy's office promptly at ten
o'clock. "Good morning, Erin," Joe said, as he shook my hand.
Then turning to Carla he did the same. "I'm Deputy Joe Cruz.
Thank you for coming in. Erin and Mike have spoken very highly
of you. I know it couldn't have been an easy decision, but we on
the trafficking task force believe that it's with such firsthand accounts as yours that we can make a significant impact on the
illicit sex trade."

A trim, fiftyish woman, with short, salt-and-pepper hair
stepped forward, and was introduced as Lucia Lopez. "Mrs.
Lopez is a victim's advocate," Joe explained. "She hates the
pimps as much as we do. And, since you don't have a lawyer
present, I thought it might be a good idea to have her here."

The woman gave us a firm handshake and a warm smile. I
was glad she was present.

Introductions completed, Joe asked, "How about something
to drink; coffee, tea, a soft drink? No? Okay, why don't we begin?
I'm going to sit behind the desk and, Carla, you take either of
those chairs opposite me so you can speak into the recorder.

And remember, we can take a break any time you feel you need one.

"I suggest it might be helpful if you just start at the beginning, where I understand you lived in Campo and, while your grandmother was in the hospital, your uncle Mateo sold you and your little sister to Nestor, his drug supplier. Then keep on telling us everything you remember from that time until you recently escaped—names, dates, locations, everything, the more specific the better.

"I will be interrupting frequently with questions, just take all the time you need to respond. Answer the questions to the best of your ability and if you do not know, just say so. When the statement is complete we have a transcriber who is standing by and will produce a typed document which I'll ask you to read carefully, and if you agree with its contents we will ask you to sign and date it. Now do you have any questions? Oh, and Carla, I just want to assure you that we will do everything in our power to get your sister back."

It was obvious that Joe was trying to put Carla at ease, but the whole atmosphere was intimidating, and, as I watched, she began twirling a strand of hair that she had worked loose from her ponytail. Our session of the previous afternoon had been so emotional. How would this one go?

Carla had raised no questions, so Joe switched the recorder on and officially began the interview. After giving the date and time he stated, "I am Joe Cruz, a deputy in the sheriff's substation, Vista, California and head of the North County Human Trafficking Task Force. With me are Lucia Lopez, a victim's advocate, Carla Flores, a minor, who is here voluntarily to give testimony as a victim of human trafficking, and Erin Bradley, Carla's temporary guardian."

Carla smiled at me when Joe said the latter. I felt a warm glow and blessed Joe for his understanding of the special place this young woman held in my heart.

* * *

For the next several hours, except for a short break, Joe prodded and cajoled and Carla ran through a variety of emotions ranging from anger to sorrow to defiance. The initial horrific story from the Campo days, when the young sisters were sold to Nestor, brought us all to tears, and it didn't get much easier from there.

Carla, though understandably a little shaky where specific dates were concerned, gave credible and riveting testimony as she recounted the cruel control exerted by Emilio, her current pimp, over her and the other girls; the beatings when quotas were not met, the hours spent in dangerous sections of Vista, Oceanside and other suburbs of San Diego County. She also described the truck stops and seedy motel encounters complete with the names of a few of the regulars who had their preferred girls, and always for her, the threat that they would see to it if she didn't behave that she would never see Serena or her grandmother alive again!

And finally it was over. "You are a brave young woman, Carla," Joe Cruz said. 'Thank you again for coming in. I'll let you know what happens next as soon as I get some feedback."

Mrs. Lopez complimented Carla as well, and then suggested that I drop by her office in the near future.

"Erin—I hope that it's okay if I call you by your first name—it seems that you're an excellent advocate and role model for young girls. And I've also read and enjoyed your articles in *The County Voice*. There are some exciting things going on right now in the fight against human trafficking and I'd love to talk to you about any contributions you might want to provide. Please give me a call when you can."

* * *

It was well after one when we finished the session but, though we were very hungry we discarded the idea of a restaurant lunch. There was, of course, the fact that the sheriff's department was in Vista, home of some of Carla's worst experiences. But in the main we were tired and the thought of relaxing in our lovely home trumped all.

There had been a text from Mike sending his love and saying he hoped the meeting had gone well and how very proud he was of his girls. "He's a nice man," we said almost in unison—a phrase that had become like a secret handshake between us where Mike was concerned. We exchanged smiles and I pulled out of the parking lot.

Carla fell asleep almost as soon I got on the I-5 going south. Poor kid, I was thinking, when I saw it in my rear view mirror. A big black car was right on my bumper. My paranoia had returned. It was broad daylight and the traffic was flowing freely. I put my right directional light on and moved over one lane, only to have the other driver do the same.

On two previous occasions I had thought I was being followed, but I was not aware of any similar incidents since. Could gang members have followed us from the sheriff's station? Too brazen even for them, I decided.

In any case, I was glad Carla was asleep. She didn't need any more fodder for her nightmares. The stalking car, as I had come to view it, kept within two car lengths as we passed the exits to Carlsbad, Encinitas, and Del Mar—sometimes falling further behind, then speeding up to pull in closer or even once closely beside me, accompanied by angry horn-blowing from other drivers.

When we turned off the freeway at La Jolla Village Drive, they were still within sight. Once on Torrey Pines Drive I had an idea, and when the busy La Jolla Country Market came into view, I turned abruptly into the parking lot, startling more than one shopper going to their car.

The sharp turn aroused Carla, but at least for now the black car was gone. As it hurtled by—much too fast for the road conditions—I heard loud music, heavy on the bass. Hopefully, just some young men having their idea of fun, I told myself.

"How long did I sleep?" Carla asked, as she awoke and looked around, recognizing her surroundings. "Oh, good," she exclaimed, as we headed into the takeout area of the bustling market. "Deli sandwiches to go. And how about including some homemade soup? I'm famished!" Mission accomplished, we headed home.

My phone began to ring just as we got in the door. "Erin, this is Malcolm. Glad I reached you. Is there any chance you can cover a special planning board meeting this afternoon? Muriel called in about a half hour ago on her way to the hospital to have X-rays taken. She thinks she may have broken her ankle. Probably fell off those spikes she wears," he added, in that way he had of trying to cover up true concern.

When I hesitated, he went on. "Anyhow, there's no one else available. Otherwise, I'd go myself, but about that time I have a meeting with some potential advertisers."

I hated to leave Carla, but Malcolm had always allowed me to have great flexibility in my position and I knew the board was going to address a controversial housing development plan. The meeting needed to be covered. "I'll do it," I said.

"Was that Mike?" Carla asked, as I walked into the kitchen where she was reheating our soup.

I explained the situation. At least I had a chance to enjoy a delicious lunch with her before leaving.

"Don't worry about me. I'll be fine," she assured me.

Of course she would. I'd be back well before dark and Mike might even decide to leave work early.


The board meeting was well attended by citizens eager to ask questions or express opinions supporting or condemning the proposed project, so there were many disgruntled attendees when, shortly after the board took care of some routine matters, it was announced that the meeting had to be postponed—something about corporate bigwigs from out of state having to cancel at the last minute.

On the other hand, I was relieved. I could only hope that Muriel's ankle injury would turn out to be a minor sprain, and that she would be back to work shortly and take over these meetings.

For the second time that day I pulled into my garage. "Carla?" I called out as I entered the house. No answer, but there was a large sheet of lined paper taped to the inside door. In her careful script she had written that she felt like getting some fresh air and exercise and went out riding her bike to get a Slurpee.

This desire was totally understandable after her stressful day, and surely there was no cause for alarm. The 7-11 was on La Jolla Boulevard, several miles from our condo, but the roads, though narrow and full of curves at times, was regularly traveled by bike riders. We had taken that same ride together several times, but still . . . I couldn't help but worry.

Fortunately for my state of mind it wasn't too long before I heard the sound of a bicycle being placed in its garage rack and Carla was safely home.

"I thought I might beat you back," she said. "It must have been a short meeting."

"It was," I said, and explained briefly.

Carla's skin glistened with perspiration. She was smartly attired in a multi-colored sports top and black bicycle shorts—a perfect ad for a sportswear catalog.

"That ride's a tester," she stated. "But I like it because it's never dull. There are green open spaces and beautiful homes surrounded by lush landscaping, and then around another turn or two are these little clusters of shops and what they call modest homes. But, in any case, the bike is awesome. I know it cost a lot of money. Once again, I can't thank you and Mike enough for all that you've given me."

"We're glad to do it, honey. And don't worry. There's no shortage of money at the moment."

"That reminds me of a question I've wanted to ask you, Erin. Mike has told me a little about his business, and you have this beautiful condo and nice cars, and you get to eat out a lot. So you must be rich. Then why do you need to work—outside the house, I mean?"

I was surprised by the question. Chance for a little feminist lecture, maybe, but I knew she was anxious to shower, so I decided to give her a condensed version.

"Before I answer, didn't many of the women you knew in Campo have jobs?"

'Yes, but that's because they *had* to or there wouldn't be enough money to pay the bills,"

"Well, I'm fortunate to be able to work because I *want* to. I like what I do at the newspaper and the bookstore. I'm good at it and it's appreciated. We don't need the money I make for daily expenses, but I like having money to spend as I wish, especially to put toward something Mike and I can both enjoy. And lastly, none of us can predict the future. A woman should always be able to provide for herself."

"Did you say the last thing about the future because you and Mike might not get married?"

"No, of course not. Are you worried about that? We've just been too busy to plan a proper wedding. You do understand that we're very much in love, don't you?"

"Oh, anyone can see that! But you *should* set a date soon. You're not getting any younger, you know, and Mike is already seeing a chiropractor for his back. You want to look good in your wedding pictures, don't you?" she asked, trying unsuccessfully to suppress a grin.

"Get out of here with your smelly clothes and your disrespectful comments about your elders, or I'll tickle you—body odor and all. I may do it anyway," I threatened as I ran after the fleet-footed Carla.

We didn't even hear Mike's car. "What the hell?" he said as he came into the room while this was going on.

"Oh, oh!" I said, as I skidded to a stop.

'We're busted," Carla added, then dissolving into peals of laughter with me before the totally baffled man of the house.

# 32

Jimmy had returned from his night out with the guys about ten that evening. Melody put aside the Ann Rule true crime paperback she had been reading while Serena slept curled up on the back seat beside her.

Melody whispered to him, "I didn't think you would be back so early. Did they give you a hard time?" she smiled. "Call you henpecked?"

"A few of them said something like that, but the truth is I *wanted* to come back. You passed up a chance to go out because of Serena, so why shouldn't I see if you needed help with her care? Does that sound too corny?"

"Not at all," Melody responded, getting that special warm feeling that came when her husband did something loving and unexpected. "I had her use the potty earlier. Hopefully, she should sleep through the night, if she isn't wakened by a bad dream. She was very intrigued by the upper bunk bed, but I'd feel better if she slept down here with me tonight. Would you mind taking the upper bunk?"

"Of course not, with the skylight open I get to look at the moon or the streetlights or whatever," he said. "Of course, I'm not sure I can fall asleep without you by my side. Do you think I could borrow Serena's stuffed animal?" he asked, feigning innocence.

"Not on your life, but instead, how about a kiss to tide you over?" Melody offered provocatively, standing up carefully so as not to wake the sleeping child. Jimmy accepted her offer by wrapping her tightly in his arms.

* * *

Melody was sure she would be able to obtain more pertinent information from Serena in the morning. She and Jimmy had to start their trip south within a few days in order for her to honor a few consignment orders in three communities along the way. And, before they did that, they needed to figure out where and how Serena would fit in with their plans.

Next morning Jimmy quietly left the camper early to spend a few hours to help a friend take inventory at his nearby hardware store located only a few blocks from where they were parked.

Before retreating to his upper bunk the previous night he had said he'd pick up breakfast on the way to work so as not to wake the child. As he left he blew Melody a kiss in the semi-darkness of the curtained camper.

When he was gone Melody retrieved the paperback from the night before and read until Serena woke up. Then she heated water on their two-burner propane stove—cocoa for the child and tea for herself. They each had a blueberry muffin as well—Serena eating every crumb of hers and licking her fingers for good measure as if she still wasn't sure there would be any more food to come. Melody vividly remembered the meal at the Buena Vista when Serena had eaten like a feral animal. It would probably be awhile before she could just relax and trust enough in her surroundings to take ordinary daily living in stride.

"How did you sleep?" Melody asked, as she gathered their paper plates and cups and threw them into a trash bag.

"Good, thank you, but I thought I was going to sleep up top. It looks like it would be fun to hang out up there—nice and cozy, and Brownie would like it too. Any chance I can check it out now?"

"Sure, for a while until we figure out what we're going to do today. The reason you slept with me on the pull-out bed down here is because you fell asleep while we were watching *Black Beauty* last night. How strong do you think I am? There was no way I could get a big sleeping lump like you into the top bunk all alone."

"Bet I can get up there myself," Serena bragged.

"Well, then, prove it," Melody challenged, standing by just in case.

Serena put one foot on top of the metal covered stove, and then, pushing off and adding her elbows for strength and balance, she threw herself safely over the upper edge of the bunk, from which she gazed down in triumph.

"Now that was very impressive," Melody said admiringly, as she reached high to hand Serena a couple of books and Brownie. "But before you get too comfortable, I *would* like to ask you a few questions."

She had noticed an understandable reluctance on the child's part when it came to maintaining eye contact with an adult—especially one prying into what must have been a painful past. This physical separation at the moment between the two of them might work to her advantage in finding out more about the child's background.

"Serena, I know you don't like to talk about your life before we met, but Jimmy and I really want to help you get back safely to your family. We can't, though, if you won't give us any more information to work with."

No response from up above. "You mentioned having a grandmother, but you didn't say where she lives or whether she knows where you are. If you have a telephone number for her or any other family member I'd be glad to make a call for you," Melody suggested.

She had obviously touched a nerve. In a sulky voice Serena said, "You weren't listening. I told you the other day that Pete let me use his cell phone to call Campo, but my uncle Mateo answered."

Nothing more was forthcoming. Melody willed herself to be patient. Mateo and Pete—who were they and how did they fit in?

Aloud she said, "Mateo sounds like he could be a bad person, Serena. Am I right?"

The child's next sentence stunned her. It confirmed Jimmy's worst case scenario. "Mateo is my uncle. He gave me and my older sister Carla to Nestor who took us far away and then the bad men came and did awful things to us and then Nestor took Carla somewhere and I've never seen her again."

Serena had delivered those words in a flat, unemotional tone. Then she started to whimper and Melody was afraid she would clam up, but fortunately the words began to tumble out; details of her time with Dion and the other girls in San Diego, including her first attempt to escape, and the subsequent beating, the long drugged-out van ride to San Francisco, her successful walk-away from a hotel room and a drunken john, while she was being held with others by a pimp called Angel,

Melody had not expected all this when she had asked for more information, but Serena, once she had begun talking, acted relieved as she unburdened herself. Melody willed herself not to interrupt.

Serena brought her chilling narrative to a close by describing in vivid detail her most recent days spent on her own—robbed, wet, and ultimately betrayed by a homeless man named Pete whom she had considered a friend! And over and over a central theme emerged—no matter where she was taken, or how farfetched her quest may have been, she had *never* given up her attempt to somehow get back with the big sister who had promised they would always be together.

Melody felt sick to her stomach. Serena's tear-stained face peered over the side of the bunk. Melody helped her down and then held her close while she crooned "You're safe now," over and over.

Finally Serena pulled away and looked into Melody's face. "You were crying, too," the young victim observed, as if that wondrous fact meant a barrier to trust was being removed.

"I was. It made me very sad to hear how those bad men hurt you. But now look—I'm smiling, because I know that will never happen to you again." Risky going, Melody told herself, but she knew that she would move heaven and earth to see that this became the truth.

"Now, I could use a good cup of coffee and the battery on the laptop needs to be recharged. Let's walk over to Coffee to the People."

"Is that the *real* name?" Serena sounded skeptical.

"It is indeed, and they have wonderful cookies. Are you interested?"

Minutes later they were seated on one of the several couches scattered about the iconic coffee shop, enjoying their mid-morning refreshments with others—regulars and tourists alike—making use of one of the numerous power outlets available.

"Serena, you mentioned that you were from Campo, but you weren't sure exactly where that was except somewhere in California near the Mexican border. I don't even know where that is, but I can show you how you can look it up yourself on Google. Do you know how to use a PC?" Serena shook her head. "If not," Melody continued, "you might as well learn how to use one starting right now. Undoubtedly they will have them for the students in whatever school you go to next year."

"You'd really let me do that?" Serena had perked up at the mention of school, as well as using a computer.

"Sure," Melody said, "and, in addition to school work, you can play all kinds of games on this. I'll show you before we look up maps."

With a few keyboard strokes they were powered up and on

Google. After checking out some game sites, an area map of Campo—about as far down as you could go in the eastern-most corner of San Diego County—was brought up on the screen.

Now at least we have that to go on, thought Melody, but we still need more information. Jimmy and I shouldn't just go down there blindly without finding out more about Serena's grand-mother, where she lives, her state of health, and so on. And then, perhaps of even more importance, is the grandmother Serena's legal guardian or not—and if not, is anyone?

And what is Serena's status as far as the authorities are con-cerned? Is she listed as a runaway, and do they know about the kidnapping and subsequent sexual exploitation? And how does Uncle Mateo fit in? Is he still around? Melody's thoughts then turned to the pimp, Nestor? Do either or both of them still pose a threat to Serena? And where is Carla?

And, Melody thought, no matter what the answers are to all my questions, we do have a missing child with us, and we may be violating any number of laws. The Campo Sheriff's Depart-ment must be contacted and hopefully we can get some answers without giving away too much about ourselves, or Serena, until we know she will be completely safe. A tall order for sure, but Melody felt, that by using her imagination, she could work it out.

She had been concentrating so hard that she hadn't realized that Serena was speaking to her. "You looked funny and I think you were talking to yourself," the child said, giving her a quizzi-cal look.

"I'm sorry if I was ignoring you, honey. Guess I just have a lot on my mind. Tell you what, I'm going to leave you to play some of those computer games while I make some calls to my suppli-ers. I'll be at that table just over there," Melody, said, pointing across the room.

*　*　*

Once out of earshot, Melody took a deep breath and prepared to make what she considered a risky call. Lying didn't come easily to her—nor did being intentionally deceptive. She was understandably nervous as she dialed the number she had gotten through Google.

A woman's voice answered on the second ring. "San Diego County Sheriff's substation, Campo, how may I direct your call?"

Melody almost shut off her cell. Of course she had no names or extensions. But she wasn't doing anything wrong either, so she said firmly, "This is not police business, actually. I have some important information for one of the citizens in your jurisdiction and am having trouble reaching her. I thought someone there might be able to help."

"'Well, if you tell me I might be able to handle it myself. I fill in here and there, but the regular switchboard operator just got back from lunch, so I'm free. I think I know just about everybody in town. My name is Dora, by the way, and if it's not a confidentiality issue, I may be able to help."

It sounded as if she might prove to be the perfect contact, thought Melody.

"Well, thank you, Dora. My name is Marlene Evans and I'm a representative for the Hartford Fidelity Insurance Company. Our firm recently bought out several smaller companies and my department is charged with getting in touch with their policy holders to alert them to the change of ownership and perhaps bring their policies up to date as well."

"But you can't reach all the people, am I right?" Dora interjected, with enthusiasm in her voice.

"That's proving to be the case," Melody replied, thinking that she better speed this conversation along before Serena got restless and came to check up on her.

"The policy holder I'm looking for is a Mrs. Renata Flores and she names a Carla and Serena as beneficiaries. Of course I'm not at liberty to share the terms of the policy except to say that Mrs. Flores had been making modest payments on a monthly basis going back for many years, but for some reason stopped abruptly awhile back. Our efforts to reach her by mail or telephone have been unsuccessful."

Dora picked up on the name immediately. "We aren't close friends or anything, but I do know that poor woman has had more than her share of trouble this past year. Last I heard she was in the nursing home out on the county road. And think about those missing grandkids of hers . . .

"There's a poster up somewhere. Rumor has it that Mateo Flores, their uncle, had something to do with their disappearance. I heard he's been in and out of trouble, but you don't want to hear all this. The person you want to talk with would be our dispatcher, Lorena, who just went into her office. Do you want me to ring her for you?"

"Dora, you've been very helpful, but I have a call coming in I have to take. I'll get back to you." When Melody hung up she was trembling at first, but relief set in quickly. Not bad for your first acting job, she thought, giving herself a virtual pat on the back.

She and Jimmy needed to get together right away and plan their next few days. She had commitments with jewelry sellers in three locations heading south, but disappointing as that might be, for now they would have to leave out their anniversary trip to Big Sur.

Serena's grandmother—that poor, ill woman, thought Melody. What she must have gone through. What she must still be enduring! She and Jimmy could at least try to arrange a joyous reunion between grandmother and granddaughter. What would happen after Campo would remain out there in the future.


That night while they were having supper at a restaurant, Jimmy gave Serena some money so she could try to snag a prize with the claw contraption on one of those machines that are such a magnet for kids. She had her eye on a red coin purse or a small stuffed animal to be a pal for Brownie, and promised to return any money if she got lucky early on. The odds against getting just what she wanted and the shoddiness of the merchandise didn't faze her a bit. Like most children, the chance to win a prize held great allure—but no such luck this time.  Jimmy would have bought out the whole inventory if that would have given Serena the result she was looking for. There was no doubt, Melody thought, that in Serena's short time as part of their lives, she was stirring up paternal feelings Jimmy hadn't known he possessed.

Melody took advantage of this rare time without the child within hearing distance to tell her husband briefly about Serena's nightmare tale and her own call to the Campo police station, However, she had to postpone filling him in fully until later that night when Serena was safely tucked into the upper bunk bed.

Standing in shadows, a few feet away from the camper, under a backdoor portico of a business, closed for the night, Melody related Serena's story to Jimmy.

She watched as her husband's kind, but usually rather bland plain face, went from disbelief to disgust to anger. "So you're saying that it looks like a family member actually sold the child to a pimp who in turn let men sexually abuse her over and over. For god's sake she must have been only ten at the time!"

"And, looking much younger," Melody interrupted. "Apparently that made her even more valuable"

"And then," Jimmy's voice was rising, "for some reason, a gang member in another part of San Diego bought her, and that same kind of abuse continued? And by then her sister had been sent somewhere else too, so Serena was totally on her own to live through this? *Incredible!*"

Melody looked around to be sure no passersby were within hearing distance. Even though she had already heard all this from Serena, she found herself experiencing profound sadness in the retelling, but she owed it to Jimmy to be as honest as possible, yet spare Serena another retelling of the past nightmarish months. One day the child would probably benefit from continuing to work through these stories during professional counseling sessions, but not now with the two people who knew her simply as a beautiful, loveable child.

It was hard for Melody to continue, but she and Jimmy had gotten in this together, and he had wanted to be told everything, so . . .

"Apparently, there are johns who prefer girls younger and younger, and also like to take pictures of them, naked or dressed in costumes. And when Serena, after a time, rebelled at this and ran away she was caught, beaten and thus, as a trouble maker, it seems, was sent up here to San Francisco to a gang-member pimp named Angel. She got away from him on a fluke when a john fell asleep in a hotel room after trying to get her to use drugs.

"And in each place she was kept, she gave me details of what the men did to her and what they made her do to them," Melody was shaking. "I can't get those pictures out of my mind. Can you imagine what she sees when she closes her eyes? But she never gave up hope, Jimmy—always believed that one day, somehow she would get back home to be with her grandmother and sister."

"It's okay, honey. Please don't cry. We'll take her down there and give her that reunion with the grandmother you spoke about."

Melody just let him hold her for a few minutes before raising the question of the anniversary trip they had planned to take to Big Sur country.

"Well, in all honesty, I *was* looking forward to spending some time with you in a luxurious room with a full shower for me and a huge bath tub for you, and a king-size bed for some serious lovemaking. And then, on the second day, a visit to one of those famous spas with a spectacular view of the Pacific. . ."

Melody broke in. "You'd actually go to a spa?"

"Don't act so surprised. I'd certainly give it a try!"

"Okay, sounds wonderful to me also, but we can always go there for some future anniversary. Anyhow, I have an idea. We need to stop in San Louis Obispo on the way down for the big order that my local seller arranged.

"I went on line and did some checking. After I take care of my business, we can check into a motel room which includes a tub, shower, and two beds, spend a few hours at one of the many spas that were mentioned, and eat at one of the town's fine restaurants. If we have more time we can check out the university and the old mission, walk on the beaches at Morro Bay and Avila, do a little hiking—whatever. In any case we'll all be clean, rested and that much closer to our final destination in Campo."

There was no problem getting Serena to hop down from her upper bunk the next morning. Melody had simply told her about the proposed trip to Campo. "We're *really* going to see my grandmother?" Serena asked for the second time as she exchanged her sleep clothes for a clean tee and shorts, and Melody began brushing her hair.

"Really, really, really," Melody assured her. "But as I told you, from what I heard your grandmother may still be very ill. We won't know until we get there. And also, there are some stops we need to make along the way, so promise you won't keep asking when are we going to get there?"

"Of course not," Serena said, indignantly. "Only little kids do that!"

Jimmy waited outside for the all clear to sound. Years in the marines had honed his morning routine to a bare bones minimum. His wife, even as one not given over to elaborate beauty rituals, needed more time. Throw in a female child with long hair and a growing fashion sense . . . but who was complaining?

Finally, Jimmy took his place in the driver's seat. "You in the back, are you belted in? Got your colored pencils and drawing pad handy—brown dog secured?" he asked, in as serious a voice as he could muster.

"Yes sir!" Serena called out. For some reason she liked it when he mentioned his days in the service and acted like the tough non-commissioned officer he had been. He and Melody guessed it had something to do with the fact that she had taken the leap of faith to literally trust them with her life. Jimmy had thus become her protector from all those bad men who had so cruelly used her. He needed to be viewed as tough.

"Then let's do it," Jimmy said, as they left Haight Ashbury behind and headed south on highway 101.

Other than making a quick stop at a McDonald's early on, for breakfast sandwiches and coffee to go, they continued driving until they neared San Louis Obispo, two hundred miles to the south.

Jimmy was proud of the way the Vanagon handled, and, though their home carried more water and possessions than would be the case if they were on a short camping trip, it kept up with the flow of traffic quite well. But how would it perform on the famous, or infamous, Cuesta Grade, heading into San Louis Obispo with its seven percent grade and impressive drop-off? They were about to find out.

Serena had fallen asleep somewhere outside of King City, but she was wide awake now. Truck traffic had been building up, the big rigs downshifting gears to increase their braking ability on the very short, very steep, downhill incline, mandated to stay in the right lane and to stick to a speed of thirty-five or less. All other slow-moving vehicles were advised to do likewise as south-bound traffic headed down the long, winding 4,750-foot decent.

"How are you doing?" Jimmy asked Melody, as he pulled the

camper in behind a huge silver-semi with Pennsylvania plates.

"Don't ask," she managed to answer through clenched teeth as the vehicle flew down the grade.

'Whee, this is fun!" Serena shouted from the rear.

And then they finally reached the bottom and resumed a normal speed on the straight-away leading into the town. Only then did Melody manage a smile of relief and, glancing to the rear, noted Serena's big smile as well.

# 33

Mike and I sat together in the breakfast nook, lingering over a second cup of coffee, while reading sections of the San Diego Union Tribune. Carla had left the table a few minutes earlier to put a load of clothes in the washer and straighten up her room.

I looked up from the paper and gazed at the man I loved. Something about this most mundane of weekend rituals reinforced the knowledge that my commitment to him was now total. And I believed his to me was the same. I fingered the engagement ring I had so impulsively taken off after the hurtful argument that resulted in our brief estrangement awhile back.

"Honey, I've taken your advice and gone ahead with some preliminary plans for our wedding," I said, waiting for an acknowledgement before continuing.

Mike mouthed, "One minute," then finished the paragraph he was reading. "Now, you were saying?"

So I told him that both Frank and Malcolm had offered use of their nicely landscaped backyards and I had already spoken to a young caterer recommended by the newspaper's food critic. A retired judge would officiate and we could write our own vows.

"Whatever you come up with is fine with me, my love. Since we are not going to elope, there are a few people I believe I should invite. When were you thinking this should take place?"

"How about one month from today?"

He calculated quickly. "Which would be my birthday. Just coincidence, or ...?"

"So you will never forget our anniversary, of course."

He leaned toward me and said, "Sealed with a kiss," before

delivering one which took my breath away.

"I'm sure Carla will want to take over as the new wedding planner," I began, remembering my previous conversation with the teenager.

"Speaking of Carla," Mike said, as he checked to be sure she wasn't around, "I wanted to ask you sooner, but there was no chance to get you alone and I didn't want to take a chance and upset her. How did your meeting with Joe Cruz go?"

"I think it went well, but even though I'd heard most of Carla's story before, it was still heart wrenching. Mike, what that girl has been through—the degradation, the fear, the pain! And the loss of her little sister, Serena . . ."

"It's hard to imagine—and I hardly consider myself naïve—but when it comes to someone you know, someone you've come to care for a lot . . ." Mike began to falter.

"It's alright to show your affection for her, you know," I said, placing my hand over his. "You know the way *I* feel. It makes it all the more important that we have a serious talk about her future."

"Agreed. We've touched on it, but it might be time to involve her fully as well. But, before we get to that, what's the next step as to prosecuting the gangs?"

"Joe is going to get back to us as soon as he knows whether the DA thinks Carla's statement is strong enough to get the grand jury to go forward with an indictment," I told him. "It seems to fit at least some of the criteria, such as being a headline grabber, having to do with rape and other sexual acts, and, of course, vulnerable witnesses with first-hand accounts who can attest that a crime has been committed against them."

"And, if they decide in the affirmative, what next for Carla?"

"As I understand it, then she will testify before the grand jury and swear to the truth of the statement she made when she was questioned in the sheriff's office."

"Did Joe mention trying to get someone to give up Serena's

whereabouts in exchange for leniency or something?"

"He did, but he stopped just short of promising that would happen. I'm not sure that Carla truly trusts in the process but Mike, from everything Carla's told me, finding her little sister is behind every move she's made, or not dared to make, since they were separated. So she really has no other option. And we can't do anything to help her and that stinks!"

We hadn't heard Carla's approach. "Ah, a true Saturday break from the rigors of the work week," she said, as she noticed us still at the breakfast table—but there was only teasing, not reproach, in her voice.

I hoped she hadn't heard our conversation. I rolled my eyes at Mike. "Darn, she caught us! And we were just getting ready to clean out the basement."

"But there *is* no basement," Carla began, "how . . ."

"'Gotcha," I said innocently. "But I'm open. Did you have something in mind to help keep us out of trouble?"

"Not really," Carla said. "I just came down to get some juice and put my wash in the dryer. And then I will continue to do a little journaling—you gave me this lovely book when I helped out at the bookstore. I try to write something in it each day."

"And I have an idea of my own to run by you both," Mike added. "What if we all head to the country club to spend some time on the driving range and putting green? Someone whose opinion I value highly suggested that it was selfish of me not to try harder to share my passion for golf with other family members."

"Oh, let's!" said Carla, smiling enthusiastically.

"You're on," I said, "but it's going to cost you. I can see lunch in the clubhouse and a stop in the pro shop to let Carla and me pick out one of those cute outfits so we can look the part. I hope they carry the Ralph Lauren line. When we were out to dinner last week your client's wife raved about some of Lauren's items she had purchased when her husband played at Pebble Beach."

Mike pulled out his wallet and pretended to check the contents. "As long as we don't have to take out a second mortgage on the condo, knock yourselves out!!"

It was obvious that Carla wasn't quite sure how to respond. But Mike and I both knew, that while I could never bring myself to pay what I considered to be outrageous designer prices for anything, he was proud that he could. He had worked hard to leave his impoverished boyhood behind, and it gave him great pleasure that now he was able to provide well for those he loved.

"We'll see," I said. "For now I'm sure we can come up with something appropriate to wear. I do have several of those visors you brought me from some of the golf courses you played." Then to Carla, "Come pick one out."

I heard my familiar ring-tone coming from the hall table. "Let me check and see who this is. I'll be right there." Then, recognizing the caller, "Malcolm, what's up?"

"Circulation, more advertisers—you name it. You have a talent, young lady, and a sense of what the public wants to read. And it keeps the spotlight on the dirty problem of human trafficking. That second article on the older sister was as good as your first. I'm proud of you."

High praise indeed! I was floating on air. "Thank you for the vote of confidence. You know it means a lot to me. Was there anything else?" I asked, hoping not to hold the others up any longer.

"No, that was it. I'll see you Tuesday."

"I'll let anything else go to voice mail," I announced to the others, "just let me make a quick bathroom stop." I was headed that way when the house phone rang.

Mike waved me on. "I'll see who that is and meet you in the car."

Five minutes later we were on the road to the Torrey Pines Municipal golf course. No one mentioned the calls. Later, I learned that Mike had spoken with Joe Cruz, who once again expressed praise for Carla's bravery and thanked Mike and me for urging her to work with the authorities against the gangs. Receiving thanks from my editor was one thing—thanks from the police was another. However, I still couldn't shake the feeling that because of me, Carla might be at risk.

But we were out to have a good time, and that we did. Carla showed great determination and some innate talent. I didn't have much of either, though I was actually able to enjoy myself, since we were on the driving range and I wasn't holding anyone up or being adversely judged. My scratch-golfer husband was the soul of patience and encouragement as he helped us with our attempts to successfully hit a helpless, stationary golf ball.

Lunch was delicious and Carla and I bought matching Torrey Pines wind jackets by Levelwear: coral for me and lavender for Carla. Very nice looking—Mike approved—and not so costly that we would be forced to take out a second mortgage on either!

Mike took a picture of us standing side-by-side in our new jackets, with our ponytails peeking through the visors. "We look just like sisters," Carla exclaimed happily.

Hardly, I thought—she with her high color and almost black hair, and me with my pale skin and strawberry blonde hair. But I knew that out there somewhere was a little sister who *was* her spitting image and in great need of help.


After we got back home Carla spent some time on the computer in Mike's study. We had discussed what kind we would buy for her use, and the necessary safeguards and rules that we would need to impose on any teenager. She might have been brutally introduced to life on the streets, but that didn't mean she had become automatically immune to the dangers posed by modern social media. Mike and I had vowed to take our roles very seriously if we were going to remain as the primary responsible adults in her life.

As was often the case, Carla brought me an article she had printed out that either held special appeal for her, or that she felt might be of interest to Mike or me.

"Look at this, Erin," she said, holding out a printed page detailing the published results of a study conducted by a researcher done on fifty-three bottlenose dolphins living in captivity in six different facilities. The article purported to prove that these mammals had amazing memories. They could also recognize the distinctive whistles of former buddies, even though separated for decades, and later reunited. "Isn't that amazing?" Carla enthused.

It would seem that Carla's dolphin infatuation hadn't waned, and that one day her dream of interacting with them in some capacity might come true.

"They are something special, alright," I answered.

"I'm going to show this to Mike," she said, holding up the paper, "and then he has promised to teach me how to play chess! Is there anything you would like me to do around the house before we start?"

I shook my head. "I'm going to call my friend, Amy, and then do some paperwork. Go have fun."

Amy was all agog about her upcoming wedding and was also very pleased to hear that Mike and I were getting closer to making plans of our own.

Call completed, I heard sounds coming from the study between the teacher and student over the chess game. I remembered that Carla had never retrieved her laundry from the dryer, so while she was busy, I decided to fold the clothing and take it up to her room.

As I went to lay the clothes down I noticed that Carla had left her journal on the bed, a fancy pen holding a page open. I didn't plan to snoop, but when I saw my name and Mike's prominently featured in purple ink on a snowy white page I had to take a look.

In essence the page was written as a letter to Serena where Carla acknowledges that there is a possibility she may never see her little sister again. Then she goes on to write how she has been totally accepted by us—me and Mike—and how much she loves me and how wonderful it is to be part of a family. And that her hope and dream is for Serena to find that same happiness in her life one day.

My eyes were so blurred with tears that I barely made it into our bedroom, quietly closing the door behind me.

.

# 34

"I could get used to all that," Melody remarked, with a contented sigh from her passenger seat, as they left the Rose Garden Inn on the outskirts of San Luis Obispo.

"Get used to what?" Jimmy asked, as he eased the camper into traffic, heading south on highway 101.

"All of it, I guess; the motel, the pool, the food, the spa. Being waited on, being pampered in general—and in such charming surroundings."

"Me, too," Serena chimed in from the back seat—her toes, painted vermillion red, peeking out from her sandals. The same brilliant color adorned her fingernails. And a professional haircut and a conditioning treatment completed her transformation from an unkempt ragamuffin into a poised pre-teen. "What I liked best were the waterfall pools at the motel and the nice lady at the spa who fixed me up like a Disney kid," she commented, happily.

"It certainly made for a nice stop," Jimmy agreed. "I wouldn't mind going back there one day when we have more time. I bet that there's a lot more to see and like about that town; that whole area actually."

"But living in here is still the best," Serena said, surprisingly, as if their enthusiasm for time spent in a motel and a spa represented a betrayal of their more modest life in the camper.

"Amen," Melody voiced her agreement, marveling yet again at the wisdom and compassion shown by this child. "We love our home away from home."

For a while there was no more conversation as Serena

worked to complete a colorful drawing she planned to give to her grandmother. Melody gave herself completely over to enjoying the ever-changing scenery of this part of the Pacific Coast, while Jimmy kept a watchful eye on the traffic. Many drivers seemed to be in a dangerous rush to distance themselves from the slower moving camper and the ever growing number of trucks.

Every so often Melody would hear Serena sigh and see her fidgeting in her seat. They still had almost three hundred miles to go until they reached their Campo destination—a very long way for their young traveling companion to wait until she could see her grandmother again.

"Anyone want to play a car game?" Melody asked, hoping to offer a diversion from the monotony of the ride.

"I do!" Serena said eagerly, laying down her drawing pad.

"I'll try," Jimmy added, "as long as I can still concentrate on the driving."

"Or if it's not too hard for a soon-to-be fifth grader," Serena threw in. "But at least I have Brownie to help me," she stated, giving her new toy companion an affectionate pat.

"That's why I thought of 'In My Grandmother's Trunk'," Melody responded, going on to explain the simple rules of this popular memory tester. "Let's practice a bit. I'll go first. In my grandmother's trunk I found an alligator. Now, it's Jimmy's turn."

"In my grandmother's trunk I found an alligator and a banana," Jimmy contributed, his usual baritone dropping into a bass register.

"In my grandmother's trunk I found an alligator, a banana and a caterpillar, said Goldilocks," Serena responded, in a high pitched cartoonish voice.

"Eating the banana, no doubt," Jimmy chimed in, eliciting a giggle from Serena.

"Very funny," Melody remarked. "It appears that we have

two comics in the car. Am I the only one taking this game seri-ously?" But, though she tried to sound disapproving, she was soon joining in with the silliness, acutely aware that the child she had come to care deeply about had made this same trip just weeks before as a virtual slave, drugged, in pain, and scared to death. She brushed such gloomy thoughts from her mind and turned her full attention back to the game.

"The practice is over. Let the games begin," she said, theatri-cally. Serena held her own for several rounds—coming up with some inventive alphabet words—but eventually only Melody was left. After her third win it was obvious that the other two players were outclassed. Neither Jimmy nor Serena would ever win a game.

"As a former teacher I think that Melody should have to do more to be declared the winner, don't you, Serena?" Jimmy called back to his young co-competitor.

"Well, she *is* the smartest," Serena answered, after a brief hesitation. "You're smart, too, Jimmy, but . . ."

And so it was agreed that under the new rules Melody would have to remember all twenty-six words in order, not just outlast her opponents if she were to be declared the winner.

The results of this modification were satisfying to all and, as predicted, playing the Grandmother's Trunk game did much to help the time pass more quickly.

But there was also plenty to see along the way as their southerly route took them straight through the coastal cities of Ventura and Oxnard, with their off-shore oil company platforms, and then on to the charming city of Santa Barbara. From there, they drove right through Los Angeles itself, then on into Orange County, eventually entering San Diego County, thus bringing them much closer to their final destination.

Melody did a fine job as navigator and Serena, reading from the legends sections of the road maps, kept them informed as to all kinds of statistics and points of interest.

"In case you didn't know," the latter began in a sing-song voice, "L.A., as it is often called, is the second-largest city in the United States with a population of over three million people living in approximately five hundred square miles."

"And about one million of them are driving in the area right now," Jimmy remarked, only half in jest.

All three travelers readily agreed that they would never choose to live in a city, though Serena did express interest in visiting Beverly Hills in hopes of seeing a movie star and also the city of Anaheim in order to spend a day at Disneyland.

They had made very good time since they left San Luis Obispo and had stopped only briefly to gas up, use the restrooms and purchase hot coffee for the driver and cold drinks for the two passengers.

When they reached Carlsbad, in San Diego County, they pulled off in the old part of town called the Village so that Melody could deliver a jewelry order—once again set up by her San Francisco buyer. The transaction took only minutes.

"There are fine beaches and restaurants here," she said, as she climbed into the front passenger seat, "but if you two agree, the clerks and a couple of customers in that boutique suggested that we go a few miles down the road to a famous café called Swami's; eat there, then go across the street to some gardens and an overlook where one can watch the surfers. Apparently Swami's Beach is world famous."

Both the funky restaurant—small, crowded, friendly, health conscious—and the surf spot, proved to be as advertised—well worth the stop. At the café, seating looked to be impossible, but a table on the tiny outside patio was soon cleared for them. A regular customer helpfully suggested that they get in line and make their selections from the simple paper menu while they waited to put in their order. Since everything was done on a first-come, first-served basis, the pace was often slow, but, they were advised, the food made it well worth the wait.

Orders were placed and picked up at a rustic counter inside and there was also a corner set-up where customers poured their own coffee, tea, and juices. Since Melody's order was easy—she had agreed to share an acai bowl with Serena—granola mix covered with blueberries, bananas, strawberries and raspberries topped with coconut and a crunchy honey topping—Melody offered to hold their table.

While she was waiting for the others to get back with the food, she picked up a section of newspaper called *The County Voice* that someone had discarded. The section was filled mostly with ads but it also contained   some letters written to the editor. She began to idly read the first one. The writer was responding favorably to a recent article, written by an Erin Butler, which had evidently portrayed a true account of two young sisters who had been sold into a human trafficking network in Southern California. It appeared as if the older sibling had been rescued, but the whereabouts of the little girl was still unknown.

Melody would call herself a very practical woman—one not given to beliefs in signs or omens—but can this be just a coincidence, she asked herself? When she saw Jimmy and Serena coming toward her—loaded down with numerous dishes, mugs, and silverware—still stunned, she folded the paper and put it casually in her lap. She desperately wanted to show it to Jimmy but did not want to include Serena at this point.

"Sorry for the wait," Jimmy apologized. "I was warned that the crew that runs this place refuses to be rushed, but I was also promised that all would be forgiven when we taste the food. Dig in. Let's see if they're right."

The chilled fruit bowl was huge and raved over by the females. Taking a suggestion from one of the staff, Jimmy had ordered the two corn enchiladas with a mole sauce combo and pronounced it to be outstanding.

Meal finished, they crossed over the highway to the lush

garden area, and joined other spectators at the railings on the bluff overlooking the surfers below. Deeply tanned men, women, and children—most wearing short-sleeved black summer wet suits, with colorful surf boards stacked nearby—also watched and commented knowingly to one another as the surfers below put on quite a show.

Lying prone on their boards, some were paddling out, as others had pulled themselves up, found their wave, and hurtled toward the shore. Many crisscrossing the waves on the diagonal, a few even doing a series of jumps—all ultimately ending up off their boards in shallow water, that is, if they hadn't been flipped further out. And then they would do it all over again; being careful not to stray into another surfer's territory.

Melody and Jim eavesdropped shamelessly and marveled at the exciting, unfamiliar spectacle unfolding below them. Serena and a young boy with curly, sun-bleached hair exchanged shy glances. Reluctantly, the threesome pulled themselves away, and returned to the camper.

"Awesome," was how Serena described their stay. It was mutually agreed that Encinitas would definitely be on a list of places to revisit one day.


"'Did that last sign read 'I-8 three miles'?" Jimmy asked, as they headed south on I-5 toward the outskirts of El Cajon and the nursing facility where they hoped to reunite   Serena with her grandmother.

"I think so," Melody replied. "But I'm afraid I wasn't paying full attention," she explained, as she put down the newspaper that she had picked up in Encinitas.

"Yeah, this is it," Jimmy announced soon afterwards as he took the exit from I-5 to I-8 East. "Now we just have to find the exit to the Golden Meadows Care Center. According to the directions you Googled, it shouldn't be far."

Minutes later they pulled onto a palm tree-lined entrance road and made a left into a visitors' parking lot. Serena had been unusually quiet the whole way down from Swami's. Who knew what she must be thinking? Melody hadn't wanted to intrude. An earlier call to the nursing facility had confirmed that Mrs. Flores was a patient, but nothing else.

"Are you ready, sweetie?" Melody asked, as she opened the sliding back door.

Serena climbed out. "Melody, I should be just happy, but I'm afraid and sad, too," she said, her woebegone face contrasting with the way she looked in her carefully chosen outfit of a navy-blue skort and a pale-yellow print shirt.

Melody held her hand. "No one really likes hospitals, Serena. It's very understandable that you are nervous about seeing your grandmother in here. But just think how happy she will be to see you."

That drew a smile. In one hand, Serena carried a plastic bag containing two kinds of Mexican candies they had purchased at a little ethnic market along the way—in the other, the rolled up drawing she had made in the camper.

Jimmy joined them and they began to walk over a short, rustic, wooden bridge which, according to the signs, led to the main entrance, a cluster of beige stucco buildings with red-tiled roofs set around a park-like area, dotted with benches and vividly-colored flower beds.

"Looks like a nice place," Jimmy remarked, as he held the entrance door open for the others.

At the information desk they asked for directions to Mrs. Flores' room. The clerk consulted her patient list and directed them to the proper corridor. "You'll have to check in at the nurses station. I know you say you've traveled a long way, but that's the critical care wing, so it's definitely a staff decision as to each patient's visitation schedule," she said, not unkindly.

Serena walked closely next to Melody. Soon, after passing a

small lounge decorated in soothing pastels, they came to the nurses station. A woman dressed in a floral print blouse and white slacks wore a nametag which identified her as a supervisor. "May I help you?" she asked.

"We're here to see Renata Flores," Melody answered. "This is her granddaughter and my husband and I are family friends."

The nurse's expression changed—inquiry replaced by surprise and pleasure as she gazed intently at the child. "Serena. Are you really Serena?"

Serena's eyes grew wide, and she nodded emphatically.

"Your grandmother talks about you a lot. I'm so glad you were finally able to visit. Just let me check on her before you go in." The nurse lowered her voice. "She has her good and her bad days. Wait here. I'll be right back." And off she went down the hall, noiselessly.

Time passed slowly. A male attendant who appeared to be monitoring a screen behind the enclosure spoke up. "I couldn't help but hear your conversation." Looking directly at Serena, he said "Your grandmother is a very nice lady. She's a favorite on this floor."

Serena smiled shyly. He continued, "Would you like to see our monitoring machine?" She eagerly accepted and soon was engrossed in learning about the system in use that endeavored to insure that a patient's needs and concerns would be addressed in a timely manner.

The supervising nurse returned. "Sorry to take so long but she had dozed off. The dinner trays will be up soon. She hasn't had much of an appetite lately. Maybe you could be of help to her, Serena. I'll have the kitchen make you up something, too, if you'd like."

Serena looked at Melody, who smiled, and said, "Go on, honey. Jimmy and I will go to the cafeteria and get something to eat ourselves. We'll visit your grandmother later."

"It's the second door from the end on the left," the nurse

said. "She's ready for you now. I don't think she believes it could be you."

When Serena had left, the nurse spoke up. "I didn't want to say this in front of the child, but I'm afraid Mrs. Flores isn't doing well. Perhaps you'd like to speak with one of her doctors before you leave so he can explain her situation more fully. She was rallying but has had several TIA episodes since she's been in the facility.

"We have an excellent Hospice program on-site which our chaplain has explained to her. I'm sure he would be glad to go over it with you as well. Now I've got to get back to work. Glad to have met you. The cafeteria is back that way, and to your right," she gestured.


Serena peeked in the door. Her grandmother sat by a window in a comfortable-looking easy chair. She was propped up by pillows and belted in for safety's sake, the child assumed. It had been less than a year since she had seen her last, but Serena was struck by the drastic changes she observed. She forced a smile and moved closer to the old woman.

"Abuela," she called. Her grandmother looked up and reached out with her scrawny arms.

"Serena," she crooned, over and over. "It's really you." And then words tumbled out in a mix of English and Spanish—also tears of joy and hugs and kisses.

Serena was glad no one was in the other bed. Mrs. Flores asked a few questions, mostly about her granddaughter's current living situation. "They treat you good—the people who brought you?"

"Oh, yes, they treat me like a princess—I have beautiful clothes and we eat all kinds of food and lots of ice cream." The latter revelation elicited a broad smile from her grandmother.

"And I get to sleep in a top bunk with my dog Brownie and

help Melody sell her beautiful jewelry and—I know you'll like them a lot. But are you getting tired, abuela? I can let you rest now."

Mrs. Flores smiled wanly—but then, having noticed Serena eyeing some snapshots which were lying on the bedside table, she grew more animated. "Here, you look. I keep them with me always."

There were candid photos of the girls from earlier, happier years—Serena at the YWCA pool, Carla in her soccer uniform, Serena in her first communion dress, both girls with their old dog—bitter-sweet memories. Serena fought back tears.

Then came the question Serena had been dreading. "Your friends brought *you* back to me, my sweet child, but do they know where is Carla?"


Meanwhile in the cafeteria, Melody and Jimmy sat at a table drinking coffee, and sharing a sandwich when Melody took the section of *The County Voice* she had carried from Swami's café and passed it to him. "Read the letter to the editor page and tell me what you think," she said, as she leaned back, and impatiently watched his face for a reaction.

Jimmy read intently then looked up at Melody. "Interesting, and certainly an attention grabber, but I'm afraid I don't get the fascination on your part. Am I missing something?" he asked, as he handed the paper back to her.

"Jimmy, the author is writing about two young sisters from Southern California who got caught up in sex trafficking!" She looked at her husband expectantly.

Jimmy mulled this over and then replied. "Honey, we don't even know for sure if these girls actually exist. This Erin Butler obviously knows about the problem—wants to fire the readers up—but do you really believe that by some miracle you were meant to find that paper and just happen to be traveling with a little girl who vaguely fits the description of the younger sister?"

Melody felt her resolve weakening, but she continued, "I know it seems far-fetched but I couldn't help thinking . . ."

Jimmy broke in. "It's just a coincidence, honey. You want so much to reunite the girls that you let your imagination get in the way of logic." When he saw the crestfallen look on his wife's face he covered her hand with his, and added, "Of course if you really want to, go ahead and try to reach this Erin."

"No, you're right. Wishing doesn't make it so." Melody stood up, and began to clear the table. "We better go back to the ward before Mrs. Flores is too tired to see us."

When she heard a noise at the door of the hospital room, Serena looked up. She turned to the old woman in the chair and announced, "They're here, grandmother," as she motioned for Melody and Jimmy to draw closer.

A wide smile lit up the lined face. "Thank you," she said, over and over in a quavering voice. "Serena tell me all about you wonderful couple. I pray to the Blessed Mother every day to bring my girls back. You are angels."

Of course they objected to any such comparison, but otherwise they accepted her thanks graciously. They exchanged a few other pleasantries, but soon noticed Mrs. Flores' head beginning to nod.

"We'd better let you get some rest," Melody said, signaling to the others.

At that Serena's grandmother seemed to startle herself into full awareness. She asked Serena to bring her a box from the cupboard under the bedside stand. When that was done she took out a few official-looking papers and handed them to Melody. A cursory look turned up birth certificates, immunization records, report cards, a deed to a house, and a brief will leaving everything to the granddaughters.

"You take good care of Serena, si? Her uncle let drugs get him. He can't do *nothing* for her. And Carla?" She rummaged in the box some more.

"Here, take this card. A nice lady who said she was a reporter came by my house awhile back. Said she had seen Carla but now she was lost again. I gave the lady a picture of her and Serena so she could show other people who might be able to help find them. Maybe you call her. I'm tired now, but you will come back? Keep in touch? Please," she implored.

"We promise," Jimmy and Melody spoke in unison.


Serena skipped ahead as they walked back to the camper. Melody whispered to Jimmy. "The name on the card is Erin Butler, the same as the letter writer mentioned. Can you believe it?"

"Make the call," he said.

# 35

Carla peered into the refrigerator and took out a handful of grapes before shutting the door. "What did we decide to have for dinner, Erin?" she asked, as I sat at the desk in my kitchen office.

"I thought we would just heat up the leftover lasagna. I don't know about you, but it seems as if I have been eating all day, what with lunch at the golf club, etcetera. What do you think?"

"Leftovers are fine with me," Carla replied, popping a grape into her mouth. "Let me know if you want a salad."

"Will do," I said, and then added, "You could ask Mike if he's agreeable. I think he went into his study to do some reading for work."

"Okay," she said, and left the room.

The house phone rang as I was looking through some household receipts. "Erin Butler?" the woman's voice on the other end inquired hesitantly.

I didn't recognize the caller's number. "Yes?"

"This is about Serena Flores. I'm calling from El Cajon and my name is Melody Miller and my husband, Jimmy, and I have Serena with us," she said.

I had been waiting for this call—praying for this call—but realized somewhere along the way I had lost hope of ever hearing those words. I think I was in partial shock so I was only aware of half what the woman said by way of an explanation, but it rang true enough for me to urge them to drive immediately to our home.

After I hung up I realized I hadn't even got her phone number—what if the directions I had given her were somewhat muddled? I felt dazed at first, but that feeling quickly turned to euphoria. "Carla! Mike!" I cried out at the top of my voice as I ran toward the study.

They greeted me part way, eyes opened wide. "What in the world?" Mike began. Before he could continue, I burst out.

"They found her! Can you believe it? They found Serena." Then I grabbed Carla in a bear hug. "Your sister is alive and well and will be here in about an hour!"

They immediately began to bombard me with questions about the call. Mike appeared satisfied that it was not some kind of hoax after he listened to some of the brief details that had been given to me.

Carla couldn't contain herself. She literally jumped with joy, then expressed concern that they might get stuck in traffic, or get confused by the directions I had given.

To help pass the time I decided to enlist Carla in more immediate practical matters; making up the convertible sofa in Mike's study, putting out extra towel sets, and deciding on alternate dinner plans since the lasagna wouldn't stretch for three more.

"Let's order pizza. It's Serena's favorite food, along with ice cream." Carla suggested. After a few minutes of helping me get ready for our guests she said, "Oh, Erin, I think I might faint when I see her! I'm going to go outside and watch for them now, if you don't mind. Did they say what they would be driving?"

"A VW camper—I think she said white. You go. I'll finish up here." What would the couple be like, I wondered. What does this mean as to Carla's future? So many questions, but for now we would just celebrate.

Several times car lights appeared in our neighborhood, only to turn off before pulling into our drive, but finally Carla called out, "They're here!" and went running down the front steps.

Mike and I watched as a smaller version, carbon copy of Carla, stepped out of the camper, and hurled herself into the older girl's arms. I willed myself not to cry. Mike offered me his hand-kerchief anyhow. I would need it later. It turned out that the woman accompanying Serena was as emotional about this reun-ion as I was. But for now it was all about joyous introductions and welcomes.

"Carla, why don't you take Serena and show her   your room," I suggested, when there was a pause in the conversation. And off they ran, hand in hand.

Melody and I looked at each other. She reached in the pocket of her skirt for a tissue and dabbed her eyes.

"You must stay with us! Can I help you bring anything in from your camper before I show you where you'll be sleeping?" I asked, as I got Mike's handkerchief out and blew my nose. "And please know that you're welcome to stay for as long as you like."

"We'll need to bring some things in if we are staying the night, and thank you for your kind offer for a longer stay, but we don't wish to intrude. This whole amazing meeting is so new," she said, as we walked outside   through the garage. "I guess I still can't quite believe it."  While she spoke she continued to dab at her eyes with the tissue, and then the warmest smile lit up her face.

The thought that she and my friend Amy could be sisters flashed through my mind. Some more nose blowing on my part and then we were hugging as if we were long lost friends—and in a unique way we were that and more.


The pizza delivered from Regents Pizzeria was a big success. We adults declined to top off the meal with ice cream, but the sisters polished off good-sized bowls of mint chocolate chip. We ex-cused them from the table as soon as they had finished. It was already quite late.

"You all set up there?" I asked Carla.

"Now that you brought in her pet," Carla responded. "I'm even going to let Brownie sleep with us."

Serena kept looking at her big sister with adoration, I noted. "We'll be up to tuck you in," I said, Melody nodding in agreement.

Carla came around the table to exchange a big goodnight hug with Mike. Serena, seeming to take a cue from her big sister, went over to Jimmy and gave him a quick kiss on the cheek. "Thank you," I heard her whisper, and I watched the obvious pleasure he received from this simple gesture.

"I don't imagine they'll get much sleep tonight," Mike commented, after they had left, then, "Can we help you with clean-up?"

"If you'd just throw the pizza boxes into the trash container in the garage, I think Melody and I can take it from here. Why don't you and Jimmy go into the living room? We'll join you soon. Not that there's any rush, but I know we have a lot of catching up and planning to do.

When we were all together again, the Millers spoke about their visit with the grandmother, the assessment given to them of her worsening physical condition, and shared with us the contents of the box they had received from her.

I told of my meeting with Deputy Wicker in Campo and his description of Uncle Mateo—definitely not a candidate to ever act as a guardian to his nieces.

We each shared the stories of how the sisters had come into our lives—of how their lives were now about to be changed forever. "And now it looks as if fate may have bound us together. And most importantly, what do we do that will be best for the girls?" Melody asked, speaking for all.

"Since they are minors it will probably be up to us to decide that, but of course, we want to take their wishes seriously as well," I declared.

Mike spoke up," I think we all know what they would prefer.

Anyone here for sharing a house—a little communal living?" he asked, adding a self-conscious laugh. "But I'm getting ahead of myself. We have a lot to consider, and need to check into the legalities, but we don't have to rush into anything."

"Speaking of time," I said, "you two must be exhausted. Sleep in as long as you want. Unfortunately, I'm part of a reporter pool chosen to cover a closed-door hearing at City Hall tomorrow, and Mike will be tied up at his office for part of the day, but we'll be back in plenty of time for dinner, and I'm sure Carla would love to play hostess."

"We *will* accept your hospitality for a day or two," Melody said, "but please, don't put your daily plans on hold for us."

Jimmy agreed. "Anyhow, we'll probably take in some tourist attractions. Take the girls with us if they are game." He yawned, and then apologized. "You're right. It has been a long day. That bed you made up looked pretty inviting. You coming, honey?"

"I'll be back as soon as I go upstairs with Erin to check on the girls."


Melody was back quickly. "Jimmy, they were sound asleep. You should have seen them. Carla's trundle bed was made up, but empty. They were snuggled up together in the queen," she related, as she began to undress.

"Your instincts were so right when you noticed Serena watching you that first day on the Green. I'll never second guess you again," Jimmy said. "Getting those two together is nothing short of a miracle."

"And it will just get better for all of us," Melody observed. "I had all I could do not to cheer when Serena gave you that kiss in front of other people. I know that there may be pitfalls ahead, but you do realize how far she has come in such a short time?"

"I admit I was surprised and very pleased when she did that" he said. "I think I'll sleep extra-well tonight."

# 36

It was still dark when I became aware that Mike was getting ready to leave for his office, trying to be extra quiet about it. "Sorry I woke you, honey. I know that it was very late when we got to bed."

I propped myself up on one elbow. "They seem like very nice people, don't you think?" I asked in a low voice, meaning Melody and Jimmy, of course..

"Very nice. Serena is a lucky girl, but not as lucky as Carla, who has you in her life," he said, leaning over to kiss me good-bye. "Now try to go back to sleep."

"I love you," I said sleepily, in response to his warm kiss.

Several hours later I awoke to full sunlight and the sound of voices coming from downstairs. I showered, dressed quickly, and went down to join the others.

"Good morning, sleepy head," Carla greeted me as I entered the kitchen. "Are you ready for some pancakes?"

Melody and Jimmy sat on counter stools, obviously well into their breakfasts. We exchanged greetings and then he got up immediately offering me his seat.

"Let's move over to the breakfast nook," I said, as I poured myself a mug of coffee. "It looks as if the diner is especially well-staffed this morning."

"It is. I have an excellent helper," Carla said, giving her sister a nod.

"I helped make the pancakes," Serena said.

"Best I ever had," Jimmy exclaimed, as he carried his plate and cup to a window seat.

Melody did the same. "This is an incredible kitchen, Erin. You must really enjoy spending time in here."

"More so since Carla arrived," I admitted, "she loves to cook. I've become quite spoiled."

Serena brought us a plate of pancakes straight off the griddle. Melody waved her off, but Jimmy speared one and I did the same. "Why don't you share your secret, Carla? After all we're..." I hesitated.

"We're all family," Carla finished. "Doesn't that sound amazing?"

"I got to beat the eggs and get the white part to stand up like whipped cream," Serena broke in, saving Melody and me a few tears, I'm sure.

"Please take your time, but I've got to get ready for work," I said, as I cleared my place.

"Erin's a reporter," Carla said, with obvious appreciation, "and she also works at the neatest bookstore. Did she tell you?"

Not to be out done, Serena piped up, "Melody makes beautiful jewelry and Jimmy was a marine for a long time and fixes things."

"I can see them opening a PR firm together," I said, laughing, then, "Have you decided where you'll go today?"

"I thought we'd visit the USS Midway Museum. Sounds as if they've turned that famous carrier into quite an interesting attraction, what with the planes on the flight deck and all," Jimmy said.

"That's well worth seeing, and the volunteer retired navy vets who lead the tours make it especially interesting. Mike should be back by mid-afternoon. I'll try to make it here by five. Now, I need to go fix my hair and put on some makeup, but if it's not against the rules, I would like to give the cooks a kiss." Which I did, and got hugs as well, in return.

\* \* \*

An hour later Melody stood in the downstairs hallway, waiting for Serena to come back down from retrieving her stuffed animal. Jimmy had gone out to get the camper ready for their trip to the Midway Museum.

"Are you sure you don't want to go with us?" Melody asked Carla.

"Thanks for asking, but not this time. As I said, I've been there before, also I want to make something special for Serena while she's out of the house. I'm not even going to tell you because I want it to be a surprise for everyone."

Carla checked to see that no one else could hear, and then leaned in close. "And Mrs. . . I mean, Melody, I just wanted you to know how happy I am that you and Jimmy found Serena. I know that my grandmother is too ill to take care of us, especially after what has happened to her. I prayed every day that my sister could one day be part of a family like I am with Erin and Mike, and now she is."

Serena came bounding into the room, her new backpack in place. "Sorry you're not going today, Sis, but having you show us around the zoo tomorrow sounds even better."

"'You're sure you'll be okay here alone?" Melody asked.

"I'll be fine. They've let me stay alone before. Besides, I'll be sixteen in a few months."

"Poor old thing," Serena teased. "Let's go, Melody. Jimmy's ready outside. We always make him wait for us."


As soon as they had gone Carla went up to the closet in the unfurnished bedroom and got out colored crepe paper, foil rolls, balloons, and the like. For the next two hours—with only a quick sandwich break—she decorated much of the downstairs; her masterpiece, a 'HAPPY BIRTHDAY SERENA' montage, complete with streamers and lots of yellow color. I know you couldn't celebrate last month, Serena, she thought. I hope this helps make up for that.

Now, she said to herself, I'd better see if I have everything on hand to make you one of your favorite meals—green chilies and beef enchiladas. A few minutes later she murmured aloud, "I can't believe I used all the chilies."

No problem. She had plenty of time and the neighborhood deli store sold them. She wrote a note and left   it on the kitchen counter for Mike to see if he returned    before she did. Door locked, key and cell phone in her pocket, helmet on, she hopped on her bike and headed out.

It was a beautiful sunny day—not too much traffic on the winding road. At the last minute, she decided to swing off to a meadow close by full of the wild flowers she always associated with the one in Campo where she and Serena had run happily with their dog. She and Erin had ridden out there a few times. Wild flowers were Erin's favorites, too—just another thing they shared that made them seem like real sisters.

A few cars passed her by and a number of walkers were out. She laid the bike down and picked some of the more colorful blooms which she put in her bicycle basket. Back on the main road, she smiled, as she anticipated Serena's delight when she saw the decorations, but the smile turned to a frown when she realized that a car had been following her much too close for safety.

She had pulled as far off to the side of the bike lane as she could, but the car still remained close behind. Glancing over her shoulder she noted it was a large black car with what appeared to be tinted windows. Fear began to take over. Should she stop? But then what? The best thing to do would be to get to the deli as fast as she could. With some relief she heard loud music— probably hip-hop—coming from the big dark vehicle. Hopefully, just some young jerks driving around harassing girls. It had happened to her before—once when Erin was with her. She sped up and rounded a corner.

The sound of an engine revving up with a roar right behind her caused her to turn her head slightly to take a look and that's when they struck her, coming directly from the rear and at full speed. A feeling of incredible pain in her back was accompanied by a sensation of floating high, floating ever higher in the air—and then—blackness.

Mike got the call. In a state of shock only certain fragments remained indelibly etched in his mind: "San Diego police Northern Division La Jolla—do you know a Carla Flores—there's been an accident—can't give you any details—sorry—the ambulance took her to— there were no direct witnesses that I am aware of, but there will be an investigation—you'll have to ask . . ."

Carla was pronounced dead in the ambulance while on the way to the hospital. There would be no visiting hours for her in room such and such. Now it was the unthinkable—a visit to the morgue to identify her body.

Mike knew that Erin would never be able to do it. The police had implied that damages to her body and face had been extensive—she had been thrown about sixty feet and landed in the midst of traffic, however, the cell phone with her home number in it had survived without a scratch.

Erin—she'd be home any minute. Mike felt panicky, he could hardly think straight. There was the sound of a car coming up the drive, but it was the camper. Serena! Mike looked once again at the beautiful decorations and thought tragically, how ironic!

The young girl burst into the room and stopped short when she saw the 'HAPPY BIRTHDAY SERENA' welcome. "Carla," she cried out, clapping her hands in glee. "Where are you?" She noticed an ashen-faced Mike standing quietly nearby. "Is she hiding somewhere? I'll go out again so she can pop out and yell surprise."

Melody and Jimmy walked in carrying packages. "A few souvenirs," Jimmy explained.

"Jimmy, I need to see you in the garage right now," Mike said quietly, taking him forcibly by the arm.

"'Oh my, will you look at this," Melody exclaimed, as she took in the decorations. "Let's use the bathroom, Serena, and then we can go select the things you want to hand out."


Much later, Mike sat at the bedside with me and waited until the pills that the doctor had prescribed took effect, then went downstairs. Melody had fallen asleep on the convertible couch beside Serena, whose heart-wringing sobs had finally allowed exhaustion to win out.

The two men sat together in the dimly-lit living room, nursing, for them, a rare strong drink.

"At times like this I almost wish I could be a woman," Jimmy said. "They're not only allowed to cry, they're expected to. I've lost a few buddies along the way. I don't think you ever get over it, but that's war, at least. Something like this is not supposed to happen. Not to that poor little girl in there who's been through so much."

"I know. I feel like I've been kicked in the gut—like a piece of my heart has been ripped out. How can I help   Erin heal, when I'm a mess myself?"

"I'll go with you to the morgue, if you like," Jimmy offered.

"I'd appreciate that,"

The ice melted in their drinks. Their eyes were heavy with sleep, but still they sat there, dreading the coming of morning.

# 37

Why was he still here? Mike lay beside me, seemingly deep in sleep. Sunshine was coming through the partially closed blinds. I was reasonably sure it was not the weekend. He must have overslept. I leaned over to check the clock on my bedside table and felt such a wave of nausea that I thought I was going to be sick.

Somewhere a phone was ringing. I'd better answer it before it woke . . . In my dream I screamed "no", over and over—silently—not silently. Mike was holding me, gently murmuring my name, but the pain and the nightmare wouldn't stop.

Did I want some coffee? Tea might be better. Toast and marmalade? How about a shower? Maybe a nice bubble bath would help. Mike looked haggard and worried. What would *I* see if I looked in the mirror?

Hours passed—day turned into night, and back again. I took the medication the doctor prescribed, but instead of helping me to sleep it made the nightmares worse and gave me dry mouth and a massive headache. I flushed the pills down the toilet.

Friends and coworkers called. They were so kind, so under-standing. We're so sorry. Can't even imagine . . . Our thoughts and prayers are with you. Is there anything we can do? Don't even think of coming in to work.

Mike took most of the calls at first, passing on the messages he felt I'd appreciate.

I went from pain to numbness and back again over and over, after the accident, as it was called. After Carla's murder—as I knew it to be—the death that *I* had caused.

Amy arrived the third day. She sat quietly by my bedside as I dozed, my body giving in to a lack of sleep. We cried together when the pain of my loss became too much, she listened to my ramblings of my love for Carla and wails of why? Why? But she refused to let me indulge in, "if only."

She made grilled cheese sandwiches for both of us. I nibbled at mine—the first solid food I was able to hold down. "Did you make one for Mike, too?" I asked.

"He's gone into the office for a few hours. You were asleep when he left. I sent him away. Looking at one glum face at a time is all I can take," she commented.

She urged me to take a shower and put on some proper clothes. "You owe it to Mike," she said. "He's hurting, too. I'll be right outside if you need me."

Dear Amy. What would I do without you? Had I said it aloud? Thanked her enough? She had a job and a fiancé, but she stayed until Mike returned.

He looked relieved when he saw me up and dressed. After he kissed me, he said, "Two of the secretaries at the office sent me home with a ton of food. They guessed correctly that I was not the star of our kitchen."

"We both know who was."

"Please don't do that, Erin."

I know he hadn't meant to be insensitive, but I wanted to lash out at someone—myself, especially. "Did Joe Cruz call?" I asked, getting up from the couch and beginning to pace.

"He did, naturally he feels very badly about what happened."

"And that's it?' I asked, in a shrill voice I hated, but seemed powerless to suppress. "Have they found the murderers—the gang members who did this?"

"There's still an ongoing investigation, but Joe said it probably can never be proved. They have a tip line, but the few people that called in only mentioned a large, black car, and none got a license number. The off-the-record view is that if the car did belong to the human traffickers, it has either been chopped up, or sent over the border to Mexico by now."

"What about the DA and the grand jury?"

"Erin, are you sure you want to talk about this right now?"

"You're saying there's more bad news? The case is probably going nowhere now that the witness is . . . I can't say it. It can't be true. Mike, it can't. It can't! I did it to her." I wanted to scream. I just wanted it to be all a dream. I put my head in my hands and began to rock back and forth.

"Erin, please," Mike begged.

"That beautiful young woman lost her life because I selfishly got caught up in some unrealistic, noble mission. You were right, Mike. All along you were right. I will never, ever get involved . . ."

"Stop, honey. Actually, I was the one who was wrong, but in any case this is not the time to make any decisions. Let's have something to eat, and then I can hold you while we listen to some music, or maybe we can find some movie to watch together. Please!"

So we went downstairs—determined to at least pretend this was just a normal evening at home. All the decorations were gone. No sign remained of Carla's handiwork. Nor were there any traces of the Millers and Serena. In my selfishness I had lost sight of the fact that a little girl had lost her sister—a child whose grief must be at least, or even deeper than mine.

How could I ever face them? Did they know how instrumental I was in persuading Carla to testify against the gangs? How my persistence in this whole trafficking issue is what probably got her killed? If so, would they ever even want to hear my name again, was probably an equally valid question.

Mike had guided me to the breakfast nook and started to get some food out for our supper.

"Have you heard from the Millers?" I asked, in as conversational a tone as I could manage—Melody and Jimmy had previously checked into a Super 8 motel that had a swimming pool for Serena.

"As a matter of fact, Melody called me at the office while Amy was still with you upstairs."

"And?"

"And, the upshot is that they are planning a memorial service in the chapel of a local crematorium, and naturally want us to be part of it. They asked if I knew who you might want to be there with you."

"Crematorium? Oh, Mike. Carla's remains being burned?"

"It seems that Serena is adamant that her sister's ashes be scattered in the ocean she loved. Anyhow, I thought we both agreed that is what we would like done with our bodies when we die."

"That's true. I just don't know if I can take part, Mike. I'll just be a blubbery mess and make Serena feel even  worse."

"You have to take part—it was Serena's choice. And remember, you're doing this for Carla. It's what she would have wanted."


So, two days later, dressed in the turquoise cap-sleeved dress Carla had said was her favorite in my wardrobe, I joined a few other mourners in a tiny chapel on the grounds of the crematorium—chosen, I guessed, out of the phone book. Fortunately, I was spared any involvement in that, or anything else to do with the body, or the procedure itself.

Frank and Malcolm were there, and Paula, the social worker from Tri-City Medical Center, as well as Judy and Dave from the Reader's Roost, Amy and Tim, Lorena from the Campo sheriff's station, and, of course, Serena and the Millers.

When she had first arrived from Campo, Lorena had related how, after the sheriff's station had been notified of Serena's rescue and Carla's recent death, she had gone to visit the grandmother.

Given the old woman's medical condition, she hadn't had the heart to tell her about Carla's death, but she did relate that Mrs. Flores had brought up the fact that it made her very happy that now her granddaughters were going to be adopted by wonderful families.

I thanked her especially for coming and the interest she had shown in general, and also introduced her to Melody and Jimmy. Lorena was pleased to see that Serena was safe and happy—at least a partial happy ending.

It wasn't a formal memorial service. I managed to say thank you to those in attendance, but when it came to saying words about Carla herself, I froze. I tried—I really tried, but . . . Mike rescued me and spoke briefly of how much she had meant to both of us. And then Serena, wearing a brightly colored print dress, was even able to bring out a few smiles by relating some happy memories from Carla's past. Minutes later the ceremony ended and the others left to return to their normal routines.


Jimmy had told Mike that Serena wanted us to be present for the scattering of Carla's ashes, and that we should meet at a nearby beach in La Jolla. When we arrived, we parked the car, and walked down a pathway to a nearly deserted stretch of beach in a secluded cove.

It was a beautiful sunny day, the sky an azure blue with just a few fluffy cumulus clouds, the sea reflecting the same color. Serena, now dressed in a yellow top and shorts, stood at the shore line, gazing intently out to sea while gentle waves were lapping at her feet. She held the urn up high with both hands. Mike and I had been told that she wanted to scatter the ashes as far out to sea as possible so that Carla could, in a way, become part of the ocean life—and she wanted to do it alone.

I tossed off my sandals, made a kind of cushion of beach grass, and settled down atop a nearby dune to observe. Seaside goldenrod and beach heather lent color to the wind-blown wall of sand—a picture postcard opportunity, I lamented.

Nearer the water, Melody stood off to one side—hands deep in the pocket of her blue denim jumper—honoring Serena's wish to do this alone, but still worried about the child stepping out into deeper water. Mike joined Jimmy, and the two men took off their socks and shoes and rolled up their pant legs. They strolled casually along the shoreline, but seemed to be keeping a watchful eye on the little girl as she began to wade into the water. Mike, at least, knew that one should never discount the possibility of riptides.

Deeper and deeper Serena went until the water was almost up to her chest—the urn held overhead in her skinny little arms. I could imagine her talking to Carla—saying, I love you and goodbye for now.

I got to my feet and started to move closer to the others. What if she stepped in a hole, or slipped below one of those steep underwater ledges? I noticed the men wading faster toward her, gesturing out to sea. Were they shouting warnings? But then I saw what had caught their attention. I must be dreaming—a Whale Rider kind of dream— because, swimming parallel to the shore and closer than I had ever seen them in the past, there appeared the distinct shape and surfacing antics of a pod of dolphins.

Serena was oblivious to any of us adults behind her. She waded in a little deeper and, in a moment that I'm sure no one present would ever forget, the dolphins swam around her as she opened the urn and scattered the ashes among them. The mammals even seemed to brush against her—perhaps nudging her gently back to the safety of the shore. And then, with a rolling salute of dorsal fins, they headed back out to the open sea.

After a moment or two, Jimmy and Mike waded back to the shore—soaked, with seaweed tangled around their ankles. They each held the hand of a radiant Serena, seawater dripping from her flattened-down hair and clothes. She broke free of them and bounded onto the beach with a look of pure joy on her face. "Did you see that, Melody?" she cried, over and over. "Erin," she shouted over to me, "they came for Carla. They are taking her home with them!"

We were all on the edge of the shoreline now. "Come, be happy with me," Serena said, reaching out her arms to all of us to embrace in a group hug. As I became part of that wet embrace I felt the first slight loosening of the constrictive band that had been across my chest since I was first told of Carla's death.

After squeezes all around, Serena, dwarfed by the adults, wriggled out of the huddle, smiled through her tears, and asked, "Any chance we could go out for lunch?"

Ah, the resiliency of youth, I thought, not for the first time. "Now that you mention it, I could eat a horse," Jimmy responded, receiving an affectionate nudge from Serena. Melody's smile was luminous.

I looked at Mike and nodded. "That sounds good to us. Got any place in mind, Serena?" he asked, and squeezed my hand.

"If there's a McDonald's anywhere nearby, I'd like to go there, if that's alright, but first I want to get out of these clothes. They feel yucky!"

I had read one of their ads that McDonald's was all about "portraying warmth and a real slice of everyday life." Going out to eat together; how pleasant—how normal. A good feeling, and the pain and guilt I'd been feeling seemed to lessen just a bit.


"There you are," said Mike, as he came into the living room late that evening and found me staring absently at the fish in our oversized tank. The only light in the room came from the enclosure itself.

"I thought you were coming up to bed," he added, as he began to give me a shoulder rub—letting one hand stray to one of my breasts.

I flinched and pulled away. "Not yet," I murmured, hating myself even as I spoke the words.

"Well, suit yourself," he said, resignation in his voice. "I understand, or at least I think I do. Anyhow, don't stay down here too long, you'll get cold."

Poor Mike. I know he's hurting too, I thought, but if he really understood how I'm feeling he wouldn't think I was ready to make love.

Yes, it was true that today's amazing occurrence with Serena and the dolphins, and our shared McDonald's meal with her and Melody and Jimmy had helped, but I couldn't just *get over it*—to put Carla's death behind me and get on with my life.

Serena had wanted to come back to our house before she and the Miller's left to move on and probably settle down. They, and we, resolved to remain in touch—hopefully forever. I had agreed to let Serena take anything of Carla's that she desired, as long as she didn't show me. I had no idea when I would be emotionally ready to go back into Carla's room.

When it was time for them to head north in their camper, I let Mike say the goodbyes for both of us. The Millers and Serena were off to start their new life together. A few bumps in the future could naturally be anticipated, as Melody had said, but they were all full of optimism. By comparison, at this point, my life looked empty and bleak.

Serena's kindness, shown to me at the funeral home and afterwards, demonstrated that she didn't blame me for what happened to her sister, but she had only been told a partial version of events leading up to Carla's death. I knew the whole ugly truth. Somehow, her reaching out to help ease my sorrow only made me feel worse. Why shouldn't she hate me? I hated myself.

# 38

I had insisted that Mike go back to work—that he did not need to be at my side all day and assuring him that I was not at all suicidal. But I have to say, that for the last few weeks, my life, at best, could only be described as murky. Some days I didn't get dressed until I knew it was time for Mike to return from work. I watched a lot of TV; the news—too grim; talk and game shows—too inane; the soaps—couldn't keep up with the plotlines and they reminded me of Carla and her Spanish language novellas. *Everything* reminded me of Carla.

I took a few calls from well-meaning friends, but ignored most of them. And I slept fitfully—though a lot. In between I read books on grief, loaned to me by Judy from the bookstore when she stopped by once with homemade cookies and a huge container of fresh fruit.

Google, as always, was helpful. One article, while emphasizing that not everyone experiences loss the same way, listed *seventeen* common feelings of grief. I saw myself in many, including a tightness across the chest, an inability to concentrate, a loss of appetite, unexpected bouts of crying, and mood swings back and forth between anger and guilt.

One night when I began to push Mike to read some of the material for both our sakes, or at least to indulge me when I felt like I was falling apart, he suggested that I look into attending a support group instead.

"You know I'm not much for reading things like that, honey, and I've been told more than once I keep my feelings to myself too much, but that's the way I am," he said. "In your case, hearing from others with a similar story might be just what you need. And if you hear something helpful and want to share it with me, I promise you I will listen carefully."


"How was your day at the office?" I asked Mike when he returned from work a couple of days later.

"It went OK," he answered, laying his briefcase on the table. "I can't believe how busy we've been lately, but that's fine by me. How were things for you?" This was a rhetorical question since I had become somewhat of a recluse.

"Actually I did get out myself. I followed through on your suggestion and went to a meeting of a group called *Compassionate Friends*. They were very welcoming and the members appeared to be quite diverse. All were grieving for a child they had loved, who had been taken from them in whatever manner, even many years ago. A few expressed feelings of guilt as well as a lingering sadness—but the reasons given for the guilt ranged from not telling the deceased they were loved often enough, or not returning a phone call, or being too much of a disciplinarian, or . . . ."

"And no one except you believed they were responsible for the death in some way? Am I right?" Mike took off his suit jacket and loosened his tie. "Erin, the gangs killed Carla! You've got to stop beating yourself up. It's been over a month since she died. I hate to see you like this!"

Words, words, words. Poor Mike. He was trying. Was I? I was dimly aware he had asked me a question—an inability to concentrate, one of the supposedly normal grieving signs from my Google list.

"I asked if you intend to go back to the group."

"I don't plan to, but one of the attendees did give me the name of a therapist she highly recommended. I'm thinking of following through on that."

"That might be a good idea," he said, cupping my chin in his hand and kissing me lightly on the lips.

Mike was right, of course. I was no good to anyone this way. I made a special effort to be upbeat that evening during dinner. We ate the last of the delicious casseroles made by one of his co-workers, and afterward we sat close together on the couch, watching a movie on HBO. I even made the first advances, which led to some tender lovemaking right where we were, while the credits were flickering by on the screen.

As we climbed into bed, Mike, obviously pleased by what he perceived as my progress, slow as it was, asked about my plans to return to work. "They must really miss you at *The County Voice* and the bookstore."

"They say that when they call. And I miss them, too, but I just have no enthusiasm for going about business as usual right now. Some days I think it would be best if I started over—doing something different where nobody knows me," I explained, as I methodically continued to rub scented lotion into my hands.

"Have you then given up on being part of the human trafficking consortium? When I spoke recently with Joe Cruz about working with the young gang member recruits, he said he hoped you wouldn't let the tragedy with Carla deter you from staying involved.

"And what happened to you and me sharing a goal with others to try and make a difference—to share a passion, as you put it?" Mike was up on his elbow now, looking into my face. "It's because of you Erin, that I'm attempting to get out of my smug businessman comfort zone."

My own words coming back to haunt me! Mike was right, but faulty reasoning or not, I couldn't get past the fact that if it hadn't been for my involvement in the human trafficking movement, Carla would still be alive. In any case, Mike had to do what was best for him.

"I *was* passionate once, but I'm not so sure it's the right cause for me anymore. I promise to seriously give thought to my future soon, but I'm tired now. Goodnight." Then I turned away from him to avoid any further discussion.


When Mike had half-waked me early next morning to give me his goodbye kiss, I apologized for my bedtime negativism. "That's alright, honey. Just so we don't let it come between us. I love you."

My "I love you, too" was especially heartfelt.

I got a call from Frank later that morning. "Where are you?" he asked, without any lead-in pleasantries.

"Where am I? Haven't you heard, I'm on a temporary leave of absence?"

"Well, it's been long enough. You should be here. You *are* a reporter, aren't you?"

"I don't know, Frank. I'm having trouble regaining enthusiasm for much of anything."

"I heard that sigh, and I'm telling you to get off your duff and get yourself down here. You're a damn good writer and you owe it to the paper and your readers to keep going—especially, for starters, to do a follow-up to the sisters' story."

"I don't think I can do that, Frank. It was my playing hot-shot reporter that got Carla killed. If I hadn't been covering that stupid meeting I would have been home to drive her to the deli for the chilies, and as for writing . . ."

"I never figured you for a quitter, Erin. Carla certainly never gave up, no matter how bad her life had been in the past. How about honoring her memory—making her death count for something?"

I got off the phone more than a little shaken. For the past few weeks people had been walking on egg shells around me— now I got a scolding, too. It stung. But there was some truth to it. And it had included that recurring comment about honoring

Carla.

More than one person from the bereavement meeting had mentioned getting involved in some activity that honored the deceased and thus made something positive come out of a loved one's death. Mike had said the same—now Frank, namely that Carla would have wanted me to keep going.

One hour later, after returning to *The County Voice*, I was sitting at my desk and began writing the first few lines on my laptop.

*Spoiler alert: If you are a person who only likes happy endings—all loose ends tied up in a nice bow—perhaps you had better stop reading here.*

The writing continued effortlessly—albeit through an occasional tear. I acknowledged a few co-workers who poked their heads in my cubicle to welcome me back, but I waved them on, discouraging conversation. I wrote and rewrote, trying to let my pain and frustration shine through, but also trying to convey the message that we needed to stay focused on the suffering victims still out there and the importance of working with the authorities and the volunteers who have refused to give up. Only by doing this could we honor those whose lives were forever changed for the worse, and especially to those who actually lost their lives.

This was the most personal and intense writing I had ever done. True, while the story reflected Carla's tragedy, there was also a glimmer of hope—after all, Serena was found and saved—but I *had* reminded the readers there was much they could do to help improve the odds. The danger to all was in doing nothing!

Before my final rewrite I took a card out of my wallet and dialed a number handwritten by the victim's advocate who had sat in when Carla had given her statement to Joe Cruz.

"Lucia Lopez, here. How may I help you?"

"This is Erin Butler. We met in Deputy Cruz's office a while ago when Carla Flores was giving her statement as a witness in a human trafficking case."

"Oh yes, of course, Erin. I was shocked and saddened to hear of her death. How are *you* doing?" she asked, and I could hear the genuine empathy in her voice.

Somewhat to my surprise I told her quite a bit about my struggle to get back to an even keel, to feel pleasure, enthusiasm, optimism once again—and, of course, about the residual guilt I felt.

She made a few encouraging comments, but mostly just let me speak. Perhaps I wouldn't need a professional therapist, after all. Hadn't Joe Cruz mentioned that Mrs. Lopez was credentialed in that area?

When I had finished, she said, "Well, Erin, I'm very happy you called, because I'm more convinced than ever that you would be a valuable asset for us. Not only could your experience work well for mentoring young women in our recovery programs, but your unique skills as a writer and speaker frankly make my mouth water at the thought of having you on board.

"Let me give you just one example. Though the California legislature passed the Safe Harbor Laws which, among other things, mandate that child survivors of commercial sexual exploitation be treated as kids, not criminals, there are still many people even in the so-called helping and criminal justice fields who are unaware of its provisions. Or, I hate to say, they deliberately choose to ignore the changes. They need to be educated and we need all the PR we can get on that one."

Before we hung up I had agreed to meet in her office at three the next day. I looked at the picture of the two sisters on my desk. Cross my heart, and corny as it sounds, I could have sworn Carla was smiling at me!

\*   \*   \*

I'll probably always feel some guilt, but Carla, I'm going to make you proud, I thought. The tight band across my chest was almost gone. Carla wasn't hurting any more. Why was I still hanging on to *my* pain? Did I really believe that made anything better for anyone?

Frank chose that moment to walk by. "Is it safe to—" he began, but before he could finish his sentence, I threw my arms around his neck and gave him a big kiss on the cheek.

"Thank you," I said, enjoying the puzzled look on his face.

"What was that for?"

"For having you always believe in me. But now if you'll excuse me, I have an important call to make."

As soon as Frank left, I dialed Mike's office. "Tell him it's Erin, and it's urgent," I said to his secretary, who screened all incoming calls.

"Erin, what's wrong, honey?

"Nothing—I just wanted to tell you that I love you very, very much, and I want to return right away to planning our wedding, and thank you, thank you, thank you."

"I love you too, Erin, but if I didn't know better I'd say you had gotten into the sherry—except we don't have any, and it's still early in the afternoon, and . . ."

"I'll explain all when you get home."


I sat there for a bit. Could something good really come from all that I had lived through these past few weeks? That old familiar tingle of mine had returned, filling me with anticipation. An unknown future lay ahead, but once again I could think of it as a future filled with wonderful possibilities.

Carla *would* applaud.

# Epilogue

Dear Erin,

As I recall, it was only two weeks ago that we spoke, but there have been a few new developments since then, and I also wanted to include a couple of recent pictures.

I'm glad we only took a three-month lease on this apartment because I think we have found the perfect fixer-upper—a three-bedroom, older home in a charming neighborhood, situated so we can walk to everything. While driving around we saw a 'for sale by owner' sign. To make a long story short, the property belongs to an elderly widower who currently resides in a senior-living complex. Apparently, he has no heirs, and isn't hurting for money. He had previously turned down several potential buyers when he found out they wanted to raze the house and build something more modern.

The owner went with Jimmy to show him around and they hit it off immediately. It turned out that as a youngster the gentleman had helped his dad and other relatives with some of the original construction. Temporarily, we will lease, with an option to buy. Very reasonable financial arrangements have been worked out, which will allow us to be homeowners in this rather high-priced real estate market. San Luis Obispo is a very special town.

As you can see by the enclosed snapshot, Serena is all set to *become Jimmy's number-one assistant. She looks so cute wearing the tool belt he bought for her at Home Depot. As for myself, I am not only watching the Home and Garden channel regularly, but I am taking notes. Hang on to this picture of the house as it looks now, because one day this will be turned into a showplace! We very much look forward to having both of you visit and see for yourselves.*

*Speaking of Serena, as mentioned to you earlier, I am home-schooling her and enjoying every minute of it. As she gets more comfortable with other children in general, and loses her linger-ing fear of abandonment, we plan to mainstream her—possibly after the Christmas holidays.*

*The therapist recommended by Cal Poly University has been a big help for her. I am toying with the idea of taking a few master's degree classes next semester, with a goal of eventually working with abused children. Meanwhile, my costume jewelry business continues to grow.*

*Jimmy has been working with a veteran's group—peer coun-seling some young returning servicemen and, also, I have reason to believe, being helped to unburden himself of some of the de-mons that he carries around as a result of his many tours of war-zone duty.*

*Serena is so excited that you asked her to be a junior brides-maid in your wedding. The check you sent was more than gener-ous. She'll have a ball picking out just the right dress.*

*Jimmy and I are loving our new family life, still taking the Vanagon out, camping on some weekends, and, at Serena's re-quest, have started adoption proceedings. Can you believe it, she wants to be a Miller? And, when I think back, on that not so long ago day when a poor, bedraggled little girl reached out to me on the Marina Green, Erin, I become so filled with emotion that it brings me to tears. That we have come so far, the three of us!*

*And whether you like to hear it or not, we have to give so much of the credit for our happiness to you and your persistence in finding the girls. I'd better close now. I'm in danger of weeping on this letter.*

*Glad to hear that you will continue to work with the human trafficking consortium—can't wait to be with you for the October wedding!*

*Love, Melody*

# Acknowledgements

The author wishes to thank Tom Holbrook, founder and co-owner of the RiverRun Bookstore in Portsmouth, NH and of RiverRun Bookstore's publishing arm, Piscataqua Press, for his consideration and suggestions. Also, Liberty Hardy's thoughtful and meticulous editorial contributions were invaluable.

In addition, my admiration goes out to the countless professionals and volunteers who provide sanctuary, counseling, and support on a daily basis to the girls and young women who have become unwilling victims of human trafficking.

To the Alicias, Taras, Wandas, Ariels, Simones, Charitys, and Tinas—the homeless, the runaways, the throwaways—may we all continue to do what we can to rescue you from the abuse and trauma of the sex trade.

And lastly, a thank you to the ever-inspiring Rachel Lloyd, whose memoir, *Girls Like Us,* encourages the reader to engage in a call to action in the fight for a better world, a world where girls are *never* for sale.

# About the Author

Lois Kenna Tripodi graduated from Boston University with a degree in Sociology, is a Licensed Certified Social Worker, and has received alcoholism and drug substance abuse training from Rutgers University. She holds certificates from California and New Hampshire in "Domestic Violence Support Services" and from the University of New Hampshire in "Social Work Counseling". In addition, she has participated in workshops at the Santa Barbara Writers Conference in Montecito, California.

A native-born New Hampshire resident, she has served in the NH House of Representatives, District 8, Hillsborough. In addition to supervising and counseling battered women in domestic violence support shelters, she was a member of the Oceanside, California, Crisis Intervention and Sexual Assault Response Team (SART).

She currently resides in New Hampshire with her husband. She is the author of one previous novel, *To Take Shelter*.